CALLING YOUR BLUFF

KATE CAMPFIELD

ALSO BY KATE CAMPFIELD

Going All In

Letting it Ride

Upping the Ante

CALLING YOUR BLUFF

CALLING YOUR BLUFF

KATE CAMPFIELD

CONTENTS

AUTHOR'S NOTE

The thoughts and opinions expressed in this work, particularly those toward goats, are fiction only.

The author holds no negative feelings toward goats, nor does she condone derogatory language toward goats, such as referring to individual goats as the Anti-Christ.

PROLOGUE
MILLER

"Can you grab me a glass of milk while you're up?" I ask innocently as Maddox stands from the poker table.

He gives me a strange look. "Milk? Since when do you drink milk?"

I shrug, keeping my eyes focused on the cards I'm shuffling. "I hear it's good for you or something. Trying to change things up, you know."

He rolls his eyes as he heads toward the kitchen.

I hold my breath, biting the inside of my cheek to keep from laughing while I wait.

Five...

Four...

Three...

Two...

"MILLER!" Maddox bellows, and I finally crack a smile.

"What the fuck did you do this time?" Blake asks from across the table, where he and Cam are wearing identical expressions of confusion.

I let out a snort of laughter as Maddox holds a glass out, the liquid inside a milky blue. "I think your milk might be bad, Maddox," I tease with a knowing look.

He places the glass on the table in front of me with just a little too much force. "Stay out of my fridge." He stalks back toward the kitchen while the rest of us try to compose ourselves.

Blake pushes a hand through his hair, still laughing. "Dude, between your pranks and Holly being all hormonal with her pregnancy, Maddox might be getting close to the edge."

I take a sip of the blue milk before I shuffle the cards again. "Just wait till he checks the fruit bowl. All the oranges have googly eyes."

This earns me a laugh from Cam, which would normally make me happy. I live for pulling harmless pranks like this, making people laugh. But even the combination of the fruit eyeballs and blue milk isn't doing it.

Look, I'm not complaining. My life is great: I have the best job in the world (playing poker), best family (my mom and Jordan are everything to me), the best friends, and I even live in Philadelphia, the best city in the world. What's not to love?

I'm just... stagnant, I guess.

I don't want to change anything, not really. Maybe just... shake it up. Maybe.

REBECCA

I tap my pencil on the desk as I re-read the question.

A three-year-old is brought to the emergency department with lethargy and vomiting. Their glucose level is 759. Which of the following cell types is affected in this disease process?

My knee starts bouncing, too. I should know this. I *do* know this. Right? The high glucose level means he has diabetes. So, something in the pancreas.

I read the answer choices once more. All of them are cells in the pancreas.

Shit.

I chew on the inside of my cheek, going through the answers in my head again. I've been studying my ass off for this test for weeks, and I have to do well, or I'm screwed. Literally.

I've already failed one of my classes this year. They'll let me make it up over the summer and stay with my class, but if I fail a second one, I'll have to repeat the entire second year of med school.

Massive tuition costs aside, I can't fathom what my parents would say.

I read through the choices again as my panic grows. *Alpha, beta, delta, epsilon, upsilon.* Is upsilon even a word? These seem more like fraternity letters than cell types. I know for sure there are alpha and beta cells in the pancreas and that they're somehow involved in sugar metabolism, so I cross out the other options.

We're down to a fifty-fifty chance of getting this right. *You can do this, Rebecca.*

Because if I don't, all my dreams of becoming a cardiothoracic surgeon like my dad are shot. My dreams of becoming *any* kind of doctor are shot.

The student next to me shoots me a dirty glare, probably because my pencil tapping has become a little loud. I tap it against my hand instead for another minute before I fill in the circle for answer A—*alpha*—and move on to the next question.

I'm sweating when I finally leave the classroom.

My sympathetic nervous system is on high alert—

the fight or flight response, with adrenaline secretion and all that. What wasn't *that* on the exam?

Hell, I know all about stress and cortisol levels.

Mine are high. All the time.

But it's how I thrive. I need a high-pressure, fast-paced environment to do my best work. It's been like that forever, and I figured it would lend itself well to med school.

But the sheer *volume* of things they expect us to memorize is insane. It's like being thirsty and trying to take a sip from a fire hydrant. Way more than you ever wanted, and you end up regretting all your choices.

I should feel lighter now that my final exam is done for the year. Most of my classmates are headed to the bar to celebrate the end of the year and the halfway point of med school.

But that's not in the cards for me, for a few reasons.

First, and most importantly, I'm not actually sure this *is* the end of my second year. At best, I'll be repeating pharmacology over the summer.

At worst, I'm restarting the entire year in the fall while my former classmates will be off doing their clinical rotations.

I've never really gotten close to any of my classmates, so it's not like my friends are leaving me behind.

I'm more of an introvert, and the competition doesn't help things at all. I'm better off just keeping to myself and studying. Because if this is the result when I work hard, imagine where I'd be if I went out to the bars every Friday night. But the idea of them all moving on without me makes the thought of failing that much worse.

I slide into my Volkswagen Jetta and pull out of the student parking lot to head home, wondering how to fill my time until the exam results are posted.

They're usually back fast; the exams get run through a machine that reads our answers and spits out the grades within a matter of hours. I should probably start studying for my summer class, but that seems like it'll jinx it.

Gym? No, that's a terrible idea. I don't even know what one does at the gym.

There's no way I'll be able to settle my nerves enough to watch a movie or read a book or anything like that. Plus, those are luxuries, things I do when my life is going well, and I'm not entirely sure it is.

When I finally pull into my assigned parking spot at my apartment complex, I realize I've spent the entire ten-minute drive stewing over things instead of actually listening to my podcast like I'd planned. I let myself into the one-bedroom apartment and slip my loafers off, arranging them by the door. I glance at the kitchen, but I'm too stressed to eat.

That's the beauty of being nervy. It keeps your weight in check, or so I can hope. I had a sweet tooth back when I was growing up, but the further along I've gotten in school and the more stressed I've gotten, it's kind of faded.

The extra layer I'm carrying around my stomach and hips, however, hasn't gone away, and it shows no sign of getting any smaller anytime soon. I grimace at the thought.

I look around the apartment. With the stress of studying for the final, I've let things slide a bit when it comes to cleaning. That's a useful way to spend my time. I nod to myself. Yes. I can get this place back in shape. I always feel better when I'm in a clean space, especially when it smells like the lemon-scented cleaner I use in the kitchen. Perfect.

I tuck my tote into the closet near the door. The vacuum cleaner is in the same spot, so I start there, running it over the living room carpet. There's something about those nice lines that the vacuum leaves. Even if the carpet wasn't that dirty to begin with, it's just so *satisfying*.

I'm finishing up and wrapping the cord around the vacuum when my phone rings. I swipe to answer without looking to see who it is—and cringe as soon as I hear the voice.

"Rebecca?" Stern. No-nonsense. Loves-you-but-judges-you in the same breath.

"Hi, Dad," I say, resigning myself to how I already know this conversation will go.

"How was the final?" he says without hesitation.

Like I do every time I'm around my parents, I fall back into my role as Perfect Only Child. "It went well, thanks. How are you doing?"

He ignores my question. "Did you *do* well?"

"I don't have my grade back yet." He doesn't know about the class I failed earlier in the year. If I have my way, he never will. Because in a family like ours, failure isn't an option.

"But how do you think you did? Did you know all the answers?" he presses.

How do I even answer that? "I think so. I'm feeling good about it."

I hate lying to my parents. But even more than that, I hate disappointing them, and if I fail my entire second year of med school, it'll be beyond disappointment.

My dad is the son of immigrants; his parents moved to America from India when he was little, and he loves to tell the story of how he went from a kid who failed English as a Second Language multiple times between first and fifth grade to a renowned cardiothoracic surgeon.

Not just a surgeon. *Cardiothoracic* surgeon. He'll correct anyone who misses that part.

But what he took from his experience is that anyone can succeed with the right motivation and persistence. So how can I tell him I'm struggling with pathophysiology?

I had every opportunity he never had, a fact he likes to remind me of often. I had the private schools, the tutors. The SAT prep courses to boost my score to get me into a top college, which he then paid for.

So, you see why I can't tell him I'm at risk of repeating a year?

"What does your schedule look like for your clinical rotations?" he asks, apparently satisfied with my responses about the exam for now. "Make sure you have your surgery rotation early in the year, but not too early. You want to have enough experience to impress them, but make it early enough to get letters of recommendation and a foot in the door for electives your fourth year."

Dad is always thinking five steps ahead while the rest of us struggle to keep up. It's why he's such an amazing surgeon. It's also why I never beat him at chess.

"We don't have our schedules yet." True. "But I'll keep that in mind." Also true. I just don't have to mention the part where my clinical rotations might not start for an entire year if I have to repeat second year.

Or ever. Fail a year twice, you're out. So, I need at least a B on this exam to safeguard my future.

B.

Beta.

Shit. It's Beta cells that secrete insulin, isn't it? I got that one wrong.

"...make sure you're still studying all the time, Rebecca. Finishing pre-clinical classes doesn't mean you're off the hook." Dad is still talking as a sick feeling fills my stomach, threatening to overtake me.

I swallow over the lump in my throat, trying to hide the fact that I'm taking a deep breath. "You've got it, Dad. In fact, I'm thinking I'll start studying now. Get a jump on internal medicine at least." I feel terrible for lying, but it's far from the first time.

And if I fail this final—and thus the class—it's far from the last time, too. But I'm on the verge of throwing up as I think about all the questions I might have gotten wrong.

I place the phone on the counter after I end the call and stand over the sink, resting my weight heavily on my arms.

Breathe in, one, two, three. Breathe out, one, two, three. I repeat the cycle until the nausea has dulled. I don't think it will disappear completely until I get the exam grades back.

Maybe not even then, depending on the outcome.

I take one more deep breath, then stand up straight and grab the spray cleaner. I pull on a pair of rubber gloves. Cleaning is mindless and methodical, so it can be almost meditative. Spray, scrub, wipe. Repeat until everything is shiny and perfect.

Because no matter how hard I try, my life isn't perfect. But my kitchen can be.

I move on to the bathroom when the scent of lemon starts to seep into my pores. The porcelain of the toilet is pure sparkling white, but I spray some cleaner in there and start to scrub with the toilet brush.

I've honestly never understood why people think bathroom cleaning is so gross. Back when I spent my summers at camp, we had to clean the communal bathrooms once a week. And *everyone* bitched about it, campers and counselors alike.

But I never minded. It's a job that has a specific

focus. There's a right way to do it, and if you follow that, you end up with a clean bathroom. Simple.

God, Camp Winnie. I use my forearm to push my hair out of my face as I think about my days at the New Hampshire summer camp. Those were the days, weren't they? A little bathroom cleaning in exchange for spending weeks in the most amazing place on earth. I even spent a few summers as a counselor while I was in college. Best job ever. Underpaid, maybe, but getting to live there for the entire summer? I would have done it for free.

Okay, maybe not free, now that I think about the time that a camper puked on my bed in the middle of the night. But the other times were amazing. I wish it were possible to be a summer camp counselor forever.

Brett managed, actually. He was a counselor when I was a Ladybugs camper—the youngest girls—and he swiftly rose through the ranks of leadership, coming back every summer. He's been the camp director for a few summers now. *Living the dream.*

While I, on the other hand, am decidedly not living in a dream, unless this is somebody's recurring stress dream. Cleaning a toilet while waiting to hear about my academic fate.

As if on cue, my phone chimes with the alert for a new email.

My stomach flips. This is the moment of truth.

Please, please, please let me pass. I send up a prayer to any god that will listen.

I open the mail app, and there it is. **Exam Results - Rebecca Patel.**

God, it's so cold and impersonal. Couldn't they add a smiley face or frown or something to give you a hint? Like, *smile emoji* *Here they are! The results you've been waiting for!* Or *frown emoji* *Sit down, love. You're going to need a stiff drink before you open this one.*

But no. Just **Exam Results**.

I sit down, just in case, chewing anxiously on my lip as I click on the email to open it.

2

MILLER

Five bucks says Cam is going to call my bluff.

I'm looking at a pair of threes and a king high. I have no business staying in this hand. But I love taking their money, and if I can do it when I don't even deserve it? Even better.

"Fold," he says, tossing his cards on the table.

I don't react, even though I'm surprised. Of all the people at this table, Cam can usually read me better than anyone. Maybe he's tired.

Sure enough, he yawns, right on cue as he leans back in his seat. "Sorry. Addie kept me up late last night." He shrugs.

I smirk as Maddox slugs Cam in the shoulder.

"That's my sister, man. Have some respect." Maddox frowns as he studies his cards and calls my bet.

Poker games like this are rare these days. It used to be that the four of us got together at least once a week to play, but since Lawton left for the police academy a few years ago, Maddox married Holly and Cam shacked up with Addie—Maddox's sister, as Maddox keeps reminding us all—our group is shrinking.

Blake and I are the only confirmed bachelors left, and I'm starting to feel... something.

It's not that I don't love my life. Who wouldn't love this? Twenty-nine, single, and making a decent living playing poker. This is the dream. No office to go into every morning. No reason not to stay out at the bars late.

I mentioned this to my mom last night. We talk on the phone a few nights a week, if not more often because yeah, I'm a mama's boy. You would be, too, if your mom was as awesome as Lori Quinlan. She's one of my best friends, and she gives great advice.

Her advice this time was to change it up. Go somewhere or do something different. Maybe spend the summer outside of Philadelphia.

She may be on to something, but I feel like our group is falling apart as the guys drop off one by one, falling to the call of true love or whatever it is they're doing. Once Blake finds a girl, it'll be just me.

Maybe that's really what's bugging me. The idea

that they could all find their happily-ever-afters and I'll be the lone guy left behind.

"You ever think about doing something different?" I ask offhandedly, studying my cards.

The three of them stare at me.

"No," Maddox says.

Cam frowns. "Not really."

Blake is the only one who looks thoughtful. I wonder if he's contemplating life the same way I am.

"Why do you ask?" Maddox pushes chips into the center of the table.

I shrug as I raise the bet again, still bluffing. "Just feeling bored, I guess. Like I need something different in my life."

"So go to Vegas. Enter a big tournament or something."

I could, but that's not exactly the change I was thinking of. "Maybe. I was thinking something... not poker related, I guess. I love the game, but I feel like I need a new challenge. You know?"

"Try convincing a girl to go out with you," Maddox mutters. "That'll take some of your focus away from the game." He spent a couple of months trying to get Holly to go out with him once they found out their parents were getting married to one another.

Eventually, she caved, and they're deliriously in love and blissfully happy.

"Go on a cruise?" Cam suggests, a smirk on his face. "Maybe Maddox has another sister that he can send with you."

The comment earns Cam an elbow to the ribs. He winces.

Play passes around the table again as the last community card is laid out, each of us getting a turn to raise or match the bet. I don't push this time, but I stay in while Maddox and Blake fold, leaving me the winner without having to show my hand.

But there's no thrill of the win. It's all just... the same. Every hand is different, but it's the same thing, over and over. Maybe that's what growing up is, though. You get good at something, and you just do it again and again and again, while you think about how much fun it used to be.

God, am I having a mid-life crisis? Can you have one of those if you're not even thirty yet?

Maddox deals another round of cards, and I study them. Once again, I have nothing.

I hate this moody feeling. I'm not usually like this. I'm the guy everyone loves—always happy and joking around, always the one to lighten the situation. I'm a fucking blast to hang out with, if I do say so myself. And I say it. A lot.

I'm not even in the mood to bluff this time. I fold, tossing my cards down just as my phone vibrates with a text. *Mom* flashes across the screen.

"I'm going to answer this," I tell the guys, standing from the table.

Maddox gives me a nod as he raises the bet.

"Tell Mama Quinlan I said hi," Blake chimes. He loves my mom. The guys all do.

I step into the kitchen and rummage through Blake's cabinets, coming up with a bag of pretzels. I toss two in my mouth as I swipe open Mom's message.

MOM

I thought of something you could do for a change this summer!

Hmm. It's entirely possible her idea has something to do with coming home, or with someone she remembers from twenty years ago, but I'll consider just about anything. And Mom has had some good ideas in her time.

I dial her number as I pop another salty pretzel in my mouth. God, these things are amazing.

"Hey, sweetie!" Mom says as soon as she picks up. "How are you doing? Am I interrupting anything?"

I swallow my mouthful. "No, not at all. I called you, remember?"

She pauses. "What are you eating?"

"Pretzels. Sorry." I should have known better than to be chewing when I dialed her number. Mom almost always answers on the first ring.

"No worries. I didn't think you liked pretzels."

I pop another in my mouth. "They're Blake's."

"Oh, shit, did I interrupt poker?" Mom has never been shy about cursing in front of us. When we were little, the rules were that we could curse, too, as long as we knew the rules: no swearing at school or at Grandma's house. We did that, we lost the privilege of using those words.

"Nah," I say between the crunching. "I folded a shitty hand right before you texted me. And I called you, remember? What's up?"

"You remember Eileen Morton?"

I do not. One of her friends from the bowling league?

"No. Why?" All the pretzels are making me thirsty. I open the fridge to see if Blake has anything good in here.

"She's part of my bridge club." Close enough. "Her son went to high school with you. Brett?"

Now that rings a bell. "Brett Morton? Yeah. We

played lacrosse together. He's a good man. How's he doing?"

"Well, he's working up in New Hampshire right now. At a summer camp. Eileen mentioned that they need more counselors for the summer." She pauses expectantly.

I'm not sure what this has to do with me, but she must have some kind of angle. "And?"

"Well, aren't you looking for a change of scenery for a while? It's a limited-time engagement, so it's not like you're committing yourself to a full-time job or something. Just a thought." I can almost picture her shrug.

Thinking, I pull a root beer out of Blake's fridge. He's got the good kind that comes in glass bottles. I twist off the top and take a long sip. "I like the thought, but I'm not exactly an outdoor type. How would I even figure out who's in charge up there?"

My phone vibrates against my ear.

"Brett's in charge. He's the camp director. Anyway, I sent his contact info to your phone. Eileen gave it to me. How's everything else going? You need any more scented candles? They're having a sale at the outlet next week."

You know the stereotype of the nagging mom, the one you can't wait to get off the phone? The one who's pushy, won't let things go? Yeah, Mom is the opposite. And I love her for it.

We move on to talking about home furnishings and scented candles while I consider the idea of summer camp. I'm not exactly an outdoor kind of guy, the ones you see in the L.L. Bean catalog wearing flannel and hiking boots and standing on top of a cliff.

But I'm looking for something different than my usual, and summer camp would certainly be that.

I'm still not exactly sold, but I do wonder how Brett is doing. I haven't talked to him in forever, maybe since college? I remember running into him at one of our hometown bars in upstate New York when we were home for Thanksgiving one year. I should give him a call to say hi.

"You coming?" Blake calls from the living room, reminding me of the game.

"Shoot, I should go, Mom. The guys are calling me back to the game. I'll talk to you soon, okay?"

"Oh, sure, honey. Can I say hi to them before you go?"

"Sure. Putting you on speaker." I bring my phone and the root beer into the living room. "Mom wants to say hi before I hang up."

"Hey, Mrs. Quinlan," Maddox says.

Cam waves toward the phone. "Hi, Mama Q!"

"Hey, Lori! I'm kicking your son's ass today. He's down to his last few chips," Blake adds with a grin. I give him the finger.

Mom laughs. "Good luck, boys. Take him for everything he's got. Miller, talk to you later." With that, she ends the call, and I slide the phone back in my pocket.

"Where were we?" I ask, slipping into my seat.

Cam deals out a new round of cards. Even though I'm staring at a great hand, a pair of queens, the usual zing of excitement just isn't there. No rush of adrenaline as I think about how best to raise the bet.

It's just cards. Great cards, maybe, but at the end of the day this is all a game.

And I'm starting to wonder if what I need in my life isn't just a change... but something more.

I light a pine-scented candle and settle on the sofa, TV remote in hand. Today's poker game was a bust. The only hands I won were full-on bluffs. I'm great at those because for some reason I don't entirely understand, people don't think this sweet face can lie.

I mean, I don't, not much. Just in poker.

I'm about to start watching HGTV when I

remember my conversation with Mom. I should give Brett a call while I'm thinking of it. I find the shared contact that my mom sent and save the number, then hit *Call*.

"Camp Winnie, Brett Morton," he answers. God, we're old if this is how we answer phones these days.

I clear my throat. "Brett, hey. It's Miller Quinlan. Your mother gave my mom your number. It's been too long, man."

"Miller? Shit, man, it's been forever. How are you? It's great to hear from you."

I stand up and wander into the kitchen while we shoot the shit. Every time I'm on the phone, I seem to find myself heading to the kitchen. I think I got into the habit at some point, and now when I talk on the phone, I get hungry.

"I'm good, man. My mom said you're working up in New Hampshire now. What have you been up to since I last saw you? When was that, college?" I root through the fridge.

"Life is good. I got married a few years ago, and we're expecting our first kid around Thanksgiving."

"No shit? That's awesome, man!" I can't believe I'm old enough that my friends are doing adult things. Maybe I really do need a change in my life. While Brett has been adulting and getting married and procreating,

I'm over here doing the same thing I used to do in the college dorms.

To be fair, back in college my winnings barely bought me a case of beer here and there, while now I make enough between tournament wins and sponsorships to fully support myself. And I'm lucky to be able to do this for a career. My recent mindset of feeling stagnant, though, is making me see things differently than I usually do.

"Thanks. We're excited. Scared shitless, but excited. What have you been up to?" he asks.

There's nothing in the fridge that looks appetizing. It's all the same.

"I'm playing poker for a living. It's been great, but I think I'm ready for a change." I push my hair out of my eyes. "Mom said you might be looking for camp counselors, actually. Think you'd have a spot for me?"

The laugh that echoes through the phone wasn't exactly the reaction I'd been expecting. "You want to come be a camp counselor? It's kind of a thankless job, man. Especially at our age. And it doesn't pay much. I don't know how much a professional poker player makes, but I can pretty much guarantee it's more than a counselor here."

I do not need to be reminded of our age. Midlife crisis and all that. "How hard can it be? I need something new in my life. A new challenge or something. And I do okay as a pro poker player. Enough that I'm not worried about the salary. More just looking for a new experience."

Brett started laughing as soon as I asked how hard this job can be, and I can still hear the laughter in his voice. "You'd be surprised. It's tough, there's no doubt about it. I mean, I am looking for a few more counselors, and camp starts in a week and a half, so I'm down to the wire here. I'm just not sure you could handle it."

"Hey, I can handle anything. Remember when I lost the bet that I could get Leah Baker to go to homecoming with me? She said no and you guys made me shave my legs. If you recall, I handled that okay."

Not my proudest moment. The fact that I'd shaved my legs made it around school by the next day, conveniently without the information that I did it because I lost a bet. My bare legs were the butt of every joke for my entire freshman lacrosse season.

And I still didn't have a date for the dance.

Brett roars with laughter. "Oh, fuck, I forgot all about that. You still shave?"

"I'm not going to dignify that with a response." And no, I do not. I manscape, but that's it. And the ladies have no complaints.

"Ah, fuck, those were good times." His laughter fades slightly. "It'd be great to see you, but here's the thing. This job is hard, and it sucks sometimes. But you think you can do it? I'll make you a bet."

My ears perk up.

"You come work as a counselor. I don't think you'll last a week. You make it the whole summer, I'll never bring up the shaved legs thing again. You bail before the end of the summer, your salary goes into the campership fund. It's like a scholarship for kids whose parents can't afford camp on their own."

Aw, fuck. That pulls at my heartstrings a little.

"So, what do you say? You going to take the bet?"

3

REBECCA

My stomach bottoms out as I blink, hoping I somehow misread the email the first time.

But when I focus on the words, they say the same thing: **Overall score: 78. Final course grade: Fail.**

No. No, no, no. This can't be happening. The room spins around me, and I'm glad I'm sitting. My stomach twists with nausea. I take a deep breath and hold it, then breathe out and repeat.

It does nothing. My heart is still racing, my fingers tingling the way they do when I'm on the verge of a panic attack.

I stick my head between my legs, the way a high school guidance counselor taught me to do when I'm on the verge of passing out. It just makes the nausea worse, though, and the last thing I need is to throw up.

God, what am I going to do?

This has been a possibility for weeks now. It's almost like I knew this was coming. So, the fact that I don't have a backup plan already in place is just one more failure.

My hands start to tingle again, and I look around my small living room. Five things I can see. The coffee table, its shiny surface. The plain, off-white walls. A pile of textbooks against one wall. My favorite armchair with its worn fabric. A sweatshirt folded on the couch next to me. My shoes by the door.

I hold another breath as I move through the exercise. Four things I can touch. Three things I can hear.

With the sheer number of coping mechanisms I've learned in order to deal with my anxiety, you'd think I'd be better at handling it by now. But I make it all the way to one thing I can taste—the coffee from earlier today—and I don't feel any better.

A text message flashes on the screen, and I tap on it, hiding the grade report for a minute. It's already burned into my mind.

STUDY GROUP

Anna: Scores are up! How'd you all do!

John: 82 *smile emoji*

Carrie: 77 but passed the class!

Anna: 85 *fire emoji*

Carrie: Wow, you go girl!

Andrew: 84. Solid work, crew.

How do I respond to this? *Do* I respond?

The four of them are all moving on to their third year. They'll have a week or two off to take their boards and then I won't see them frequently, if at all, once they start their clinical rotations in July.

Maybe I can just quiet-quit the group. It's not like they need me for their studies at this point. Would they even miss me?

I wait for one of them to ask me directly how I did, or to message me outside the group chat, but nothing comes. Maybe they assume I'm away from my phone, at the bar or celebrating somewhere like most of our class.

But there's a part of me that wonders if they actually ever liked me or if they just put up with me. Maybe they don't really care at all. Either way, it doesn't really matter. I'm on my own now.

The four of them are moving on, and no one in my new second year class will want to involve themselves in a study group with someone repeating the year. Maybe it's not fair, but that's how it is.

Med school is kill or be killed, and no one is going to hitch their rope to a sinking ship.

One glass of wine isn't enough to make me forget the disaster that is my life right now. I eye the bottle beside me with pursed lips, considering a second glass, but I've never been much of a drinker. Two glasses would just give me a hangover.

I slouch back on the sofa with my phone in hand. There has to be something I can mindlessly scroll through to make me feel happier. Pictures of Golden Retrievers, maybe. Kittens?

When I open my phone, however, I find myself searching for Camp Winnie. The days I spent there as a camper and counselor were the happiest of my life. Just looking at the pictures can bring back some of those feelings, and I need that now, more than ever.

But as I scroll through the website, something comes over me, and before I know it, I'm dialing a phone number.

"Hello, Camp Winnie, Lois speaking," a pleasant voice answers after a few rings.

And it's a voice I recognize, one I've heard so many times over the years that I almost dissolve in tears right there.

Lois has been the front office person for years, if not decades. She's the face of Camp Winnie in so many ways—the person you see when you check in, the voice on the other end of the line when you call.

I swallow the lump in my throat. "Hi. Could I, um, speak with Brett?" I cross my fingers. I'm not even sure if Brett will even remember who I am.

"Oh, of course, love. May I tell him who's calling?" A faint scratching noise in the background suggests that she's working on paperwork while answering calls.

"It's, um, Rebecca Patel. Becca."

"Oh, Becca!" Lois chimes, immediately recognizing the name, the same way she remembers everyone. The scratching comes to a halt. "How are you, honey? It's been too long since we've seen you here. How are things going for you?"

"Good," I lie. Lois doesn't need to know all the dirty details. "How are things up there?"

"Oh, you know. It's always a cluster the few weeks before summer starts. I'll get Brett for you. He'll be just tickled pink to hear from you." Lois puts me on hold.

I consider just hanging up. This was a stupid idea. I

have no idea what possessed me to call in the first place. Camp Winnie is my happy place, the place I think about when I'm searching for comfort. Maybe I was trying to get closer by dialing the phone. But now I'm not sure what I'm going to say.

Plus, Lois knows it's me, and there's a good chance that if I hang up, she'll find my number and call me back.

Before I have a chance to make up my mind, a deep voice comes through the phone. "This is Brett."

"Hi, Brett. It's Becca Patel." Camp Winnie was the one place I ever went by a nickname. It was like it was my secret identity.

His voice conveys his ever-present smile. Brett is scary as shit when you're a camper in trouble, but he's a big teddy bear to those who know him. "Becca. It's been too long. How are you?"

"Oh, I'm good. I, um..." How do I explain this? I'm not sure I even know why I'm calling. *I fucked up at med school and now I need something to do over the summer to keep my mind off my shortcomings. Or, I need to go back to the place where I feel most like myself. Or even, I need to be somewhere I feel in control.*

Brett, being Brett, seems to understand me without the need for words.

"Well, it's great to hear from you. Any chance

you'd be interested in coming up here for the summer? Even a few weeks, if you could. Even a week would help me out. We need a few more counselors."

My heart leaps. There it is. My opening. But my body freezes, and I can't respond.

How am I going to explain my summer plans to my parents? Or to anyone else, for that matter? I hadn't even figured out how I was going to tell them I'd be starting my third year late, spending the first six-week rotation redoing my pharmacology class.

Now, I don't even have that to occupy me this summer. I'll just be biding my time until it's time to start second year all over again.

But maybe this is my out. I can hide away at Camp Winnie for the summer and keep my failure to myself until I'm ready to deal with it.

Rebecca may be in deep shit. But *Becca* can go have a rockin' summer.

"Becca?" Brett says, jerking me back to reality.

"Sorry. Lost in my thoughts for a minute there. You were saying?" *Smooth, Becca.*

Brett chuckles. "I swear, with all the last-minute things I'm trying to get done, I'd lose my head if it wasn't attached. I was just trying to convince you to come help us out for a few weeks. I know it's totally out of the blue, and I'm sure you have plans."

"You know what?" I take a deep breath and let it out slowly, feeling better already, more in control. "I'd love to come up for the summer. I'll do whatever you need."

"Seriously?" Brett's voice rises an octave in his excitement. "That's honkin' amazing, Becca. Seriously."

I'd forgotten about the weird camp words. The ban on cursing while campers are around has led to the development of some creative adjectives over the years.

"Staff week starts in... a week? And then the campers will be here shortly after that. I can email you the contract and all that jazz. When can you start?"

I scroll through my calendar while I think. I can definitely be there in a week. Honestly, I'd kind of like to be there as soon as possible. "I can be there... maybe not tomorrow, but the next day, actually. Would that be okay? I'm happy to help out with preseason, setting things up, all that."

"That would be awesome if you can swing it. Counselors are staying in the Ladybugs cabins for staff week. You can just claim your spot early. Send me a text when you know for sure. I can't wait to see you! Any questions?"

I shake my head, then realize he can't see me. "No, I don't think so."

"Cool. Now, I have another person who's going to be coming up, too, I think. He's new to camp. If you both decide to join us for the summer, would it be cool if I give him your number? It would be great if he could benefit from your years of experience here."

"Yeah, sure. I'll let you know soon, okay?"

"Awesome sauce. Talk soon, Becca." With a beep, Brett ends the call.

I feel like a weight has been lifted from my shoulders. Everything about school can sit on the back burner for a while and I can just *relax*.

At some point, I'm going to have to talk to my parents, let them know that I'm repeating my second year. But I just can't bring myself to do it yet. We don't talk often, so they wouldn't find it strange that they haven't heard from me in a few days, or even a few weeks, which will buy me some time to accept it myself.

I'll deal with what I need to over the summer. I'm not going to stick my head completely in the sand. But I'll relax, focus on something completely different from medicine for a while. And when I come back to start second year again, I'll be ready to start fresh.

I nod to myself. This is a great idea.

Knowing that I'll be in the Ladybugs cabins as soon as I get there adds to my excitement. That's always been my favorite unit on camp. Not only is it where I spent three amazing summers as a counselor—Ladybug Cabin 2, all three years—but it's close enough to the lake that you can see it from the window and hear the gentle waves of Lake Winnipesaukee along the shore.

Plus, the Ladybugs are near the swing. Everyone on camp knows the swing, and almost everyone who's worked at camp has a memory involving it in some way.

It's a bench swing suspended between two pine trees with a clear view of the lake. My first memory of the swing was taking a cabin photo there when I was... nine? Ten? Four of the girls squished together onto the swing itself, while the rest of us stood around it. I think I still have that photo somewhere.

Then as a counselor, sitting there in the dark while the campers were falling asleep. I even had my first kiss on that swing when I was fourteen. It was as romantic as you'd imagine two fourteen-year-olds can be, and we were interrupted by the counselors almost as soon as his lips touched mine.

As the memories rush back, I know what my decision is. I think I knew what I was going to do as soon as I called Brett, honestly. Excited, I type out a text.

BRETT

> I'm in for the summer! I can't wait to get there.

> *thumbs up emoji* *sunglasses emoji* Yes! Can't wait to see you.

God, I can't wait. I find the camper packing list on the camp website, because that's always a good place to start, and head into my bedroom. In a flurry, I pull a large plastic bin out of the closet to use as luggage. It'll hold tons of stuff, and it'll double as an animal-safe storage bin to hold snacks after my clothes are put away.

I fold my t-shirts and shorts carefully as I stack them in the bin, then add some long pants, a couple sweatshirts, and a jacket. It's summer, but it gets cold, especially toward the end of the season.

I peek at the packing list to make sure I'm not missing anything. Hiking boots, check. I set them next to the bin along with a few water bottles and a travel mug. Two pairs of flip flops, one for the shower and one for the beach. Swimsuits and towels, check, check.

I'll need sunscreen and bug spray, but I can pick some up along the way.

By the time I load it up, the plastic bin is so heavy that it's tough but not impossible to carry to my car. I shove it in the backseat of my Jetta and wrestle with it for a few minutes before it fits. I'll need to pack up my toiletries in the morning and probably bring a laundry bag with some of my dirty clothes to wash up there, but we're mostly finished packing.

I slam the trunk with satisfaction. Day after tomorrow. Camp Winnie, here I come.

4

MILLER

There are about a million reasons to say no. My life is here in Philadelphia. My friends.

Plus, I have no fucking clue how to be a camp counselor. But I said I was looking for a challenge, right? And I'm not one to back down from a bet.

"Hell, yeah," I say. I hope my enthusiasm masks the slight panic in my voice.

Brett laughs. "Oh, man. This is going to be great. I can't wait to see you, and I have a feeling that this is going to be a shitshow. Staff week starts in a week. Can you be here by then?"

Let's see, between my schedule of doing nothing and doing more nothing... "Yeah, I can make it by then."

"Awesome. Text me your email and I'll send you some paperwork and stuff. I can't wait."

Something occurs to me. "So, uh... what do I bring?" I'm imagining shorts and flip flops, but I'm sure there's more to it than that.

Brett's chuckle doesn't do much to assuage the feeling that I'm in way over my head. "Oh boy. I'll send you the camper packing list. Just... multiply by a few weeks. There's a laundry room the staff can use, so factor that in."

"Okay. Thanks. This is going to be fucking amazing. I can't wait." Blind enthusiasm is better than fear. Always.

Right?

"I'm going to give your number to another counselor who's going to be coming up for the summer, a late addition to the staff just like you. She hasn't been here in a few years, but she's a veteran. She can give you all the information you need. And Miller?" Brett pauses, and I wait for him to give me some advice, some pep talk or something. "You can't swear at camp."

———

"What the fuck do you mean, you're going to go work as a camp counselor?" Blake stares at me in disbelief from where he's standing on the other side of my bedroom. The bed between us is covered with clothes and other things I think I'm supposed to be bringing on this little adventure.

I snatch the packing list out of his hands, giving him a pointed look. "Exactly what I said, dingbat. And I can't swear on camp property apparently, so we're going to practice using alternative words."

"The fuck does that mean?"

I roll my eyes. He knows exactly what it means. "Like, say *what the heck does that mean*, or maybe *what the hoppin' toads does that mean*? Words other than fuck. I think you and your PhD can come up with an extensive vocabulary."

Blake wanders into my kitchen without answering and comes back with a beer. "My PhD is in economics and game theory, you anus. I didn't exactly read the classics while I was in grad school."

"I think *anus* might be considered to be on the same spectrum as *asshole*."

"I'll work on it." He takes a swig of Yuengling with a scowl, one of his more frequent expressions.

I stare at the packing list, trying to make sense of everything.

T-shirts, short and long sleeved
   Shorts and long pants
   Sweatshirts

"What do you think I need a sweatshirt for? It's eighty-five degrees, for crying out loud." I hold the paper toward Blake.

He shrugs. "Maybe it's just in case? It can't hurt to bring one, right?"

I roll my eyes. I don't need a sweatshirt. I'll be fine. I keep working my way down the list.

Hiking boots
   Shower shoes
   Sneakers

Why are there so many damn shoes on this list? Just sneakers will be fine. If I survived the high school locker room after lacrosse practice without getting athlete's foot, I think I'll be okay in the camp bathrooms. And hiking boots? Who owns those? Again, sneakers will be fine. I mentally check off all footwear.

Flashlight

Unnecessary. What are we, going cave exploring?

> *Water bottles*
> > *Laundry bag*
> > *Raincoat*

I toss an umbrella into the duffel bag that's open on my bed. Do I even own a water bottle?

"Go get me a water from the fridge," I tell Blake.

"What's this for?" he asks as returns from the kitchen and hands it over.

I pack it into the duffel bag. "The list says water bottles."

Blake looks doubtful. "I don't think they meant Dasani."

I ignore him. I may not be an expert on summer camps, but it's not like Blake is, either.

The rest of the page contains an exhaustive list of toiletries. Toothpaste and toothbrush, got it. And bug spray and sunscreen. I can probably get a grocery delivery with those before I leave. Or just have it delivered to the cabin or tent or whatever we live in at camp. And maybe I'll even order a new pair of sandals for the shower, if I must.

Also, snacks. If I'm living in the woods for the next few weeks, I'm bringing Doritos with me. And maybe some Swiss Cake Rolls.

I pull on the zipper, which gets stuck halfway. I

drop the bag on the floor anyway. There are still some things left to pack, and not all of them will fit in the backpack I plan to bring, so I'll need to shove a few more things in the duffel. "All set. Want to see if Maddox and Cam can go out to the bar tonight? I'm leaving in the morning."

<hr>

"So what are you going to do? Like, teach kids knot tying or something?" Maddox leans back against the booth and tips his beer bottle to take a sip. His wife Holly is home tonight, apparently dealing with morning sickness. From Maddox's description, it does not sound pleasant.

"I don't know. Maybe. I could teach them poker, I guess. Or lacrosse." I shrug and lift my own drink to my lips.

I didn't look into whether we were allowed to have alcoholic beverages at camp, but given Brett's stance on swearing, I'm guessing it's also anti-alcohol.

Anti-good times, more like.

Cam pushes a hand through his hair as he sets his soda on the table. "Are you sure you know what you're doing? I mean, just think of how things went when I agreed to help Addie babysit. I'm just saying."

I snort with laughter as I pop a handful of peanuts into my mouth. "I don't think these kids are in diapers. God, I'd give anything to have video evidence of you changing that kid's diaper."

Cam frowns, probably remembering the little gremlin who peed on him. "I'd give anything to forget that. The whole idea of kids freaks me out, honestly. I can't believe you're about to voluntarily take this on."

I'm still on the fence about whether this is a good idea at all. Fortunately, Blake saves me from having to respond.

"Well, let's wish the fucker luck. Better him than us, right? Miller, we'll miss you, and we expect frequent updates. Got it?" He raises his beer in a toast. "Cheers."

We clink our drinks together. I'll need all the luck I can get.

It's only 10 p.m. when I get back to my apartment. I never go to bed before midnight, but I'm going to be getting up early to beat traffic, so it might make sense to tuck in sooner tonight.

I look at the duffel bag on my floor, its zipper gaping open and the Dasani bottle sticking out the top. Maybe I could use some advice, honestly. I pull my phone out and add the number Brett sent me to my contacts, then send a text.

BECCA CAMP PERSON

Hey, Yoda. This is Miller. Brett gave me your number. I'm coming up to camp soon, and I hear you know all the things. Teach me your ways.

Um. Hi.

No ways to teach me?

Not particularly.

Well, aren't you just a ray of sunshine.

Do you have a question for me?

What color underwear are you wearing?

There's no answer. Geez. It was a joke, woman.

Mine are plaid, for the record. Real question is just about packing. What do I really need to bring?

Bring what's on the list.

That's surprisingly unhelpful. I wonder what wisdom Brett thought this delightful creature could impart. I can't wait to meet her now, see what she's like in real life.

The picture I have in my head is less than flattering, but you never know.

I plug in my phone and set it on the nightstand next to my favorite candle. It smells like cherries and citrus and was a Christmas gift from my mother last year.

I don't usually question my mom because her ideas usually turn out to be good ones. Like this candle, for example. Cherry and citrus sounded like a terrible combination, but it works somehow. This whole camp thing, however, might be a disaster waiting to happen, even if it was her idea.

What the fuck do I know about being a camp counselor? I'm way too old for this. I have no idea what I'm doing. This is going to be a hot mess.

When the sun finally peeks through my blinds, I'm pretty sure I'm making a huge mistake, but there's one thing I'm not doing, and that's being a quitter. I don't back down from things, which, to be honest, has caused me some problems in the past.

But the point is that I've never quit something important, and I'm not going to start now.

And Brett said he was short on counselors. He needs me, which means these campers need me. And I can get through anything if it helps people.

I toss my toothpaste, toothbrush, and a couple of razors into my backpack along with a phone charger before I zip it up and sling it over my shoulder. Blake is going to check in on my place while I'm gone, since I'm not sure exactly how long it will be. I'm planning to stick it out for the whole summer, but if things really go downhill, I could be back sooner.

I toss the duffel bag into the backseat of my Wrangler and set the backpack on the front passenger seat. I love this car. Maybe it's a little much for city driving, but now that I'm doing this camp thing, it seems like it lends me a little credibility, like maybe I've eaten some granola in my day or scaled a mountain or two. Maybe even shit in the woods.

None of those are actually true, but there's a first time for everything.

I call my mother as I pull onto the highway, loving the hands-free function.

"Hi, honey. How's it going?" she answers on the first ring.

I flick on my turn signal and shift lanes. "Good. I'm headed up to camp."

Her laughter fills the car. "I still can't believe you took him up on it, Miller. I'm sure it'll be good for you, and God knows they're lucky to have you. But if I could be a fly on the wall!"

Mom's been using that expression since we were little. Usually, it means she thinks we're about to do something that she imagines will become a shitshow. I guess her and Brett have that in common.

"Hey, have some faith in me. I'll be a good counselor."

"Oh, I know you will. I have no doubt. I'm more worried about the campers who have to deal with you. Does Brett know you still love to pull pranks?"

I grin, thinking of all the things I'd love to pull this summer. "Nope."

Mom laughs again. "Oh, heaven help that poor man. He has no idea what he's getting with you, does he?"

"Nope," I say again. It's true. One of my favorite hobbies is planning elaborate pranks. My mom has been the target of many of my jokes over the years, but who do you think I learned it from?

She snickers into the phone. "What are you thinking of doing first? Want me to call him and tell him you broke both your arms and you need someone to help you for the next few weeks?"

I roll my eyes. "Nah. He won't buy it. I was thinking more like putting his boxers up the flagpole some morning. Something classic and harmless. I think the kids would get a kick out of that one, too."

The underwear-up-the-flagpole prank will be a solid choice for the first week.

Maybe the second week I can get someone to help me steal all the forks from the dining hall or something. Benign but annoying.

"Hmm. Low-level, but yes, classic. I like it. Well, if you need help, let me know. I'm also here if the kids need to be threatened. Remember how I used to call Santa and the Tooth Fairy when you were little, and they'd threaten you into behaving?"

Yeah, I remember. It was terrifying to think that I'd pissed off Santa, until I got old enough to read and realized the number she'd dialed was for Uncle Jack.

"I'll let you know. Anyway, just wanted to let you know I'm headed out. Tell Jordan I say hi and I'll call him Tuesday, okay?" My weekly call with my brother is set in stone, not to be missed by either of us. He has Down Syndrome, so he's mentally younger than his twenty-two years, and routines are important to him.

I hit my brakes as traffic slows in front of me.

"Will do. Love you!" Mom chimes before ending the call.

I do my best to focus on the road. As I get further outside the city, the traffic begins to thin, and my mind wanders to all the things I read in the camp handbook that Brett helpfully forwarded me, along with the ridiculous packing list.

I make a mental note to remember to pick up bug

spray on my way. That's one of the few things that seemed actually necessary on that list.

According to the handbook online, we'll be separated into cabin groups by camper age—the groups are named almost too cutely, things like Ladybugs and Dragonflies—and then the counselors are also assigned to a department for activity times. Arts and Crafts, Sports, Swimming, Boating... what was the last one?

I tap my fingers on the steering wheel, trying to remember.

Anyway, I'm hoping for Sports. I was a decent lacrosse player back in the day, but I've also dabbled in soccer, tennis, and football. I even tried basketball for a few years in high school, since the coach saw me in the hall and assumed the tall kid would be a good center.

It turned out that my height, six-foot-three back then before I put on another inch in college, wasn't quite enough to overcome my inability to shoot.

The drive takes a solid seven hours, even though I shaved off the extra sixteen minutes my GPS estimated at the start. It's almost 3:30 when I finally turn onto the dirt road.

Well, I wanted a change, right? Looks like this is it.

A smile crosses over my face as I see the sign, welcoming me to my next adventure.

WELCOME TO CAMP WINNIE.

5

REBECCA

The mist rises off the lake as the sun peeks over the mountains. The slight chill in the air at this hour sends a shiver through me as I curl further underneath the blanket that I've wrapped around myself and lean against the corner of the swing, holding my coffee mug just below my chin.

I take a long breath through my nose. The early morning dew mixes with the deep aroma of the coffee. *This* is peace.

Most of the staff should be arriving today. The last several days it's been a skeleton crew holding things together, the few of us who couldn't wait and volunteered to help set things up. We've spent our time cleaning cabins, hauling the docks back to the lake, and dragging canoes and sailboats out of their winter storage.

I'm already feeling more at ease. This is what I've needed—a chance to do something useful, where there's a clearly defined job to do and outcome needed.

No studying everything that may or may not be on some exam, or that I may or may not need in the future. No guessing at what professors are thinking when they ask you some vague question.

It's blessedly simple. The docks are here. Move them there. You're done when they're all in the new spot.

There's a part of me that's nervous for the rest of the staff to get here, which is also part of the reason I'm up so early. At this hour, everyone else is sleeping, other than the two girls who get up to go jogging every morning.

And aside from them, it's just me right now. Me and the swing and the lake.

Adding to my nerves is the fact that most of the staff that will be working as counselors aren't even here yet, which means I haven't even met the people I'll be spending the most time with.

Meeting new people makes me nervous. I'm always so focused on making sure they like me that I think I end up being weird.

Actually, I know I come across weird. I review the interactions in my head in excruciating detail after the fact, which makes me even weirder. I wish I had a way to just turn my brain off sometimes.

I think that's why I love camp. Because when I'm in a defined role, it's easier somehow. It's not this nebulous, poorly defined social interaction like most things in life.

It's why I was looking forward to starting third year, actually. Beyond the fact that it's that much closer to what I want to do with my life, when you're on your clinical rotations, you have a particular role to fill, so there's less gray area to be weird.

I frown to myself. I might have been stranger than usual over those text messages. What was the guy's name? Miller? Odd name, if you ask me.

But to be fair, he wasn't the most normal with his texting, either. My underwear color? Seriously?

The steam from the coffee hits my face as I take a sip. I hope I can avoid him for the summer. I know I wasn't the most open and friendly over our short text conversations—give me a pass here, I was kind of in a mood—but he came across... cocky, almost. There was something about him that grated on me, even with just a few messages. My money is on him being an obnoxious prick in real life, too.

I take another sip of the bitter brew. I love coffee all year round, but there's something extra special about the chilly mornings before a hot day. Like Mother Nature throwing us a little something out of the ordinary, just for those of us who are willing to get up early to experience it.

I stare at the shimmering lake while I finish the coffee, and for a few extra minutes while I hold the empty mug.

With a resigned sigh, I force myself to get up and walk back to the dining hall to return the mug. I'm the only one here, too, in the rustic cabin-like building where all the meals are served and where coffee and hot chocolate are available throughout the day. I set the mug in the bin with the dirty dishes and turn to head back to my cabin.

The remaining mugs stacked along one wall catch my attention. The camp mugs have changed since I was last here, although some, like the one I grabbed for my coffee this morning, are still the old style. They all used to be the standard camp logo, printed in a different color from the ones available for purchase.

The newer ones still have the camp logo, but with **STEALING IS WRONG** printed in bold lettering beneath it. Apparently, too many counselors didn't return the mugs.

The thought makes me smile slightly. I have one at my apartment that I appropriated during my first summer on staff, actually. It's one of my most prized possessions. The added text actually would make it kind of funny if people still stole them. I wonder if the addition has helped or made the mug stealing worse.

I walk back to my cabin, waving at Andrea as she and Bridget pass me, finishing up their morning run, their identical blonde ponytails swaying behind them. They're in charge of the Swimming and Arts departments this year; I remember them both from when I was a counselor and they were counselors-in-training.

It makes me wonder how many more of my direct supervisors for the summer are people that I was once in charge of.

The two of them reach the cabin before me—so far, there are only six girls who've arrived, and we're all staying in Cabin One—and when I pull the door open, they're both wrapped in towels, headed for the communal bathroom.

"You guys have a good run?" I ask, holding the door for them.

Andrea nods, wiping sweat off her freckled nose with one hand. "It was good. Perfect temperature for a few miles."

"You should come with us one of these days,"

Bridget adds as the two of them head down the cabin steps.

"Maybe one of these days!" I haven't run in forever. Like, since third grade when we ran a mile in our jeans during gym class. I wonder if it would help my stress levels. It could go either way, actually. The running might help, but the proximity to people I don't know well could make it worse.

Then again, it's hard to get to know people well when you don't want to hang around with strangers. It's a vicious cycle.

I tiptoe into the cabin, doing my best not to wake the three girls that are still sleeping in their bunks. Maybe this summer I can push those fears aside and make a few new friends. You know what? That's my goal. That's what I'll do.

It'll keep me occupied enough to keep my mind off school.

"Winnie-winnie-hoo-ha! Winnie-winnie-hoo-ha! Rah, rah, rah!" I clap my hands along with the rest of the staff as we yell the camp cheer again, all of us packed into the seats of Meredith Hall—or M-hall, as we all call it.

The large building, named after the closest town, serves as an auditorium, dance hall, and general indoor space during rainstorms. It's practically identical to the dining hall other than the two-story design, and while the dining hall is filled with tables and chairs, this one's space is taken up by rows of benches. Right now, the staff take up about three rows, but when the campers come, it'll be so full that some of the youngest will end up sitting on the floor.

When I was a camper, I assumed the rabid enthusiasm the counselors displayed was just for our benefit, that things were much more muted when it was just staff. I was floored when I showed up for my first summer on staff and realized that nope, all the counselors were just as excited as I was.

Looks like things haven't changed where that's concerned, which is comforting.

One by one, staff members have arrived today, settling into the four Ladybugs cabins we'll be staying in for staff week; two for the boys, two for the girls.

The non-counselor staff that were in my cabin up until this morning—Andrea and Bridget included—have moved into their summer accommodations, spread across camp in little cabins and tents tucked out of the way. It's just the counselors in this unit now.

There are a few familiar faces. I cringed when two

of my former campers came up and gave me hugs. Not that I have anything against hugging, or against them, of course. It's more that... I should be further along in my life, or something. This is their turn to be counselors, but I'm still here.

But this is just to relax. Remember? I'm here to reset and avoid reality. It doesn't matter that I have a good four years on most of these kids.

"This is so much fun!" The brunette next to me hooks her arm into mine, giving me a broad smile. "Isn't this a blast?"

I smile back at her. What was her name?

As if reading my mind, she says, "I'm Vivien. You're Becca, right?"

I'm about to correct her—it's REbecca—but I always went by Becca at camp. And I'm here to be anyone *but* the Rebecca who failed her classes. New scenery, new me. "Yep! Becca. Nice to meet you."

"First time on staff?" she asks. Her arm is still entwined with mine, and it appears she has no intention of letting it go. Strangely, I don't mind it.

I shake my head. "No, I was actually on staff a few years ago. I've been away for a few summers, but I just missed it so much, you know?" I explain.

She nods. "Oh, I get it, girl. Last summer was my first on staff. It was so random, since I never went to camp as a kid, but my mom told me to try it out. A friend of a friend's kid was obsessed with this place or something. Long story short, I fell in love."

We both join in for the "Rah, rah, rah!" chorus.

"With the camp," she clarifies as the yelling dies down.

I flash her a smile. "I know exactly what you mean," I say. "I feel like sometimes I'd fantasize about this place. It's such a blessing that I was able to figure out a way to come back for this summer."

"What do you do outside of here?" she asks.

I knew this question was coming, but it still sends my insides plummeting. "I—"

Fortunately, I'm saved from answering when the next cheer starts up. *Saved by the crazy chanting.*

We sit through Brett's welcome and brief reminder of key rules—no smoking, no drinking, no swearing—and then he tells us to split into groups of six for an icebreaker.

"Come on!" Vivien says eagerly, tugging me with the arm that's still looped around mine.

I follow her as she grabs another person, then drags both of us along to approach two other people who are standing together, looking lost.

"Want to be part of our group?" Vivien asks, solidifying her stance as the extroverted group leader.

They agree, and we take a seat in a circle on the floor. Besides Vivien and me, there are two other girls and one guy, all of us dressed in the standard camp attire of shorts, worn t-shirts, and sneakers. Vivien's shirt is emblazoned with a University of Maine logo, making me wonder if that's where she went to school or if she just knows someone who did.

"The game is Two Truths and a Lie," Brett says from the stage. "Go around the circle and each person gets a turn to say their name, then tell two true things about themselves and one lie. The rest of the group has to figure out which is the lie. Ready? Go!"

I look around our little group. What should my lie be?

This is a super common game we play here, and it's almost always the least exciting thing that's the lie. I'm terrible at lying, so I'm pretty bad at it no matter what lie I come up with.

"Anyone want to go first?" Vivien asks, looking around the group.

No one volunteers.

"Okay, I'll go. I'm Vivien, of course, and let's see..." She thinks for a minute, tapping her finger against her nose. "Okay. I have four brothers, I'm in grad school studying chemistry, and I played soccer in high school."

Hmm. Any of those could easily be true. It's either the brother thing—maybe she has three brothers, or a mix of brothers and sisters—or she played a different sport. I'm hoping the grad school thing is true, because that means she's on the older side for a counselor, like me.

"You didn't play soccer in high school," I guess.

She smiles.

"You don't have four brothers." The blonde girl she tugged into our circle rubs her palm against her knee as she thinks.

The other two take their guesses. Two votes for soccer, two for brothers.

Vivien's smile grows wider. "I do have four brothers. James, Kyle, Ben, and Tyler. And I played midfield on the high school soccer team."

"So, you're not in grad school?" I ask, deflating a little that she may not be as old as me.

She shakes her head and winks. "I am. But I'm studying biology, not chemistry." Vivien gently elbows me. "You go next."

"Okay. I'm Becca." The nickname is feeling more comfortable now that I'm in camp mode. "How about... I'm originally from upstate New York. I love crossword puzzles, and I'm an only child." I look around the circle, trying not to laugh. It's so hard to lie.

"You're not an only child?"

"I think you're not from upstate New York."

"Hmm. The crossword puzzle one is too easy. I think that's the lie."

I let a few giggles slip out. Only one person—a guy across from me, whose name I haven't gotten yet—correctly guesses that I'm not from upstate.

"I'm from New York City originally. I live in upstate New York now, though," I say. I'm not sure how long I'll live there, to be honest. There's nothing for me there other than school.

We move on to the girl next to me—the blonde one, who introduces herself as Lillian—and I learn that she just finished her freshman year of college, is on the downhill ski team, and this is her first summer on staff.

I'm not sure I'll be able to remember all of the facts people shared, but I'm doing pretty well with names as we wrap up. Drew, Lillian, Vivien, and Mary. Got it. They all seem like fun.

And so far, none of them turn out to be an obnoxious asshole named Miller.

6

MILLER

Holy shit.

I know I'm not supposed to swear on camp property, but that was in my head, okay?

And it deserves a *holy shit*.

Because I've barely made it onto camp, just parking my Jeep next to the cabin I'll be staying in so I can unpack before I move my car to the staff parking lot, and I'm already in love.

Seriously.

The most drop-dead gorgeous girl is sitting on the steps of the cabin across the way, her brown hair, so dark it's almost black, shining in the late afternoon sun as it falls around her shoulders. Her skin is tanned, a shade darker than I'd expect from the sun this early in the season.

Her features are defined, almost sharp, but from what I can see, her body is the perfect set of curves and softness.

Exactly my type.

And while a lot of the counselors that are milling around look like they could be campers—okay, I get it, I'm old—she's not as young as they are. Maybe mid-twenties or so.

She doesn't look my way as I head into my designated cabin. I'm told these will be the girls' cabins once the campers get here, but we all get to stay together this week to get to know one another or something. I drop my sleeping bag, backpack and duffel bag on one of the bottom bunks.

"Hey. I'm Dave."

I look across the cabin to see a guy with short dark hair lounging on one of the other beds. "Hey. Miller. You working as a counselor this summer, too?" I ask.

He nods and gets to his feet. "Yeah. Third year here. This your first time?"

I chuckle. "That obvious, huh? I have no fu—no stinking clue what I'm doing."

Dave tosses his head back in a laugh, and I like him already. "You got the memo on swearing, huh?"

I nod sheepishly. "It's going to take some getting used to. I tend to drop f-bombs like they're candy. It's my mom's fault."

"Well, when it's just staff in the cabins, you can say whatever you want. Most of us try to get into camp mode so we don't swear when the campers get here, but no one cares if you swear this week. Maybe Brett, but don't piss him off." Dave grips the back of his neck with his hand. "I made that mistake last year. He's scary as shit when he's mad."

I can't exactly picture Brett as scary. "Well, I went to high school with Brett, so he doesn't scare me. I'll try to play by the rules, though." I unzip my duffel and dig through it, realizing as I do that I never picked up that bug spray. Darn it. "Speaking of rules, what are the guidelines for hooking up with other staff members? Someone may have caught my eye on the way in."

"Just make sure the campers don't know. That's the big thing here. Campers are here for fun and to make friends and learn new things and all that shit. They're not here to hang on counselor gossip and see who is hooking up with who. But after lights out and on your days off, you're free to do whatever. Or whoever."

I definitely like this guy. "Nice. Want to show me

around this place?"

<hr>

The girl is gone when we head out of our cabin, but I make a mental note to point her out to Dave the next time I see her. He seems to know the ropes around here, no pun intended, but he did walk me by the ropes course and tell me all about that. So I'm sure he can give me the dirt on any of the other staff members.

This place really is gorgeous. It's a huge change from Philadelphia, in a good way. The air smells like pine and something sweet, and there's all this nature everywhere—trees and a lake and squirrels and stuff. It's gorgeous.

The lake and trees, that is. Not the squirrels.

I'll be honest here: I'm not exactly an animal person. I mean, I like pets. But not weird little rats with fluffy tails. Like, what are those tails *for*? They seem like they're just for looks, and I for one think it's a bit extravagant. That's all.

I look over the playing field appreciatively as we walk by the Sports department. The grass is cut short and even, and a large, green-painted shed sits to one side, where I imagine all the equipment is stored.

There's a baseball diamond in one corner, tennis courts off to the side.

I take a deep breath through my nose, smelling the fresh-cut grass, and it's almost like I'm back in high school getting ready for lacrosse practice.

"This looks awesome," I say, motioning to the field with one hand.

Dave nods. "The Sports department is amazing. It's my favorite, but I'm biased. I've worked in this department the last few summers." He glances over at me. "What department are you going to be in?"

Huh. I didn't think to ask. "I don't know, actually. Brett offered me the job last-minute, so I guess it's wherever he needs me. Hoping for Sports, though."

Dave gives me a fist bump, and we continue on our tour, meandering past the field to find a large red building with some fenced areas around it. I take a step back when a goat comes trotting right up to the fence.

"Don't like goats?" Dave asks as he looks at my face.

"What's to like? They seem evil. Look at those horns. Why are there goats, anyway?"

Dave laughs. "This is the nature barn. It changes every year but this year I think they have a goat and maybe a sheep or two. There are usually some rabbits. I heard something about an alpaca this year and maybe a pony. So, not a nature lover?"

I make a face. "Let's just say I'd rather do Arts and Crafts than Nature."

A few hours after I arrive, we assemble in M-Hall, which apparently stands for something, but I've already forgotten what.

I peruse the other staff members as we grab our seats. They all look way, way younger than I am. But they're mostly welcoming, and all of them so far have laughed at my jokes, so I've got that going for me.

Brett goes through some introductions after a camp cheer that was frankly disturbing. Something about a hoo-ha. And it was yelled at a volume that I'm sure people across Lake Winnipesaukee could hear. My ears are still ringing when we split into groups to play something called Two Truths and a Lie.

I look around for the girl from earlier, hoping to finagle my way into her group, but she's been dragged into a group of people by another counselor.

I wind up sitting in a circle on the floor, criss-cross-applesauce like we're in preschool. Besides me, my group consists of Dave, who in the past few hours has solidified his position as a new best friend; two other guys that are sharing our cabin; and two girls, both of whom look at least a decade younger than me.

We go around the circle, sharing our two true facts and one lie about ourselves, and I do my best to remember names. There's Dave, Jackson... and others. I'll remember them eventually. Probably.

I end up going last, which means I had more than enough time to plan my facts.

"I'm Miller, first timer here at Camp Winnie. Three things about me... well, I play poker professionally. I've gone sky diving twice. And I have pictures of Brett from when he was in high school. And stories." I end with a smirk.

The group appears intrigued but skeptical.

"No way does he have pictures of Brett."

"He looks like he's Brett's age. Sorry, man. But it might be true."

I shrug off the reference to my age. I don't really care how old they think I am, honestly. But I'm loving the debate that's going on, with me firmly at the center of it.

"Two minutes," Brett announces from the stage.

"Place your bets, ladies and gentlemen," I say, waggling my eyebrows suggestively.

There are two votes for poker, one for skydiving,

and two for Brett. The nice thing about a poker face is that you can lie your ass off and no one can tell.

"It's skydiving, actually," I confess. "I've gone three times, not twice. And ask me later about those pictures of Brett."

When we head back to our seats—yes, I groaned a little trying to get up off the floor—the rest of the group follows me and sits close by. I grin to myself.

First friends made. Check.

This time when I look around for the hot girl, I catch her eye. I give her a wink, and she blushes slightly and looks away.

Game on.

I'm seated near the back of the room, so when we're excused to head to dinner, I'm the first to the door. I wait patiently for the girl to walk by me and fall into step beside her.

"Hey," I say.

She offers a polite smile. "Hi."

"I'm Miller."

Her expression hardens, completely confusing me. How the fuck did I manage to piss her off with just my name?

Her lips are set in a thin line. "Becca."

Ah. She's Becca. The one who hates me already. And while I was already planning to get to know her just based on my physical attraction to her, the fact that she hates me has my competitive spirit firing.

I can get anyone to like me. Just watch.

"Nice to meet you, Becca. This is my first year on staff. Trying to get to know some people, although I think I've corresponded with you before." I grin, hoping to soften her up.

"Nice to meet you." She does not soften.

If anything, she looks like she hates me even more, which is not something I'm accustomed to.

"What do you do the rest of the year? Are you in school?" I go for small talk, which seems safe. The school thing seems like a safe assumption. Most people who are out of school don't get their summers free to do things like work at camp.

But instead of answering what seems like an easy question, she somehow seems to get even stiffer, if that's possible. "I need to catch up to Vivien. It was nice meeting you."

I don't even have time to respond before she quickens her steps to join the dark-haired girl she was sitting with earlier. Vivien, apparently.

I shake off the clear rejection as Jackson falls into step next to me.

A challenge. This is going to be fun. And the thrill of the chase makes me want to win her over even more.

"You know Becca?" Jackson says, raising a brow.

"Getting to know her," I answer honestly. Maybe Jackson has some information on the new object of my affection. "Was she on staff last year?"

He shakes his head. "I remember her from a few years ago when I was a CIT. Counselor-in-training," he clarifies at my confused expression. "But she hasn't been here for a few years. I'm glad she's back."

Me, too.

I follow the crowd to the dining hall, which is set back a little ways from the beach. From the windows, you can see the lake. I wonder if you get a sunset from this direction, or if it's sunrise. Maybe I'll get up early and find out tomorrow.

The tables quickly fill up, and I spot Becca sitting with a table of girls. There's one chair left. I practically push a guy out of the way to get there before anyone else can claim it.

"This seat taken?" I ask, sliding into it before they answer.

Becca's lips purse slightly, but she doesn't say anything as I settle in. She's the one to fetch the tray of food from the kitchen, and we all share family-style as I learn the other girls' names.

"So are meals like this when the campers are here, too?" I ask Vivien, reaching for a dinner roll.

She nods. "Lunch and dinner, anyway. Breakfast is a buffet. But the unit heads will assign counselors to tables to make sure there's always at least one of us at the table, and we're the ones who get the food. Campers can go up for refills but not the first big trip." She frowns slightly. "Actually, what unit are you going to be in? It's really only the Bumblebees and Dragonflies who are allowed to get food from the kitchen. The younger kids aren't allowed."

Something else I hadn't thought to ask. "Not sure. Wherever Brett needs me. How about you?"

Vivien smiles. "Oh, I'm with the Ladybugs. Best unit at camp, if you ask me."

"Those are the younger kids?"

She nods. "The younger girls. The younger boys are the Fireflies."

This sparks a little recognition. Dave and I walked past a set of cabins that had a Fireflies sign, not too far from where we're staying in the Ladybugs cabins.

Seriously, who named these units? An entomologist?

"Well, I'm not sure yet where I'll be. I was kind of a

last-minute addition to the staff, so I'll be filling in wherever Brett needs me."

Vivien forks a bite of breaded chicken into her mouth and chews thoughtfully. "Nice. Well, maybe I'll see you over by the Arts department. That's where I am this summer. Becca, what about you?"

Becca takes a sip of water and swallows before answering. "I'm also last-minute but I was always a Boating counselor. Up to Brett, though."

"What's up to me?" a deep voice says.

I look over my shoulder to see Brett standing beside the table. "Hey! How are you, man?" I stand from my chair and offer my hand.

"Good to see you, Miller." He clasps it, giving it a shake.

Vivien clears her throat. "Miller and Becca are wondering what units and departments you put them in. The rest of us already know our assignments, other than cabins."

Brett points to Becca. "Ladybugs and Boating, your usual."

A smile immediately spreads across her face. Fuck, she really is gorgeous. I cross my fingers that I get an assignment that puts me somewhere I can spend time with her.

I'd do almost anything to get her to smile like that at me.

"And Miller, Fireflies."

The younger kids? Huh. I hope they don't wet the bed.

"And I need you in the Nature department," Brett finishes.

"The goats?" The words pop out before I can come up with a more coherent response. Fuck, I hate those things.

Vivien snickers at the expression on my face. "You don't like goats?"

Brett folds his arms over his chest. Yeah, I can see how he'd come across as terrifying to a kid. Or to anyone who didn't know him back when he was struggling to grow a mustache in junior high.

I don't want to get a reputation as someone who isn't a team player. I'm here to help Brett out, so I swallow a sip of water while I pull myself together. "Uh, goats are cool. Just surprised."

Goats are *not* cool. Goats shit on things and eat things and, I believe, head-butt things.

I am not looking forward to this. Paddling a fucking canoe around the lake would be better than this.

"Good. Have a good night, you guys. See you

bright and early for first aid training." Brett moves on to the next table.

And my mind is hard at work figuring out how I can spend more time with Becca.

Because if she gets to know me, she'll love me. Everyone does.

But seriously, goats?

7

BECCA

Why won't he hold still?

Miller planted himself next to me on the bench in M-Hall at the start of the lecture on safety rules, despite my glare, and he won't stop moving. He's bouncing his leg, messing with his blond hair that frankly looks like it needs to be cut, doing some weird thing with his hands.

Seriously, just sit still and pay attention.

Yes, I had a preconceived notion of what Mr. *What-color-underpants-are-you-wearing* would be like.

And lo and behold, looks like I was right.

His easygoing demeanor—*too* easygoing, if you ask me—and the unkempt blond hair are right in line with what I expected, which was a guy who didn't take anything seriously.

I may not have pictured the piercing blue eyes, or the way his eyes crinkle at the corners in the most adorable way when he smiles, or the way my body would react to his broad form, but those are hormones. I'm an educated woman. I don't fall for hormones. I make decisions logically, and I'm picky about who I spend time with.

Miller is not the kind of person that I want to be associated with.

I do my best to focus on the speaker. I've heard this talk so many times I could practically give it myself. Camper safety is of the utmost importance. Parents are trusting us with their most prized possessions. It's important. It's the same from year to year, so it may not be the most riveting, but I can sit still and pay attention. Unlike *some* people.

I glare at Miller again to get him to stop fidgeting, but he just gives me a wink.

Oh, no, sir. Do not implicate me in your shenanigans. And why are you latching on to me anyway?

Maybe when we have a break, I can find somewhere else to sit. Camp is where I know what I'm doing. I'm a damn good camp counselor, no matter what else in life I've failed at. I don't need to look like I'm not taking this seriously.

"Okay, we'll take a five-minute break and then start first aid," Brett says from the podium.

I stand up so fast Miller's going to think my seat is on fire. I beeline to Vivien, who is sitting in the back row.

"Want to go to the bathroom?" I blurt out. It was the first place I could think of where I know for sure Miller won't follow us.

Vivien and Lillian join me in the bathroom, which is more or less pristine despite the twenty or so girls using it this week. Next week at this time, we'll be fixing clogged toilets on a daily basis.

"How's Miller?" Vivien asks from the stall next to me.

"Ooh, he's hot," Lillian adds. "I love tall guys. And he's *tall*. What do you think? Six-three? Four?"

I roll my eyes, even though they can't see me. "He's annoying is what he is."

Vivien laughs. "How? We're in a lecture. It's not like he's talking to you."

I finish in the stall, then join Lillian at the sinks to wash my hands. "He won't sit still. It's distracting." I have no opinion on his hotness.

Is he attractive? Empirically, yes. But I'm not in the

market for a relationship or even a hookup. I'm here for the camp experience: the woods, the campfires, teaching kids how to sail and to appreciate nature. All the things I got from my time as a camper.

Vivien flushes and joins us at the sinks. "Well, I think he's hot. You should hit that, Becca."

I roll my eyes again, so they can appreciate just how interested I am in that option. If it even were an option, which is unlikely. Guys like him don't go for girls like me.

We link arms as we walk back to M-Hall, and I take a moment to appreciate just how amazing this place is. Not just the scent of pine trees, the soft dirt below our feet, and the breeze off the lake. It's more than that. It's what I mean when I say the camp experience: the fast friendships that go deep and last long.

I sit in the back with Vivien and Lillian this time, ignoring my natural urge to sit in the front of the class. I scan the benches for Miller but don't see him until he slides onto the bench next to me.

I bristle. How does he *do* that? Just appear out of nowhere like some ninja?

"Hey," he says, sliding a little too close to me.

I'm not entirely sure what he's doing. Why does he want to sit with me at all? He's already making friends even faster than I am. Everyone on staff seems to be enamored with Miller, especially after last night's antics, where he convinced everyone to play flip cup using protein shakes.

I did not participate, in case you're wondering, but virtually everyone else did. And it turns out that protein shakes, especially those designed as meal replacements, are not meant to be chugged. Shocking, I know.

But he established himself as the life of the party, the big man on campus. Or the big man on camp, as it were. So, any number of people are probably clamoring to sit with him, which makes me wonder, again, why he keeps sitting with me.

"Hi," I finally force out. I'm not sure what else to add.

Hell, I'm not even sure there's an actual conversation to be had here, even if I did want to get to know him. He's like my polar opposite: outgoing, confident, funny. I tend to come out of my shell more here than anywhere else, but it usually takes the campers arriving for me to really get in the groove.

"Excited to learn some first aid?"

I shrug, and I'm saved from having to elaborate by Brett raising his hand at the front of the room to get our attention.

"Okay, this is John Warner, your first aid instructor. I expect you to give him the same respect you give me. More, probably. I'll see you all at lunch." Brett steps to the side, and a man who looks like he's ready to hike the Appalachian Trail, hiking boots and all, takes his place.

John goes through the basics of applying pressure to bleeding wounds and how to splint, then tells us to pair up to practice splinting and making a sling.

I turn to Vivien, but she's already heading off with Lillian. Traitor. I look around desperately for someone else, anyone else, but everyone is pairing up.

The voice I was hoping to avoid speaks up from behind me. "Looks like it's you and me."

I turn around reluctantly. Miller has a smirk on his face, like he planned this.

He probably did fucking plan this. I'm trying to be chill, but I feel like he's not going to take any of this seriously.

"Come on. Let's go over here and I'll splint your arm." He tugs on my arm.

I have no choice, so I follow him to a spot on the grass. "I'll splint first. Give me your arm."

Miller obediently holds his arm out, and I take one of the bandanas that John is passing out and fashion it into a sling. I slide Miller's arm into it while he watches me with a smile on his face.

"Your arm is too big for this sling," I say when I can't fit it into the small bandana. I've never had trouble with first aid before. Why does he have such big biceps?

And it's not hot. It's not. I don't care about his stupid arms.

I grab a second bandana from the pile and adjust my sling until his stupidly large arm fits, then tie it around his neck. "There. You're splinted."

"I feel better already," Miller says, grinning wider. It's almost charming. I'm sure that's the intent, at least. But he's nowhere near winning me over. If anything, I'm more annoyed with him than I was earlier today, when he was busy fidgeting in his seat. "What about you? Which arm is broken?"

I offer him my left arm.

He pulls the sling I fashioned off and unties the knots, then looks at the two bandanas, frowning. "Hmm. I think maybe it'll work better if I..."

I should look away, but somehow, I can't avert my gaze as he grasps the hem of his grey University of Scranton t-shirt and pulls it up and over his head, revealing toned pecs and abs that no one has a right to have other than models and maybe movie stars.

Jesus. What does this guy do for a living? Work out all day? Unbidden, the image of a shirtless Miller covered in a sheen of sweat and lifting weights comes to mind.

He clears his throat, and I shake away those thoughts and meet his eyes. The expression on his face makes it clear that yeah, he knows exactly how good he looks. It's cocky as hell, and it pisses me off even more.

"Was that really necessary?" I ask, my words coming out almost in a hiss.

My anger doesn't seem to faze him. "You have a broken arm. I'm just using what I have at my disposal to help you out," he drawls as he ties a knot in one corner of the shirt, turning it into an actually very functional sling. Dammit.

He wraps the material around my arm. I refuse to think about how soft the shirt is or how good he smells. Is that his deodorant? Or does he just smell all manly like this by himself?

No. No, I don't care. Because Miller is using this class as an opportunity to flash his pecs instead of actually learning. I just need to get through this part so I can find another partner for the rest of the day.

"Nice job. Good use of resources," the instructor says as Miller adjusts the sling.

I hold my breath until Miller takes a step back.

"Thanks. Figured it makes sense to practice with what we might have available in an actual emergency, you know?" Miller flashes that smile again, the one that I can tell gets him out of every possible consequence, and the one that's starting to get on my nerves. "Plus, I got to show off the goods to Becca, so win-win."

He winks at the instructor, and *no he did not.*

John laughs as he moves to the next group. Why does everyone fucking love this guy?

My face heats as I pull the sling off me and shove Miller's shirt back at him.

"Here. Put this on."

Miller tucks the shirt in the back pocket of his jeans. "Thanks. It's getting hot out, don't you think? You're looking a little flushed yourself."

I'm going to murder him. How did he get this job anyway?

We make it through one more exercise, practicing a pressure dressing to stop bleeding, before we break for lunch.

I catch up with Vivien and Lillian as we all head toward the dining hall. "How could you leave me with him?" I ask under my breath, peering over my shoulder.

Lillian laughs. "Aw, it was cute. And man, those abs. I want to lick them."

Vivien nods. "Same. Just wait till lifeguard training this afternoon. There's a guaranteed shirtless Miller."

If there's anything the last day and a half has taught me, it's that Miller enjoys attention. I'm pretty sure he'd take off his shirt for no reason to get attention, and apparently it works on some girls.

Some. Not me, obviously.

I'd actually almost forgotten about lifeguard training. It's not the full course, just a refresher to make sure we're all up to speed on things, and we practice the different rescues. You don't have to even be a lifeguard to come to the training, and you can opt out of it if you don't work on the waterfront. So I'm crossing my fingers that maybe Miller won't be there. Since I'm spending another summer in Boating—I do a happy dance in my mind—I have to do it, and I can't wait.

Lunch is grilled cheese, one of my favorites, and I eat one too many sandwiches before remembering I'll be in a bathing suit in thirty minutes.

But again, I'm not here to impress anyone. I don't give a fuck if people see my little food baby.

I take one more half a sandwich and take a huge bite, savoring the taste of the off-brand Kraft singles on white bread. It's not gourmet, but I'm not sure I've ever found a better grilled cheese.

"You want to be my partner for lifeguard training?" Vivien asks.

I'm ready to agree, but this time she's looking at Andrea, who's nodding. Lillian appears to be pairing up with Bridget.

My anxiety starts to mount, and I hate that even in my happy place it's getting to me. I hate being left out, always the one picked last at dodgeball and every other sport on the school yard. It's not like I was bad at sports, even. I was just the quiet kid that everyone kind of forgot about.

I take a deep breath. I'm not Rebecca right now, queen of nervous energy who's wound so tight no one wants to hang out. I'm Becca. Relaxed, confident Becca. Or at least I can fake it for now.

"Aw, no one wants to be my partner?" I say with a laugh.

Vivien gives me a side hug. "You feeling left out, chica? I figured you were partnering with Miller again."

Over my dead body.

"Wasn't really planning on it," I say.

She gives me a knowing smile, then looks at something over my shoulder. "I think *he* was planning on it."

I follow her gaze. Miller gives me a wink.

Why is he always just... *there*? Doesn't the man have anything else to do other than watch me? What's so goddamn interesting about me, anyway?

"Well, he's out of luck. I'm going to find someone else." I look around the dining hall.

There are a ton of people. Someone else will be my partner... right?

But as I check in at a few tables, looking for unpartnered people, it looks like I might be the one out of luck.

8

MILLER

Once again, *holy shit*. When I catch a glimpse of her on the beach, my world comes crashing to a stop.

How is this girl single? She's gorgeous, and her body is perfect. She's wearing a navy one-piece bathing suit that sits high on her hips, showing off curvy thighs. Her round ass and cute little swell of a tummy are impossible to tear my gaze away from.

And her tits. God, those tits. I want to bury my face in them.

Something occurs to me as I'm picturing her naked. *Is* she single? I didn't exactly ask. But with the cold shoulder she's giving me so far, I feel like she would have brought it up as a brush-off.

We'll look into this, I decide, nodding my head to myself before sauntering over.

"Hey, partner," I say, casually slinging my arm around her shoulders. She comes up to my shoulder, fitting perfectly, even if she stiffens at the contact.

It seems to be her default state around me, her back ramrod straight and her muscles so tight it looks painful. Maybe I can offer her a massage to help her loosen up. I trail a finger over the soft skin of her arm, pleased at the goosebumps that rise in its wake.

"How come you're doing lifeguard training? Do you even need it?" she asks, shrugging my arm off and taking a step to the side. I don't think I'm imagining her breathing getting quicker.

Ooh, she's prickly, even though her body can't hide her reactions. It's interesting, because I've watched her with her friends. She's quiet, but even in one day she's warmed up and is laughing and talking with the other girls.

She's only like this with me. My own little hedgehog.

I'll keep that one to myself. Somehow, I don't think she'll like being referred to as a hedgehog. The thought almost brings a grin to my lips.

"It's a good skill to have, right? Even if I'm hanging out at the nature barn, I can still spend time at the waterfront." And I plan to, if that's where Becca will be. I wonder what the structure of the camp day looks like, how much free time the counselors get. I doubt the schedule is made with the intent of maximizing counselor flirting time, but one can hope.

Becca's jaw clenches.

A tall girl in a bright red bathing suit announcing her status as **LIFEGUARD** blows a whistle. "Okay guys, listen up. I'm Jana, waterfront director this summer. Let's warm up with some laps and then we'll move into practicing rescues."

We splash into the surprisingly cold water. I like to think I'm an okay swimmer. My technique may not be pretty, but it gets the job done.

Becca, however, is way above decent. She glides through the water like a dolphin, the sun glinting off her wet arms as she moves them in a perfect crawl stroke. I tread water for a minute, watching her.

"Dude!" Dave's head hits my shoulder. "Move it along."

I grin and shift back into a cross between a crawl stroke and a doggie paddle.

Jana keeps us swimming laps for what feels like a long time, but according to her was only ten minutes. I probably would have gotten more laps done if I hadn't stopped every time I hit the edge of the swimming area to look at Becca. I just pretended I needed to catch my breath.

To be fair, I did need to catch my breath. I'm not exactly one for cardio. I do spend my fair share of time at the gym, but I mainly lift.

Jana taps her fingers against her hip, watching while we get out of the water and sit on the beach. The sand coats our legs as she goes over the basics of some rescues.

"First, we'll do an active drowning rescue, where the victim is conscious. Anyone want to demonstrate?" she asks the group.

My hand shoots into the air. I have no idea how to rescue anyone, but I'm pretty sure I can drown like nobody's business.

"Okay, you and your partner go for it and show us how it's done."

Becca does not look pleased, but she stands up alongside me as I walk into the water.

"You rescue me first," I say, then swim out into the center of the swimming area where it gets deep and start flailing my arms dramatically.

Becca glares at me from the shallow water while Jana hands her the red lifeguard floaty thing. I figure I'm too big for her to really rescue, but it'll be fun for her to try. Honestly, I'm probably too big for anyone in this group to rescue, so it's not like I'm putting her on the spot. More just making fun of how big I am.

Becca keeps her eyes on me, brows still furrowed as her eyes shoot daggers in my direction, and swims toward me with the red float under her arms. I grin at her and splash some more, ducking under the water for a minute. This is going to be fun.

But when I surface, she's gone. Where did she—

Smooth arms come up under my armpits and before I know what's happening, she has me on my back, red floaty under my shoulder blades, and she's expertly swimming me to shore.

Holy shit. This girl is amazing.

"Good work, Becca," Jana calls when Becca reaches the shallow end and unceremoniously dumps me off the float. "Now, everyone saw how she approached from the back and pulled Miller onto the tube, right?"

So that's what the floaty thing is called.

Everyone nods, and then Jana watches as three pairs at a time practice.

"Do I get to save you next?" I ask Becca.

She doesn't answer, but Jana looks at us and gives the signal.

Becca sighs, defeated. "Just don't let me actually drown."

With that, she wades out to the deeper water.

I slip the strap of the lifeguard tube over one shoulder and hold the red part in front of me. I think I'd be good at this lifeguard thing. Just stand here with this floaty and get tan.

"Go save your partner," Jana orders.

Right.

I swim out to Becca, who is calmly treading water.

"You're supposed to be drowning," I say.

She gives me a pointed look. "Then rescue me."

I take a few strokes closer, then without warning, she lunges forward and grabs my arm.

"Approach from the back so your victim doesn't try to grab onto you," Jana calls from the beach.

I wrestle Becca off of me and try to swim around behind her, but she spins so I'm still staring right at her face.

And her tits, which are right at water level.

Focus, Miller.

We play this game for a few minutes while I swim in circles around her and she toys with me.

Finally, Jana blows her whistle at us. "Becca, give him a chance."

Thank you, Jana.

Becca shrugs and lets me swim up behind her this time.

I awkwardly manage to pull her onto the tube.

Now what? When Becca rescued me, she held me with one arm across my chest and used the other to swim. I look down to gauge the feasibility of that move, which only gives me a very clear view of her tits.

And her hard nipples.

Fuck. Me.

"Don't even think about it," she says from her victim position. "Use your legs to pull us in."

Probably for the best. I keep my gaze off her chest as I pull her to shore. Mostly. I steal a glance or two at her gorgeous tits. I'm not a saint.

The tube is supporting her upper back, but the rest of her body is floating below it. What she apparently failed to consider when ordering me to swim like this—both arms under her armpits, swimming backward, instead of holding her across the chest the way she did to me—is that with this rescue her ass is *really* close to my crotch.

I hadn't really considered this aspect of lifeguard training. It's both the best thing ever—having her perfect round ass brushing up against me—and the worst, as I try my best not to get a boner. I'm glad the water is as cold as it is. It's helping keep things in a low profile.

By the time we get to shore, her cheeks are flaming again. The blush is subtle against her tan skin, but it's there. Is it that she's embarrassed by being the center of attention? Or is it me?

God, I hope it's me.

"We'll do passive drowning next, then a submerged victim," Jana announces.

Becca is easier to rescue as a passive victim. She can't fuck with me when she's pretending to be unconscious.

As I get her onto the tube to rescue her a second time, she cracks one eye open. "Keep your hands to yourself," she mutters.

"Go back to being unconscious." I grasp her one-handed this time, my forearm across her chest. This turns out to actually be easier for a few reasons. First, it lets me use my other arm to swim, and second, I don't have to spend the whole time thinking of my mom to avoid a boner.

When we switch, Becca manages to knee me in the leg while rescuing me, which I'm not at all sure is accidental, despite her muttered, "Sorry."

Both of us successfully rescued from drowning for now, we sit together on the beach watching the other pairs practice. The sand clings to her legs, and I watch as she pushes a wet strand of dark hair out of her eyes and tucks it back into her long braid.

"So, tell me about yourself," I say, trying to crack her icy exterior.

She looks over at me and furrows her brows. Is she offended by my attempt at small talk? Or maybe it's just my entire existence that bothers her.

"Not your whole life story. Just like, one thing about you." I give her a nudge with my elbow.

There's a mix of emotions playing in her dark eyes as she watches me before shrugging her shoulders. "Fine. I'm from New York City originally. I came here as a camper because my mom worked here as a teenager. I fell in love with camp, just like she did."

"I love that. She must be proud of you."

Becca doesn't respond. I know she's capable of having a conversation. Hell, I've watched her have plenty of discussions with Vivien and Lillian just in the last day. She's even seemed animated through some of them. So it's either that she's shy around me, or she hates me.

Based on our interactions so far, I'm thinking it's the latter option. Actually, it's definitely that. She's not exactly been subtle about her distaste for me.

And while most normal guys would probably take this as a signal to back off, it just makes me more determined to win her over. Even if it's just as friends.

I mean, I don't want to be just friends, but you've got to start somewhere, right?

Everyone loves a good friends-to-lovers story. Or enemies-to-lovers, which might be even better. I'm definitely a fan of both.

What, you don't think a guy can be into romance novels? I'm confident enough in my manhood to admit it. My mom's book club competes to see who can choose the spiciest read each month, and she passes them on to me when she's done.

Let me just say, those slow burns... when they get to the good stuff? *Totally* worth the wait.

"So... what's your favorite animal?" I ask. That should be a benign subject, right?

"Um. Probably... panda bears? Or maybe penguins." The corner of her lips quirk up in the tiniest of smiles. "I love how they look like little cocktail waiters in tuxedos."

I laugh out loud, picturing penguins carrying trays of drinks. "Love that."

"What about you?" she asks, tracing a line in the sand with her toe. "Do you have a favorite animal? You must, cause you're in Nature for the summer, right?"

I wince slightly, remembering the goats. "Hedgehog." Maybe someday I'll tell her why that's my favorite.

A whistle blast pulls our attention to Jana. "Okay, guys, last drill. Submerged victim again, but this time you need to bring your unconscious victim all the way onto the beach enough for your team to save them. Not just dump them off the tube once it gets shallow." She blows her whistle again.

I want one of those. I wonder if they stock them somewhere or if she brought her own.

I consider where I could buy my own whistle while Becca rescues me first. I'm amazed once again that she's able to pull a 250-pound, six-foot-four guy off the bottom of the lake and all the way to shore. I guess the water buoyancy helps, but still. It's really fucking impressive.

She drags me along the sand until my shoulders are all the way out of the water. I do my best to stay unconscious and ignore the sand that's making its way into my ass crack. I'm taking a long shower after this.

Partly for the sand, but after being this close to Becca for a couple of hours, a cold shower seems like it might be warranted. *Down, boy.*

"There. You're saved."

I open my eyes to find Becca leaning over me, her face blocking out the sun. "Aw, you rescued me," I say.

She heads back into the water. "Come save me so we can be done."

We're just getting started, if I have any say in this.

I follow her out into the deeper water and do my best to scrub away the sand with my palm. God, it really gets into your crevices, doesn't it?

I'm getting a little better at this after practicing all afternoon. It only takes me two tries to pull Becca up to the surface of the water and onto the tube, and she plays the part of the unconscious victim as I pull her into shore. I feel a little bad, knowing she's probably getting sand in uncomfortable places as I pull her further onto the shore.

"Don't worry, victim," I say, leaning over her. God, her lips are so close, deep pink and soft. I'm itching to run my thumb over her full lower lip, to tug on it until her mouth opens just enough for me to press my lips against hers. "I'll save you." I bring a hand to her face and cup her jaw.

Her lips part on their own, just slightly, and there's a sharp intake of breath just before she opens her eyes to meet mine.

9

―――――

BECCA

Miller's breath is soft against my lips. He's barely a few inches away, so close that if he were someone else, it would seem like he was about to kiss me.

And it has to be that thought, the idea that someone *else* would be close enough to kiss me, that makes my heart race and my breath hitch in my chest. I force my eyes open, trying to break the spell, but all I see are the deep blue eyes with gold flecks in them staring into mine, his pupils dark with something I can't read.

And then he lifts his head enough for me to see the smirk that says he knows exactly how his closeness affected me, and *fuck,* do I hate him.

It's not enough that he humiliated me by making

us demonstrate a rescue, that he takes nothing seriously and just wants to fuck around all day. Now he's embarrassing me on this beach in front of half the summer staff.

My face burns as I clench my jaw and cross my arms over my chest to hide my nipples, which have completely betrayed me by growing hard. "I'm alive. Thanks."

He settles back, his butt on his heels as he studies me. "You good?" he asks.

Um, no, I'm not good. I want to murder you. And then disappear.

"Fine," I manage. "Just covered in sand." I lift myself up on my elbows and look at Jana. "Are we done? I'm dying for a shower."

Jana dismisses us, and I practically run to the showers. I stand under the hot spray, scrubbing myself furiously with a bar of pink Dove soap to wash off the sand, along with whatever bullshit made my body react the way it did.

I'm better than this. I'm smart, or at least I used to think I was.

I managed to get into medical school, for whatever that's worth, my recent class performance aside. So I'm not the kind of girl who just melts into a puddle when some asshole puts me on the spot and brings his—admittedly hot—body near mine.

What's wrong with me?

I wash myself twice. Because there has to be something in the air if my body is completely betraying me.

I take a deep breath as I rinse the suds from my body, admiring the tiny tattoo just below my hipbone. It's a tiny ladybug, strategically placed to be invisible in even a bathing suit.

I actually got it when I was a camp counselor up here, the summer after I turned eighteen. It was a small act of rebellion, and I loved having a part of camp with me—both the ladybug symbol that I chose to represent the Ladybugs section of camp that I love so much, and the tattoo itself.

My first summer on staff was the first time I'd been away from home for so long and on my own. It was nice to have something for myself, something uniquely for me.

And so far, no one but me has seen the tattoo.

Another deep breath. I hold it for three seconds, then let it out slowly. Campers will be here the day after tomorrow, so I only have to deal with Miller for the rest of today, which is really just dinner and the socializing after. Most of tomorrow will be spent getting the cabins ready.

I can handle a few more hours of him.

I can handle anything.

We'll find out our co-counselors after dinner tonight. I turn around under the spray while I mull over the other counselors that I know are in my unit, wondering who I'll be paired with. Even as a late addition to the staff, I'm considered a senior counselor, so I have some pull in the way we'll do things in the cabin.

As I turn the water off, I'm already thinking of decorations and cabin games and icebreakers and all the things I want to do with the campers. I can't wait.

Dinner is spaghetti, and I manage to snag a spot with a bunch of the girls, far away from Miller. I catch a glimpse of him from across the dining hall. He's grinning, and the entire table is laughing. He's managed to get a bunch of the guys under his spell, apparently. Actually, most of camp, as far as I can tell. It seems like I'm the only one who's not swayed by his charm.

"Nice view, huh?" Vivien winks at me and nudges me with her elbow.

I roll my eyes. "Um, right. No. I'm just trying to figure out what's so stinking funny over there."

She giggles. "Probably something Miller said. He's

hilarious. How was being paired with him for lifeguard stuff?" Vivien and some of the other non-waterfront staff opted out of lifeguard training, so at least it wasn't the entire staff that witnessed my humiliation.

Just most of them. I hold back a grimace at the thought.

"Annoying, mostly. He doesn't take anything seriously." I pick up a slice of garlic bread from the plate in the center of the table. "Like, lifeguarding is serious. I don't know why he can't just focus for a few hours. Why he needs to be the center of attention all the time."

And why he needs to drag me into it.

"Well, he's certainly got my attention." Vivien twirls some spaghetti on her fork.

I'm not sure I have a reply to that. Fortunately, I don't have to say anything, because McKenna stops at our table.

"Hey, ladies. Want some cabin assignments?" our unit leader asks.

We all turn to her with rapt attention. Your co-counselor factors heavily in how your summer goes, especially these first few weeks. You live with them, work with them, lean on them when things get tough. I cross my fingers that I'll get along with mine.

McKenna looks at her clipboard as she lists off

names. "Lillian, you're with Sophia in Cabin 1. Grace and Liz, Cabin 4. Cabin 3 is Madison and Abby—they're at that table over there if you haven't met them yet. And Becca and Vivien, congrats, two senior counselors in one cabin. Cabin 2."

Vivien gives me a side hug with a little squeal. I return the gesture with a grin.

"Can you believe we're together?" she asks, a little breathless from excitement. "Having two seniors together is going to *rock*. I can't wait."

I'm thrilled, too. It's not just that Vivien has become a friend in the short time I've been here. Having her as a co-counselor takes some of the stress off me, too. Junior counselors, the ones who are in their first year on staff, usually need more oversight and mentoring. Being with another senior, though? We both have experience to draw on.

I can trust her to manage things, and she can trust me. And of all the people I've met on staff so far, she's the best one I could have picked to spend the next weeks living with.

"What's everyone's plan for tonight?" I ask, looking around the table and back to Vivien as I take another bite of food. "Maybe we can get together and talk about things for the first week. I'm so excited!"

Vivien looks thoughtful. "Well, I don't think

they're going to play flip cup anymore after Jackson almost threw up. Campfire at like eight, then maybe we just hang out in the cabin? I want to make a list so we can run to Target tomorrow for things we need."

I love the way her mind works.

"Perfect. Let's chat after the campfire."

I'm so excited that I wake up as soon as it starts to get light out. The only ones that I know who wake up as early as I do are Andrea and Bridget, and they're now living in a tent across camp with a few of the other leaders. The remaining girls in my cabin are still snoring softly as I wrap myself in a blanket and head to the dining hall for my morning coffee.

The mist is doing its thing coming off the lake, and the swing is covered in a fine layer of dew, but the blanket is thick enough that I'm still cozy. I make a list in my head while I sip on my coffee of the things I want to do today.

Target run, make a poster with the rules for the cabin, decorate the cabin door with the campers' names before they show up tomorrow.

Tomorrow. My heart gives a happy little leap.

I haven't been this excited in a long time.

At one point I thought my love of kids and working with them as a camp counselor would translate well to being a pediatrician if the whole surgeon thing didn't work out. I understand kids, relate to them well. I figured med school was just a stepping-stone to get there.

I never imagined I'd be wondering if I'd be able to finish.

My stomach twists as my thoughts stray to my parents. God, what will they think?

At some point, they're going to want to know how third year is going, since my former classmates should be starting their first rotation this week. I can only pretend to busy for so long before I'll have to admit that I'm spending my summer up here, trying to regain some sense of control in my life, and that I'm redoing my second year.

I push off the ground to make the swing rock back and forth as I curl my feet up next to me.

No more thoughts of school. We're not at school. We're going to focus on camp and the campers for the next six weeks, and then we'll deal with all the shit waiting for us back in New York.

I hold the coffee to my lips and savor the scent.

"How's it going?"

I startle but manage to only spill a few drops of

coffee on the blanket. I turn my head to find Miller walking up to the swing. My swing.

"This is a great spot," he remarks, coming to a stop beside me. "Mind if I join you?"

There are very few polite responses I can think of for that. *Fuck off* would not be considered camp appropriate, nor would *there's no chance in hell I want to spend time with you voluntarily*. Perhaps *over my dead body*.

While I contemplate the best way to tell him to get lost, Miller slides onto the end of the swing opposite me. I'm curled up with my feet on the swing, and Miller's body is wide enough that my toes push into his hip.

"Um," I hesitate, unsure what one says in this situation.

Miller gives me that signature smile of his. "Perfect time to hang out, right? No one else is up. This is beautiful."

I give him a short nod. Yes, it's beautiful. No, it's not a good time to hang out. It's a good time to be alone, Miller.

"Did you get your cabin assignment?" he asks, putting a hand on the back of the swing, his arm so long that his fingertips brush my shoulder. I hate that the air crackles with electricity between us. "I'm Fire-flies 2 with Dave. Should be fun."

Fireflies 2 is just through the woods from Lady-bugs 2. Our cabins are the two closest ones between the units, with their own little path between the two buildings.

But I don't think I'm going to mention that to Miller. The last thing I need is him bugging me more than he already is. With a deep breath I try to hide from him, I force myself to unclench my jaw.

"What are you doing out here?" I finally ask.

His eyebrow quirks. "Felt like having some quiet time. But I saw you out here and thought it would be nice to hang out. What are you doing out here?"

Having alone time sounds like a bitchy answer, so I shrug. "Just enjoying the view."

He nods and looks at the lake in silence for a few minutes. "So, what's your cabin assignment? You like your co-counselor?"

He's being nice, and I have no reason to be a bitch other than wanting to be alone. And the way he humil-iated me yesterday, but there's no one around now. I've thought about it more—of course I did, my anxiety working overtime and keeping me from falling asleep —and I realized that *maybe* it wasn't about me. Maybe he just likes being the center of attention.

The only other reason to push him away is the way my body is reacting to him, and I'm just not going to acknowledge that. I can't, for about a million reasons.

And I may not like him, but I can be polite. "I'm in Ladybugs 2 with Vivien. I'm excited, actually. Can't wait to move in and start decorating today." I shrug.

He tilts his head, his brow creasing. "Decorating what?"

"Um, the cabin. We're going to cut out pictures with the campers' names on them, so they feel welcome. Like, maybe a cloud with Vivien's and my names and then the campers on raindrops. Or a bunch of flowers, or something."

Miller looks even more confused. "Why? Don't they tell the campers which cabin they're supposed to go to?" he asks.

"They do, but it's... more to make them feel at home, or something. You don't have to, I guess. I don't even know if all the guys decorate to quite the extent the girls' campers do. Or at all." I sip at the coffee, which is starting to get cool.

We sit in silence again while I hold the mug at my lips, sipping slowly. As I drain the last drops, Miller turns away from the lake to look over at me.

"So, aside from decorating the cabins, is there anything else should I know about camp, Yoda?"

I meet his gaze. Even with his smile, there's something in those blue eyes that makes me nervous. It's like he sees something inside me. Like he knows too much. Or like if I'm not careful, I'm going to share too much.

"Nope. Just like sitting out here." I pop the *p* for extra emphasis. The last thing I need is for Miller to see my secrets and insecurities. My anxiety rears its ugly head, telling me that he'd just use them for a laugh. And I'm intellectual enough to know that's probably not the case, but even so, I'm going to keep some things to myself.

He doesn't push, and we sit together in silence until the camp bell rings to signal that it's time to wake up and start the day.

10

MILLER

MOM

Camp is excellent.

Glad to hear it. How are the campers?

Not here yet. But there's a girl here and she's HOT.

How old is she?

shrug emoji Old enough.

As long as she's not still in college. You need someone mature in your life.

wink emoji That's why I have you.

eyeroll emoji Jesus, you need to get laid.

Don't we all?

Need me to send a care package with condoms?

Think I'm good for now. But I'll take some brownies.

I'll work on it. Let me know how things go when the campers get here. Can't wait to hear all about it. And the girl.

CARD SHARKS

Blake: You quit the camp gig yet?

No chance of that. There's a girl here.

Cam: Please tell me it's not a camper.

Maddox: You're one to talk about hooking up with someone off limits.

Cam: Um, stepsister much?

Thanks for the vote of confidence, you assholes. And no, it's not a camper or my stepsister or any of your sisters. The campers get here tomorrow.

Cam: I was kidding. Mostly. But… details.

She's… well, there's something about her. She's smart and feisty and it's like there's so much more to her that I haven't figured out yet. Pretty sure she hates me, but she'll get over that. So I'm here for as long as it takes.

I just need to figure out how to jerk off in the shower without the campers hearing. I'm not going to last long without some relief, but I also don't want to end up as a sex offender.

Cam: Admirable goals for someone working with children.

Shut up. Maddox, how are things with Holly?

Maddox: Good so far. The first ultrasound was weird. The baby looked like a gummy bear.

Looks like its dad, huh?

Maddox: That's my kid, you asshole.

Blake: Calm down, boys. Good luck tomorrow, Miller. You're gonna need it.

11

BECCA

"You want some bacon?" Vivien holds her fork out, a slice dangling from the tines.

I shake my head, shuddering slightly. "Nah. Bacon and I don't get along."

Vivien looks personally offended. "Bacon is delicious." She pops the meat in her mouth with a satisfying *crunch*.

Breakfast is usually my favorite meal of the day. There are sweet and savory options, and all of them come with coffee. Win-win. French toast is my favorite, with the crisp edges and soft inside and buttery taste like heaven when you bite into it. I like almost everything breakfast-related. Pancakes. Cinnamon rolls. Eggs and toast. Cereal, even.

Just not bacon, and the smell of it is enough to dampen my excitement of the whole meal.

Bacon is one of those classic foods that everyone seems to like. It's fatty enough that it's a little taboo to eat too much of it. And the people who don't eat it usually have some reason, like keeping kosher and avoiding pig products, or being plant-based and avoiding all animal products.

I, on the other hand, just... don't like it. It's one of those small things that just sets me apart from the crowd, and not in a good way. I've tried enjoying, but I just can't. Sorry.

I take a sip of my orange juice to get the scent of bacon out of my nose as Vivien swallows the last of hers.

"So," she says after washing her mouthful down with water, "what do you think about door decorations? You want to do something with camper names, yeah?"

The other staff at our table are also engrossed in one-on-one conversations with their co-counselors, too. Since we got our cabin assignments last night, the focus has shifted to the imminent arrival of campers and getting ready. Other than interrupting my alone time this morning, even Miller has been scarce, spending his time planning with Dave.

I nod as I swallow and place my cup on the table. "Yeah, I always love doing that, and changing it up each week. Any thoughts on theme for this week?"

Vivien taps her empty fork against her mouth. "I feel like we should do something that represents us, you know? What do you do for work? Or are you in school?"

At the breakfast table wasn't exactly where I'd hoped to spill my guts on all this. But Vivien is a grad student, too—she's in a PhD program, and this is the last summer she managed to wrangle a few weeks off to come to camp. She'd probably understand more than most about the stress of failure.

Carefully, I force the words out, "I'm in grad school. Kind of a long story, actually. I'll tell you more when we're fixing up the cabin." I cross my fingers under the table that she lets it go.

Vivien picks up her water glass. "Kay. You want to drive us to Target after breakfast or should we take my car?" she asks.

Topic changed. I breathe a sigh of relief.

We definitely should have taken my car. Vivien isn't exactly a *bad* driver, but she sees road signs as loose suggestions rather than binding rules to be followed.

"Oops!" she says again, throwing the car into reverse. "Didn't realize this was one-way."

I bury my head in my hands as she backs down the row of the parking lot, the driver of the oncoming car looking directly at us. "Just park somewhere, Viv. I think Brett will be pissed if both of us die and he has to find more counselors by tomorrow."

She laughs as she pulls into a spot. "Fine. We can walk a little. Think we should stock up on snacks or candy for the campers, too?"

We both slide out of the car. I round the sedan to stand beside Vivien as she clicks the key fob twice to lock the doors. "A little candy, sure. I have a plastic bin that we can store it in to keep the squirrels out."

We spend an hour browsing the store. Ultimately, we end up buying construction paper, markers, and tape to make decorations for the cabin, candy and some dried fruit, two sets of matching t-shirts, and a pack of bandanas for the campers.

"Ooh!" Vivien picks up a stuffed bear, giddily holding it out for me to see. "Talking bear?"

The idea of 'talking' anything is to have a way to keep all the kids from talking at once. One person holds the talking stick—or talking bear—and they're the only ones who should be speaking.

I consider the bear, pursing my lips in thought. It could work, but I have visions of it covered in mud and the other gunk that seems to accumulate on everything in the cabins. Resigned, I shake my head.

"Let's do a talking stick instead. I bet we can get Bridget to give us some glitter and feathers and stuff to decorate it," I suggest.

Vivien claps her hands after putting the bear back. "YES. Love it. So much glitter."

We toss ideas for the week back and forth as we drive home. Vivien ignores the **NO TURN ON RED** sign as we swing onto the road that leads toward camp.

"Oh!" she says as we make another turn onto the dirt road. "Did you want to talk about grad school now that we're alone? Is everything okay?"

Leave it to the PhD candidate to sniff out trouble.

I let out a sigh. I can't keep this to myself forever, and if you can't trust your co-counselor, there's no one at camp you can trust. "Sure, but I'd kind of like to keep this between us, okay?"

She nods seriously.

"I'm in med school. I'm supposed to be starting my third year, but I failed a couple classes, so I have to repeat the year. I'll start up again in August, but I just needed some time away from it all." I feel a little of the weight lift as I say the words out loud.

"Oh my God," Vivien exclaims, and my stomach drops. "You know what this means?"

That I'm a failure. That you're smarter than me. Probably any number of things I've told myself over and over, but she doesn't wait for my answer.

"We're both science-y people. So we *have* to have a science theme for the week!" Vivien looks at me expectantly.

I just blink. *That's* what she took from my revelation?

She returns her gaze to the road, slowing as the **CAMP WINNIE** sign comes into view. "What do you think?" she presses.

"I-I love it, Vivien. I just figured you'd have something to say about the failing part."

She pulls into a parking spot that's as close to the cabins as we can get in the staff parking lot. "Dude, grad school is tough as shit. I can only imagine how tough med school is. I'm impressed that you got in, because God knows I wouldn't make the cut. And having to repeat some stuff isn't a big deal. It's only a big deal to you because you've spent your whole life being the smartest one in your class." She laughs at my expression as we get out of the car, her hair falling around her shoulders. "Let's go make some beakers and test tubes to put campers' names on."

Our cabin looks flipping amazing. The door is decorated with ten cutout pictures of a variety of science things—an atom, a beaker, a test tube, lab goggles. We tried to make a Bunsen burner, but that pushed our artistic skills a little too far.

The back wall boasts a poster on which we've written the rules in multi-colored, swirling handwriting, reminding campers to keep their feet on their beds during rest time and to use kind words. Along with the talking stick, the candy bin is also decorated with glitter, thanks to Bridget in the Art department, and is now tucked under my bed.

Vivien sets an old-school CD player on the floor next to her trunk. "Look what I found at Goodwill! No internet required." She piles some CDs next to it with a wink.

I look through the options, picking up a Beatles CD. I slide it into the machine and hit play.

Vivien and I sing along to *Come Together* as we organize our clothes by the beds that will be ours for the next few weeks. I stack a few books under the bed, then line up my sunscreen, bug spray, and moisturizer along the shelf above the pillow.

As *Octopus's Garden* starts to play, Vivien grabs a broom. "Care to join me in cleaning?" she asks, twirling around with a laugh.

I grab the other broom, giggling as we sweep away the dust that's accumulated since last year. Vivien stops every few minutes to sing along to the chorus, using the top of the broom as a microphone. On the last chorus, I join her.

This is the person I want to be all the time. This carefree woman whose only concern is the cabin being all cutesy for a bunch of eight- and nine-year-olds. Who isn't worried about passing pharmacology or what impact a bad grade will have on the rest of my life.

I set the broom in one corner and adjust the pillows on one of the bunk beds as another song starts.

Vivien sets her broom next to mine. "So, what's up with you and Miller?"

I focus on making sure the pillow's corners are unwrinkled. Who cares that the campers will all bring their own pillows and that these will end up under the beds by tomorrow?

"Nothing," I finally say, when I turn around and find her staring at me.

"Hmm," she says, refolding a wool blanket that's likely to meet the same fate as the pillows. "It seems like there's something there."

There is nothing there. If anything, there's an annoying guy who won't leave me alone.

I move to the next bed and focus all my energy on this pillow. "He's not my type," I insist, smoothing a hand over the pillowcase. "I think he just likes annoying me, honestly. He's like my complete opposite. He doesn't take anything seriously. I don't trust him."

"Yeah, but he's hot," Vivien says, like I don't have eyes of my own, and like his physical attractiveness somehow negates his entire personality.

When I don't answer, she moves on to another topic.

"Let's go over the camper list and figure out the best get-to-know-you games," she suggests.

I give up on the pillows and join her on her bed, where we sit cross-legged and pull out the packet of papers Brett dropped off earlier. There are eight pages, one for each of the girls that will be in our cabin this week, with a list of names on the front. All ten-year-olds.

Vivien splits the pile in half and hands me four pages. I leaf through them quickly.

"I have four two-week campers here," I say, holding them up.

The families have the option to sign up for one- or two-week sessions when they register for camp. Most of the younger kids end up doing only one week to start, so this many two-weekers is a lot.

"I have two in my pile. Looks like in total we have six two-weekers, and only two staying for one week." Vivien holds up two pages.

I look more closely at mine. "Probably because they're on the older side. One is almost eleven," I remark, glancing back up at Viv.

"I kind of expected younger in Cabin 2, but I'll take it," Vivien says, turning a page over. "Ten-year-olds are usually sweet as pie." She grins.

Usually is the key word here, and we both know it.

We read through the information provided by the parents and the campers themselves, then swap pages and continue reading. There are three that are first-time campers, five that have been here before. Two from the same hometown and requested to bunk together.

I start to form a picture in my head of the dynamics I'm expecting from the descriptions.

"Hey, did you see this?" Vivien holds out one page. It's one of the first ones I read, a girl named Maya.

From the information she supplied, she seems young for ten, even though that's the age listed at the top of the paper.

"What?" I ask, reaching for it.

"Look at the bottom of the page. The part the parents filled out." Vivien points.

I follow her finger. I'd skimmed the parent information, focusing more on what the girls think of themselves and how they want to present themselves.

The parents have an idea of their children that are formed from watching their kids grow, and sometimes campers want the chance to reinvent themselves.

Maya's parents seemed overprotective when I skimmed through their sheet, focused on making sure their daughter would be supported. It seemed a little out of proportion to her age, but when I see what Vivien is pointing at, I realize what I skipped over and why they came across that way.

"She has Down Syndrome?" I say. It comes out as a question, even though I'm just reading the information on the sheet.

Vivien taps a finger against her lips. "Let's go through some of the games we have planned after this. I want to make sure she can participate in everything and we don't end up excluding her."

I'm thankful, for about the hundredth time since

we got our assignments, to have Vivien as a co-counselor.

When we finally drop into bed that evening, the last night with a quiet cabin for a while, I'm filled with excitement for the week coming up. I focus on the crickets chirping outside the cabin window as I drift off.

This time, I don't wake up until the morning bell. But I don't need my alone time at the lake today or an extra cup of coffee to wake me up before breakfast.

The excitement alone is enough to get me going.

Campers come today.

12

———

MILLER

*D*ing-ding-ding-ding.

The camp bell reverberates through my head as I force my eyes to open. How is it morning already?

I'm usually pretty good at being a morning person. I like the silence, and also the opportunity to set up pranks before my friends have had their coffee. Yesterday, it worked out in my favor when I ran into Becca on the swing by the lake.

Hot, smart, *and* a morning person. Who could ask for more?

Sure, it seemed like she was contemplating ways to get rid of me, but any attention works. I just need time to grow on her.

This morning, though, I'm dragging. Dave and I

spent yesterday cleaning the cabin—it still looks and smells a little musty—and figuring out things to do with the campers.

We even decorated a little after Becca gave me the idea, cutting out shapes of construction paper and writing campers' names on them. I mean, they're just shapes, because artistic skills aren't exactly our strong suit. But I'm proud of our hard work as I look at the door with its colorful decorations.

I started to get swept up in the excitement as we planned, but all the moving things around and sweeping and shit has me feeling like an old man this morning.

I groan out loud as I swing my legs over the bed and feel around the floor for my sandals. Just need to make it to the dining hall for some coffee. Then I'll be a functional human.

When thinking about coming up here, I didn't exactly anticipate this little gem, which is that unlike in my apartment, the coffee isn't within a few steps. It's across camp, in the dining hall. I have to put clothes and shoes on and trek all the way there to get a little caffeine, and in the mornings, it's *cold*.

Maybe I should have brought the sweatshirt the packing list recommended.

I push a hand through my hair, studying the row

of cabinets that form a small divider between my bed and the bunks where the campers will sleep. They make a nice countertop. Dave and I should figure out a way to put a coffee pot in here. Even a small one would get the job done, and our campers are all eight and nine years old, according to their paperwork, so it's not like they'd be stealing it.

I think. Kids that age don't drink coffee, do they?

I pull on my favorite faded Philadelphia Firebirds t-shirt and a pair of jeans, then slip my feet into the Birkenstocks knockoffs. Good enough to make it to the coffee.

I roll on some deodorant just in case I run into Becca, too.

The morning goes by in a flurry of last-minute cleaning, setup and other things, punctuated by two more trips to the dining hall for coffee refills, and before I know it, someone knocks on the cabin door.

"Hello?" a woman calls. "Is this Fireflies Cabin 2?"

Dave practically jumps off his bed, beaming. "Sure is! Are you our first camper?"

I force myself to my feet from where I've been lying on my bed, daydreaming about Becca's tits. I'm excited about the campers too, but the rabid enthusiasm on Dave's face is hard to match.

"This is Liam. It's his first year at camp, and he's so excited!"

"Right on, man! Put it here." Dave holds his hand up for a high five, which the kid reluctantly returns.

In contrast to my co-counselor, Liam is doing a remarkable job of hiding his excitement.

Dave gestures at me. "I'm Dave, and this is Miller. We're Liam's counselors. Liam, you want to pick a bed? Since you're the first one here, you get first dibs. Your mom can help you get your stuff set up once you choose."

Liam's mother leads the way into the cabin and waits, sleeping bag in hand, while Liam weighs the merits of a top bunk versus a bottom bunk. He settles on a top bunk just as another kid appears at the door, walking in like he owns the place.

"I'm Noah," he says without any preamble.

I look around for his adults and finally spot them several yards away. I give them a wave as Noah walks into the cabin and selects the top bunk opposite Liam.

The two campers so far seem like polar opposites, and I realize I hadn't considered this possibility. What do we do if they don't get along?

Before I can worry too much more about it, two more campers arrive at the same time and take the final two top bunks, settling the question of whether top or bottom bunk is more popular. Looks like top wins in a landslide.

As campers three and four—Mason and Oliver— settle in, Liam and Noah have started discussing their favorite Pokemon characters, and Liam seems to be coming out of his shell as he defends the superiority of Charmander over Squirtle.

"Miller?" I look over to find Mason peering at me, his little legs crossed.

"Yeah, buddy?"

"Where's the bathroom?"

He couldn't have gone while his parents were still here? They left like three minutes ago. I stand up from the bed, where I finally sat down all of thirty seconds ago. "I'll take you." I raise my voice slightly. "Anyone else need to use the bathroom? Or want to come along to see where it is?"

I lead the way to the bathroom—also far away from the cabin, just like the coffee—with four small boys following behind me like I'm the Pied Piper. I direct them to the stalls and lean against the counter while I wait.

"Miller?" A small voice comes from one stall.

I'm starting to hate the sound of my own name, and it's been less than an hour. "Yeah?"

"The toilet won't flush."

I knew I should have sent Dave on this little bathroom expedition. Fortunately, I like to keep things clean around my house, and I know just how to fix a clogged toilet. I just don't like to.

"Okay, just finish your business and I'll take care of it when you're done."

Ten minutes and one toilet plunger later, I lead the boys back to the cabin.

"What took you guys so long?" Dave asks, a furrow to his brow. There's another camper setting up his bed on one of the bottom bunks.

"The toilet got clogged and Miller had to unclog it," Noah pipes up.

Dave chuckles. "Good for Miller." He motions to the new camper, who's sitting cross-legged on one of the bottom bunks. "This is Caleb. Make him feel welcome, guys. We have three more coming and then we'll go to the swimming area so they can see what level you should all be in."

This thought perks me up somewhat. Not because I'm that excited about swimming, but because Becca's campers will have to do their swim test, too.

I cross my fingers that we'll end up at the swimming area at the same time.

The three remaining campers—Jack, Ben, and Grayson—show up just before the end of drop-off time. They get settled in while the earlier arrivals change into their bathing suits.

"Okay, guys. Everyone have a swimsuit on?" Dave is taking charge of everything today, and I've never been more grateful to not be the center of attention. I'll get back to that eventually. I just have no clue what I'm doing, so I'm content to fly under the radar for now.

The campers nod as the last few pull their swim shorts on.

"Okay, friends. Let's go. Shoes on and bring your towels." Dave exits the cabin and stands by the door, and I follow along with the campers. I probably have just as much experience as they do at this point.

"Miller, are you swimming too?" Ben asks.

A spark lights in my mind. There's nothing I love more than acting like an idiot, and something tells me these kids will eat that up. Here's my opening. "You know what? Yeah, I am." I duck back into the cabin and pull on a pair of swim trunks before Dave and I herd the campers down to the waterfront.

Jana and Andrea are standing on the floating dock, lifeguard tubes strapped over their shoulders as campers splash in front of them.

The sight of the bright red floats reminds me of lifeguard training. God, having Becca up against me was the heaven I didn't know I'd been missing. I wonder if we'll get to do something like that again later this summer.

The two women hand out wristbands of varying colors to the campers as they make their way out of the water. Once another cabin's worth of dripping kids are standing on the sand, Jana motions to our group.

"Come on in," she says, gesturing.

Dave gives two of our boys a little nudge. "Go ahead, guys. Leave your towels on the sand."

They drop their towels in a heap and splash into the water. I wait until they're waist deep, focused on Jana, then charge into the lake.

"Cannonball!" I yell, launching myself in front of them. When I come up to the surface, they're giggling and seem a little more at ease. I flick my head to get the wet hair out of my face.

Even Jana is smiling slightly. "Okay, guys. I need the campers—and Miller, if he wants to—to swim out to that rope there"—she points—"and then back to me. I'm going to watch to make sure you're safe swimmers, and then you'll each get a wristband that tells you how deep you can go in the lake. Reds can swim to the first rope just past this dock, blues to the second, and green can go all the way to that dock out there." She points to the square floating at the far corner of the deepest section.

She blows her whistle, and the boys set off in a flurry of arms and legs and splashing water. I lean up against the dock and watch them. I'd hoped that Becca would be here with her campers, but I'm having fun anyway.

Jana and Andrea hand out wristbands after a few more laps, with all of the campers receiving blue or red. Dave waits while the nine of us splash back to the beach and towel off.

We stick our sandy feet back into sandals for the walk back to the cabin. There's a remaining drop of disappointment that Becca didn't get to see my antics, but there's always dinnertime.

***

Four hours later, I'm drained. Being a camp counselor is *hard*. Not any one thing specifically; I can handle swim screening, taking kids to the dining hall for dinner, helping them pick their classes for the week, settling them around the campfire on the beach, and keeping them from throwing sand at one another, even plunging two more toilets while they brush their teeth. It's more the fact that it's *nonstop*.

Just when I start to feel proud of myself for getting the campers safely through something, it's either time for another scheduled activity or something has cropped up that I need to deal with.

On the plus side, and I give myself a pat on the back for this, none of the kids have gotten injured today. I may have learned about first aid last week, but I don't want to have to actually *use* those skills.

The campers look tired, too. In fact, only Dave actually looks like he could stay awake at this point. Which is fine for the kids, since it's 8:30, but that seems a little early for me to be ready to pass out.

"What was your favorite part of today?" Dave asks as the boys snuggle down into their beds.

"Pizza for dinner," Liam mutters into his pillow.

"Swimming," Ben says, prompting a nod from two other boys.

Noah sits up in bed. "The best was when Miller cannonballed into the lake!"

I hold back my smile, hoping he'll lie down and go to sleep, but when he finally does, two more kids sit up, too. It reminds me of whack-a-mole, except I don't think we're allowed to actually whack them.

"Yeah, that was the best! Miller, will you do that again tomorrow?" Caleb asks.

"If you guys go to sleep, I'll think about it," I say, letting the smile spread over my face. Hell, I'm not above bribery. I just didn't think they'd offer up the leverage so easily.

The two that are sitting slam their heads onto the pillows with terrifying speed.

"We're asleep," Noah assures me, his voice muffled.

"Glad to hear it, little man," I say, still smiling.

Dave and I walk around the cabin, stopping at each bunk to offer a high five and make sure each camper is all set. Once we've both gotten to all eight boys, Dave stands by the cabin door.

"Goodnight, boys. Sweet dreams," he says. "If you need anything, wake one of us up. It doesn't matter even if it's the middle of the night, okay? If we're not in our beds, look for one of us right outside the cabin. Goodnight!"

Dave flips the light off, leaving just the soft glow of a nightlight that he somehow knew to bring, and the two of us step out of the cabin.

"Well. Solid first day, huh?" he says after shutting the door with a grin.

I'm almost too tired to respond, but I manage to nod my head.

"Only one counselor needs to stay close by for the campers, so one of us can go hang out with other staff in the dining hall until curfew. You want me to hang out here tonight so you can socialize?"

I ignore the mention of curfew, because there's no way I'm abiding by that. But also, there are more important things to focus on. Like the fact that Becca might be down at the dining hall, too.

And I don't want to miss my chance to spend time with her.

13

BECCA

I hold my breath, expecting a tiny voice to pipe up or the rustling of someone shifting in their sleeping bag on the bunk bed, but there's just silence. I let out a breath. They're finally asleep.

I close the door silently behind me, leaving eight campers and their sweet dreams behind in the cabin. I'd almost forgotten just how taxing this job can be. It's amazing, don't get me wrong, but it's also physically and emotionally draining.

I lean my head to one side, feeling the stretch along my neck.

I'm proud of myself, and it's a strange feeling. I haven't felt like this in a while—maybe even since the day I started med school, or even college. In academics, no matter how well I do on a test, there's always something I could have done better. Lately, in med school, there's a lot I could do better.

But today, I felt like I found my groove again. I know who I am here at camp and what my role is. Maybe that's what I've been missing. And I know how to engage a group of kids.

It's a skill that I've known I've had for a long time, to the point where I realize now that I've taken it for granted. The skill isn't exactly useful when my goal is to memorize the layers of the abdominal wall or the innervation of the cranial nerves.

But when a group of ten-year-olds looks up at me, their faces nervous and uncertain? That's when I really shine.

It only took two icebreaker games before they were giggling, and one more before they were hugging one another and laughing uncontrollably. Ha-Ha will do that. It's one of my favorite icebreaker games, where each girl lays her head on the stomach of the one next to her and they say "ha-ha" one at a time, creating ticklish vibrations that roll through the group.

It starts slow, but it brings kids together in record time. A few rounds of that and they were even excited for their swim tests, which normally cause a lot of anxiety.

I might have been the one most nervous to head to

the swimming area, actually. I've been preoccupied with camper arrivals all day and managed to keep thoughts of Miller out of my head. Fortunately, he was nowhere to be seen when we finally made it to the swimming area—the last group of the afternoon, according to Jana.

I mean, not fortunately. I don't care. At all, actually. I don't want to see him, or care what he's up to. He just annoys me.

"I can take tonight," Vivien says as we make our way to the picnic table, her flashlight illuminating the ground ahead of us.

I glance back at her. "You sure?"

Each cabin needs one counselor to stay within view of the door, but when there's two of us, one gets to relax a little. I don't mind being the one to stay, since Vivien knows more of the staff members from her recent summers here and is probably dying to socialize.

She gives me a nudge with her hip and sets the flashlight on the picnic table. "Go. I'll go tomorrow. You were amazing today, for what it's worth. I was already psyched to be your co-counselor, but I can tell it's going to be an amazing summer. For us and for the girls."

I manage a smile as heat rises in my cheeks. "Thanks. I'll be back well before curfew."

The lights are bright in the dining hall as I approach. I used to love these nights, hanging out with the other staff members and hearing all the stories of the crazy things the campers did. But I find myself walking past the door, even as the mix of voices filters out through the windows that are cracked open to let in the cooler evening breeze.

I slip my shoes off when I reach the sand. The air is starting to cool, but the sand is still warm from the hot day. I wiggle my toes to dig them deeper into the grains.

Out on the lake, the water is as smooth as glass, making the full moon reflect in a long line that leaves me in awe. I take a deep breath and close my eyes. The smell of sand and pine trees, the gentle breeze on my face, the sound of the tiny waves lapping at the shore. It's everything I love.

I gaze across the glistening lake as I walk along the shore, loving the contrast between the cooling air and the still-warm water as my feet find my way to my favorite spot.

But as I approach the swing, I'm pulled out of my reverie. There's someone there already, on *my* swing, their body moving it back and forth in the moonlight.

A few steps closer and the mess of blond hair gives it away. My face twists into a scowl.

Miller has taken over my spot.

A rush of frustration fills me as I turn around. My almost meditative walk is ruined, and any plans I had of some quiet time alone on the swing is shot to hell. I start back toward the dining hall, debating whether I should work up the energy to socialize. Maybe I'll just head to bed.

"Becca." His voice is soft, and I almost don't hear it against the sounds of lapping water and the breeze. "Becca," he says again, a little louder.

I finally look over my shoulder as his footsteps approach, uneven on the sand.

"Hey," he says, catching up.

"Hi." I don't have much else to say. *Stay off my swing* sounds petty, and to be fair it's not exclusively my swing. I just happen to love it. And *you're the last person I want to see right now* sounds even worse. And it's not even true. I just enjoy my quiet time.

Miller falls easily into step next to me. "Sorry if I startled you. I was just hoping for a quiet minute, you know? It's been nonstop today with the campers."

I do know, and the fact that Miller is seeking the same solace I am is somehow jarring, since I've settled into the idea of him being my polar opposite. "I thought you'd be chatting it up in the dining hall," I admit.

He shrugs, a lopsided grin spreading over his face. "I like hanging out with people, but I like the quiet sometimes too. Plus, I wanted to call my mom. Tough to do that with all those people around."

He talks to his mom voluntarily? I call my parents when required and do my best to not disappoint them in the few short minutes I spend on the phone with them. It's not that I don't like them—not at all. They're wonderful parents. But that's what they are. *Parents*. Not friends, necessarily, and I think they made that choice consciously. They're of the mindset that your children have plenty of friends, so what they need from you is a parent. Not a friend. I've never minded it, but sometimes I wonder what it would be like to have a parent I wanted to share things with all the time, to joke around, to just hang out.

"That's nice," I manage. I'm struggling to reconcile the Miller in front of me, the one who craves silence and likes to talk with his mother, with the loud, obnoxious guy I know.

He pushes his hair out of his eyes. "So, you can have the swing back if you want. I'm going to walk for a little. It's kind of a perfect night."

He's giving me an easy out, but something is

different about this Miller. He's not the guy who's been making me question myself all week. The idea that he's close to his mother softens him somehow. I'm not sure he's a classic mama's boy, but there's more to him than his frat guy exterior.

I'm not ready to be *friends* just yet, but maybe, just *maybe,* I want to know more about him.

"I think I'm going to walk a little, too," I say after a minute, grasping for more topics of conversation. "You talk to your mom a lot?"

He nods and shoves his hands in the pockets of his cargo shorts. "Almost every day. Or we text. She's one of my best friends." He smiles a little.

"Wow." The idea is a foreign concept to me.

"I know. It's weird, right? But she's cool, I swear." He drops his voice to a whisper. "Sometimes I like her more than my group of best guy friends. She's the one I tell everything to, cause she gives better advice."

I grin despite myself. "That must be nice." My mom gives good advice too, but somehow I don't think she or my dad would exactly understand the situation I'm in right now.

He nods, and we walk in silence for a minute. "So how are your campers? They seem cool?"

I'm glad we've moved on to a topic I'm comfortable with. "Yeah, they seem like fun. Most of them are staying two weeks. They warmed up to one another fast and seem like they're having fun already." I look at the lake. Miller's heavy steps shift the sand by my feet, a constant reminder of his presence. "There are going to be challenges, I'm sure, but so far it's going well."

"Yeah?"

It feels good to talk to Miller right now. He's different in this one-on-one space than he is when he's in a bigger group. He's open and safe, and something about this conversation is just... comfortable.

Maybe it's that I've had a long day with the campers.

Maybe it's the moonlight, or the fact that I'd let my guard down when I started walking alone.

In the back of my mind, I also wonder if maybe I got him wrong the tiniest bit. I'm not interested in being friends, and I'm definitely not interested in something more, but maybe he's not *quite* as... whatever I thought. Cavalier, maybe.

I push a stray hair behind my ear and smooth my French braid down with my fingers. "I have one camper, Maya. She has Down Syndrome, and I was worried the other campers were going to treat her differently. But so far, they're being really accepting."

"I think if you treat her the same, it'll set the tone

for the cabin. If adults treat her differently, that'll prompt the kids to do it, too."

I look back at Miller, expecting his expression to be mocking, or at least slightly sarcastic, but he looks sincere.

As I think about it, I realize he's right. "That's... actually a really good point."

He grins. "You seem shocked that I had a good idea."

I am, but I don't think I should tell him that. It's just that this level of seriousness seems so different from how he normally is with me. With everyone. I just shrug.

"I have a brother with Down Syndrome," Miller says, surprising me again.

I'm not sure why it takes me aback. Maybe it's because I'm only seeing him here, alone, and I never thought to wonder about his family. Or maybe it's the unexpected level of opening up he's doing.

"If you have questions, I'm here," he adds, then blows out a breath as he looks out over the lake. "It really is beautiful at night, isn't it? Anyway, how are you keeping up with your campers? Mine have boundless energy. It's fun, but it's draining. It's making me feel like an old man."

I'm thrown by the abrupt change in topic, but I

laugh, because Miller is older than me by a couple years —I may have asked around—but at twenty-nine, he's the furthest thing from an old man.

"I'm actually not sure," I say honestly. "I think their enthusiasm kind of rubs off on me somehow, and I take my cues from them. When they get comfortable and start to really be themselves, it's just... I'm not sure there's a word for it. But it's an amazing feeling, and it keeps me going." I study his face again, waiting for him to make fun of me, but it doesn't change.

"Makes sense." He looks at me, expression earnest. "You're good at this counselor thing."

Heat rises in my cheeks, and I peer back at the lake to gather myself for a minute. I've never been good at taking compliments. Growing up, my parents were proud of me, sure, but it was rare that they actually *said* it. Between that and my ever-present anxiety that tells me I'm not good enough, I have trouble believing compliments when I do get them.

And getting one from Miller is completely throwing me for a loop.

Except his next words ruin the moment completely.

"Want to help me put Brett's boxers up the flagpole?"

I snap my gaze back to Miller. "What?"

His lazy grin is back, and the serious, sincere Miller is gone so fast I wonder if I imagined it. "I've got a pair of his underwear. I'm going to swap it with the flag. The campers will love it."

"You don't take any of this seriously, do you?" I throw my hands in the air, exasperated. For a minute I almost thought there was more to him than the joker in front of me, but turns out the joke was on me. Pun intended.

Miller shifts, coming to stand in front of me, so close the air gets too thick to breathe. "I take lots of things seriously."

I step back, and Miller mirrors my movement, stepping closer. I open my mouth, searching for words to tell him off. He's too close. My heart beats faster, so loud I'm sure he can hear it.

I step back again. I need to take a breath, because the pull toward him is too strong. The sand shifts beneath my feet and I stumble, almost losing my balance before a strong arm wraps around me, a large hand pressing into my back. It's firm and warm as he holds me steady. The heat spreads through me as I stare up into his face.

"Give me a chance," Miller says softly. He pulls me the tiniest bit closer to his body. My hands find his chest, pressing against him. I'm not sure if I'm pushing him away or pulling him closer to me.

His free hand traces my jaw, a line of electricity left in its wake, and an unfamiliar feeling pulses in my stomach.

14

MILLER

In the moonlight, her pupils dilate, making her deep brown eyes look almost black.

I lean in, close enough that she would only need to move a few inches for our lips to meet. Close enough that my intentions can't be misunderstood.

But I wait, needing her to make this move. I've been waiting for her to let me in, and this could be our chance. Holding myself still is torture when her lips are this close. A couple of inches is all that separates me from what I've been dreaming of since the first day I saw her.

All I want to do is pull her in, crush my lips to hers, and make her mine.

But she needs to make this decision, not me. I can't take this from her.

Becca's sharp intake of breath has me closing my eyes, waiting for her lips to meet mine.

But instead of her warm lips, cool air brushes my face.

I open my eyes to find Becca stepping back from me. Her gaze is on the ground, avoiding my eyes as she shakes her head. "I'm sorry. I should go."

I take a step back too, giving her space. What just happened? "That was—I'm sorry. You don't have to go. Walk with me?"

I need to salvage this somehow. Maybe I got carried away, tried to move too fast. What did I think, that a few minutes of walking in the moonlight was going to change her entire opinion of me?

Yeah, that's exactly what I thought. I opened up, showed her the part of me that I keep hidden from the rest of the world. I thought that maybe if she saw that part, she'd understand. That she'd give in to the attraction that's been growing between us.

It's obvious, at least to me. Can't she feel it?

Becca hesitates, indecision written across her features.

My voice is soft, like I'm speaking to a scared

animal, because that's exactly what she reminds me of. A shy creature who's about to bolt. "I want to know more about you. What made you decide to come up to camp for the summer? What do you do the rest of the year?"

I hold my hand out, palm up. I'm hoping she'll take it, like a peace offering as I try to transition the conversation to something that's not as emotionally charged as the moment between us was.

Patience, Miller. Give her time. Give her space.

But instead of taking my hand, she stiffens into that posture I'm getting to know so well, the one where she puts up walls between herself and the rest of the world. Between us.

Her face shutters, all emotions disappearing from view.

"I-I have to go." She stumbles as she hurries across the sand toward the dining hall.

I watch her, stunned. That seemed like a benign question. I wanted to engage her in small talk, not scare her off.

How did that send her running even faster than my almost kissing her?

Clearly, there's something I don't know, and I'm going to make it my mission to find out. Because Becca might think that her blowing me off tonight made me less interested, but all it did was pique my interest even further.

I need to know more. I need to know everything about this girl.

Becca walks quickly past the light of the dining hall, disappearing into the shadowy night. My phone buzzes in my pocket, and I pull it out as I turn back toward the beach.

MOM

How's it going? Can't wait to hear about my future daughter-in-law!

I roll my eyes as I type out a text back. My mom has always offered her unwavering support for anything I say I want to do, no matter how improbable or poorly thought out my goals might be. I tell her I have a crush on a girl? She starts planning the wedding.

Crash and burn this time. There's something there that I can't quite figure out with her.

Keep trying. Mama didn't raise no quitter.

Thanks. You know I will. Jordan still up?

I wait, and a minute later Mom sends a thumbs-up emoji to indicate that Jordan is up for talking. I make my way back to the swing.

Sitting here to call my mom earlier might have been a little bit of a calculated decision. I was hoping to see Becca, and since I know she loves this spot, I took a gamble and hung out here. But the spot is growing on me for its own merits. It's the perfect place to sit and relax without distractions.

I settle in against the smooth wood before scrolling to the contact for my mom's house phone and dialing the number. Even though Mom has had a cell phone for years, she'll never give up her house phone.

"Hello?" Jordan's voice comes through the speaker as the call connects.

"Hey, Jordan. It's me. Thanks for talking on a Sunday." Jordan loves routine. Sometimes he'll just refuse to talk if I call on a day other than our usual Tuesday.

"It's okay. I was playing a video game, but I'm done now."

"Mario Kart?" That one's his favorite. Mine, too. It's an old classic that we discovered when the

Nintendo Classic came out and we ended up loving it more than any of the more modern games we had on our other systems.

I used to be able to beat him easily at almost any video game, but it didn't hurt that I'm seven years older, and that my motor skills were more advanced, since his Down Syndrome delayed some of his skills. He's gotten better with lots of practice, and now we're pretty evenly matched.

"Yeah. Do you like camp?" Dishes clank in the background. He must be in the kitchen, maybe cleaning up after dinner. Or getting a snack.

My stomach rumbles at the thought of food. I wonder if the campers would wake up if I dug out some of the snacks I have hidden in the cabin in a bag under my bed. The chips might make a lot of noise, but there are other options in there. Gummy worms might hit the spot.

"I do like it. It's really fun. Maybe you can come up and visit sometime this summer. I'll stop by on my way home at least and stay with you guys for a few days so we can hang out. Are you taking care of Mom?" I push off the ground, making the swing sway gently.

"Yeah. We had spaghetti for dinner tonight." Jordan's favorite. Even though he lives with Mom primarily because of his disability, he really does take care of her, and he's damn proud of it. The two of them split the cooking and laundry duties; Jordan does the grocery shopping and Mom does the driving.

Over the years since he's finished high school, they've settled into a steady routine.

"With marinara? My favorite. Hey, how's work? Did they make you employee of the month again?" That would make it... six times, now, in the four years he's worked there?

We chat for another twenty minutes about Jordan's job as a bagger at the grocery store.

I wish everyone could see what I see when I look at Jordan. His hard work and dedication, unwavering loyalty to friends and family, his unbridled optimism. So many people just see his disability.

He had some health challenges when he was young, so it wasn't always the easiest growing up with him for a brother, but it's shaped me into who I am in lots of ways.

"Did you do any pranks yet?" Jordan asks, as the subject turns back to camp.

I can imagine his blue eyes shining, mirror images of mine. When we were little, he was the best sidekick for the pranks I'd pull on Mom.

Still my favorite by far: the time Jordan and I tried to switch places and trick Mom into thinking he was me and I was him. It was mostly Jordan's idea, and we weren't exactly convincing when he was nine and I was fifteen. The identical blond hair and blue eyes only go so far.

I chuckle. "Not yet. I borrowed a pair of my friend Brett's boxers. Thinking about putting them on the flagpole. Think that'd be funny?"

He howls with laughter, which gives me my answer. Jordan has always been my target audience for my pranks if he's not involved in them in the first place. He loves things that are generally funny and harmless at the same time, so that's always the goal.

"Underwear on a flagpole! That will be funny. Will they say the Pledge of Allegiance to them?"

I smirk at the idea. "The Pledge of Underwear, maybe."

This sets Jordan off again. When his laughter finally dies down, I pull the phone away from my ear to check the time.

"Hey, Jordan, I have to go. It's almost curfew. We have to be in our cabins by ten." It's a stupid rule, if you ask me. I'm twenty-nine and usually stay out at bars past ten. I don't need to be told when to be in bed.

But if I get fired over a stupid rule, I'll lose any chance to win Becca over. I wouldn't put it past her to block my number. Here at camp, she's stuck with me.

"Okay. Talk to you later. Love you, Miller!" Jordan hangs up the phone.

I head back toward the Fireflies cabins, making a detour by the flagpole to attach Brett's boxers to the line and hoist them until they're flying like a flag at the top. He chose well with the ones he offered up; these have hearts all over them in shades of red and pink. The campers will love them.

Like I said, my pranks are meant to be harmless. I didn't actually steal Brett's boxers. Who would do that? I asked him for a pair for exactly this purpose. The campers will think it's hilarious, and since Brett is in on the joke, no one will get hurt. I'm not an asshole.

The entire funny-guy, easygoing, jokester personality was carefully curated back in the day to give people what they want. And no one wants an asshole.

I use the phone's flashlight to guide my way through the woods to my cabin. When I reach the bathroom that the Fireflies share, a text message flashes on my screen.

CARD SHARKS

Blake: You survive the first day?

Barely. But it was fun.

Maddox: Told you it'd be too much.

Cam: We talked about this. Don't be a dick.

Maddox: Right. Sorry. You've got this, Miller.

Blake: So, are the campers cool?

Exhausting, but yeah. I get a kick out of them.

Cam: How's the girl?

I thought we were getting somewhere. We walked on the beach tonight.

Blake: Moonlit walk on the beach? Very romantic.

Yeah, except then she bolted.

Cam: Did you show her your dick?

I'm too confused right now to even address that. But no. I just asked her what she did when she wasn't at camp. How is that a touchy question?

Cam: Maybe she's in the Mafia.

Maddox: Witness protection?

Cam: Owns a money-laundering front?

Why would she have the summer off from the money-laundering front?

Blake: Honestly, she's probably in school.

Cam: Or a teacher. Addie has the summer off.

Maddox: Holly says maybe she got fired from her job.

Why are you reading our texts to Holly?

Maddox: She thinks you guys are hilarious. I don't understand why.

Does she have any advice?

Maddox: She says to take it slow and take your cues from her, but I think that's terrible advice. If I backed off when Holly didn't want to go out with me, we wouldn't be where we are now. Just keep showing up and talking to her and eventually she'll give up and marry you, like Holly did with me.

Maddox: This is Holly. Maddox has lost his phone privileges. Just be a nice guy and let her take the lead a little.

Man, she's got you by the balls.

Maddox: Still Holly.

Should I at least text her?

Cam: Sure.

Blake: Can't hurt.

Maddox: NO LEAVE HER ALONE
WHY DON'T YOU GUYS EVER
LISTEN TO ME.

Good luck, Maddox.

Maddox: Holly threw the phone at
me and says she hates you all.

Holly might think Becca needs me to leave her alone, but Maddox has a point. He didn't give up on Holly, even after she tried to date half the city trying to find someone better than him.

Addie lusted after Cam for more than a decade before they finally got together.

So maybe Holly thinks she's giving good advice, but what I've learned from watching my friends is that persistence pays off. I consider this as I tap out a text message to Becca, trying to smooth out whatever damage I did tonight.

BECCA

> Hey. Hope I didn't say something I shouldn't have or make you uncomfortable. Glad you had a good first day with your campers. Sweet dreams.

When I wake up in the morning to the sound of the camp bell ringing, there's still no answer.

15

BECCA

*S*hit. *Shit, shit, shit.*

That was too close. Not just physically, although God only knows what I was thinking with that, too. I knew how big he was—I've seen him with his shirt off, after all, and he "rescued" me while we were doing lifeguard training, so I've been pressed up against his body before.

But this was different. My heart wasn't beating this fast any other time, and I wasn't so... *aware* of him. Though, that's not even the part I'm kicking myself about.

I almost opened my mouth and blurted out everything: how I'm a fuck-up at life, the whole mess with med school and how I can't tell my parents and how I'm hiding away here.

He was so sweet and sincere, and it almost had me spilling everything.

And that story is not something that anyone can know. Even Vivien doesn't know the entire thing, and she knows more than I planned to share with anyone in the first place. If I share this with Miller, I'm scared that it'll just be a matter of time before his big mouth blurts it out to everyone.

I shake my head as I slip between the trees, my feet making their way along the dark path by memory. I need to get a grip here. Play my cards close to the vest.

And stay the hell away from Miller.

"Eww!" Lena groans. The tiny blonde has established herself as the ringleader of our group of campers, and most of the time, I'm all for it.

But she's currently leading them all in rebelling against the simplest thing: cleaning the communal bathrooms.

It's not a big deal. It's not. Cleaning bathrooms is a part of life, and it's a part of camp. Every cabin group gets assigned a day to clean, and today is our day. Otherwise, we'd have paper towels everywhere, mirrors covered in a film of God knows what, and overflowing toilets.

Well, we have the overflowing toilets pretty regularly. Little girls tend to use way too much toilet paper. But we do our best.

I plant my hands on my hips while I wait for them to get their protests out. When the volume dies down, I hold one hand in the air.

"This is happening, ladies. We all do our part. Here's how it's going to go. Each of you is going to come over here and pick a job out of this cup. No redos, no tradesies. If you all do the jobs you pick without complaining, I'll take the toilets." I shake the cup.

This gets an immediate reaction, like it always does. Faced with the prospect of having to clean the toilets and the chance to avoid it, the girls snap into action, practically falling over themselves to try to get a job like sweeping or cleaning the mirrors.

They each take a folded slip of paper and set off to do the job listed, while I pull the cleaning supplies out from underneath the cabinets and pick up a toilet brush.

"I love that," Vivien remarks as she pulls on rubber gloves alongside me. "I've never thought of doing it that way. They're so excited to avoid toilets they'll do the rest of it. Genius."

We each take a stall and start to scrub as the campers wipe down sinks. The campers may hate doing the toilets, but if you ask me, this job is about a million times better than cleaning toothpaste spit off the mirror.

"So how was last night? You went to bed pretty fast after you got back." Vivien flushes the toilet she's working on and moves on to the next stall.

I scrub a bit more firmly at the ring of hard water in the toilet bowl. Or maybe it's built-up poo. Best not to think about it. "Yeah. It was okay. I just walked along the beach for a while. I was going to go sit on the swing, but... someone was there."

"Yeah? Anyone special?" Her voice carries across two stalls.

I turn around to see Mollie and Savannah grinning at me, their ears perked up at the hope of gossip. "Not really. Get back to cleaning, girls."

Relationships between staff members aren't discouraged, exactly, but Brett makes it clear that the campers shouldn't know anything about it. Plus, the last thing I need is a bunch of ten-year-olds sing-singing *Becca and Miller, sitting in a tree, K-I-S-S-I-N-G!*

For the record, we weren't. And we're not going to.

"Hey, did you see the thing at the flagpole this morning?" Vivien changes the subject.

I flush down the suds of the cleaning solution and move to the next stall.

"I just saw some people gathered around there this morning. What was up?" I can guess, but I'm not going to admit any knowledge here.

Vivien appears behind me, grinning. "Someone put a pair of boxers up the flagpole instead of the flag. A real *Salute Your Shorts* moment, right? Classic."

The campers giggle.

"I heard it was the camp director's underwear," Lena offers, turning from the mirror she's wiping down. "It was boxers with little hearts all over them. Do you think Brett really wears those?"

"Why would they put his underwear on the flagpole?" Maya looks genuinely confused as the other girls snicker.

I peel off my gloves and tuck the toilet brush back into its holder. "Someone thought it would be funny, or maybe they thought it would be embarrassing. But is it really funny to embarrass other people?"

The laughter dies down as heads shake around the room.

"I bet whoever's underwear it was felt sad," Mollie says, and Lena and Maya nod.

"We should do something nice for Brett. Or for whoever's underwear it was," Savannah adds.

This is taking a turn I'm not exactly prepared for. "Well, I think we—"

"Good idea, girls!" Vivien winks at me. "How do we know whose underwear it was?"

"A bunch of the Fireflies boys were standing around the flagpole this morning. Maybe we can ask them."

The other campers nod at Lena's suggestion, while I rack my brain for a way to say no. Because I know exactly who has the real scoop here, and I do *not* want to get mixed up with Miller and his campers.

"Let's just finish cleaning, okay?" I need to regain control here.

Bathrooms, not boxers.

Vivien hoots triumphantly behind me. I turn to see her sliding her contraband phone back into her shorts pocket. "Fireflies 2 is playing kickball in the field after this. And Dave says they *know something*. So clean hard, girls. We have a mission."

"Strike one!" I hear Miller's voice before I see him.

Other voices carry through the trees, getting louder as we get closer to the Sports field.

I've never seen campers clean a bathroom so quickly. I did my best to waste time so we'd have to abandon this mission, but it was spotless in record time as they all worked together, their focus on their upcoming scheme.

As the branches part in front of us, I take in the scene. The eight boys from Miller and Dave's cabin are lined up, taking turns kicking the rubber ball as Miller pitches, rolling it toward them at varying speeds.

"Hey! A worthy opponent," Miller says when he sees us, raising a hand in greeting.

We're *not* here to play. Get in and get out. "We just came to ask—"

Lena plants her hands on her hips, taking charge. "Whose underwears were those on the flagpole?" she demands.

I try to hide my smile at her use of the word *underwears* in reference to a pair of boxers.

The other campers follow suit, little hands fisted on their hips. It's about as intimidating as a group of ten-year-olds can look. Which is to say, not very.

Miller grins as he rolls the ball toward another camper. "Brett's."

My campers aren't amused.

"He probably feels bad. We're going to make him feel better," Mollie announces, after Miller's camper sends the ball soaring across the field with a strong kick.

Miller pauses. "Oh. Well, that's a very nice thought, but he doesn't mind. I asked him if I could do it. So, if you don't need to comfort him, we'd love to invite you to join us in our kickball game."

Huh. I could have sworn he said he *stole* the boxers, but maybe I'm remembering it that way because of my mindset when we were talking. It certainly makes the prank more harmless if Brett was in on it.

"Sounds great!" Vivien says, following the girls as they stream onto the field. "You guys kick first. Becca, do you want to pitch?"

I do not, in fact, want to pitch. I don't even want to be here, anywhere close to the man who was *this close* to getting me to spill way too much. Plus, I don't need him to blurt out that he's the one I was talking with last night.

I just... I need to get us into another situation. Preferably all the way across camp.

Maybe across the lake. Sailboats?

"Becca?"

I jump, realizing that the three other counselors are

all staring at me. Shit. "Sorry. Lost in thought for a second. I'll take the outfield with the girls. Vivien, you pitch."

Vivien is a ruthless pitcher, or at least her skills outmatch the bunch of eight and nine-year-olds in Miller's cabin. One gets on base, one strikes out, then another on base. Vivien walks a little guy who looks vaguely afraid of the ball altogether, loading the bases.

While kickball is the same in theory as baseball—just with a ball you kick, not throw—there's very little action for the fielding team at this level of play.

Most of the girls just stand there, grabbing the ball when in bounces slowly toward them well after the other team is already on base. When the ball goes any measurable distance, it falls to the counselors to chase after it.

We don't keep score, at least not officially, but Vivien lets a couple of the boys cross home plate before she strikes out another camper and we switch sides, giving the girls a chance to kick.

"We're going to dominate!" Lena announces, making me smile as the other girls cheer.

I love her confidence and general optimism. I hope for her sake that the rest of these girls have more sports skills than I do, because I certainly can't carry the team. Not like Miller, who seems like a natural athlete with the way he jogs out to the pitching mound and juggles the ball in his hands, then with his feet.

Furrowing my brows, I try not to gawk. Where do people learn to do things like that?

I arrange my campers into some sort of batting—kicking—order. There's no sense of strategy here, more just trying to keep them in a line.

"He looks good up there, eh?" Vivien mutters under her breath as Miller pulls his arm back to send the ball rolling toward our first kicker.

I ignore her, even when she elbows my side. I have no opinion on how Miller looks out there, his white t-shirt just a little too tight across his chest and showing off his pecs. His corded legs extend from board shorts, muscles rippling as he pitches.

So, he has muscles. Who cares? Not me.

Miller pitches to two of our campers, each of them getting one base, before he motions for Dave to come over.

He hands off the ball as Dave takes his place on the pitching mound, shifting the ball from one hand to the other.

"You want to head to the outfield?" Dave asks.

Miller shakes his head. "Keep playing; I'll be right back. I just have to ask Becca something," he says, jogging toward me.

No. No, he does *not*.

I do my best to ignore him, instead focusing on cheering for my team. Dave rolls a slow ball toward Maya, who kicks with all her might and runs toward first base, making it safely. My heart warms at the smile that spreads across her face.

"Hey. I wanted to talk to you about—" Miller starts.

"Go, Lena!" I cheer as our next camper heads up to kick. I cross my fingers that we can get Maya in for a home run.

"Becca," Miller prompts.

Lena connects with the ball, sending it soaring toward first base, and I turn to face Miller. "What? Sorry, I'm trying to focus on the campers for now."

He winces. "Sure. I just wanted to see if you were okay."

"I'm fine." As far as he needs to know.

He doesn't look convinced. "Anyway, if you need someone to talk to—"

He breaks off as someone yells from across the field.

We both look up just in time to see the disaster a second before it strikes.

16

MILLER

When Becca's eyes go wide and she lets out a gasp, I forget what I was about to ask her. I follow her line of sight. I'm not fast enough to see how it happened, but it's pretty clear from the aftermath.

The kickball bounces sadly on the field, while Maya sits on the ground, the other girls rushing to her as she holds her hand to her face. Even from this far away, I can see the blood seeping through her fingers.

My stomach drops. Maya is in one of the classes I'm teaching in the Nature department, and she's the sweetest kid. She reminds me of my brother when he was younger.

"Maya!" Becca rushes toward her.

I run a hand down my face. This is not going well.

I should have been out there with my campers. I could have blocked the ball, maybe.

My campers are all over the place, as are the girls. Two of the boys have followed Dave toward the injured camper. Five of them are shifting from foot to foot in their spots on the field, looking like they don't know what to do with themselves, and Liam is still standing in his position between first and second base.

From the guilty look on his face, it doesn't take a rocket scientist to figure out that he must have been the one to throw the ball.

A few of Becca's campers are still on the sidelines, staring at the scene and talking in hushed voices. The one blonde—Lena—who kicked the ball toward Liam is hesitantly making her way to first base, looking uncertain about whether she should finish her run or stop.

"Okay," I say, putting my serious voice on and raising the volume. "Fireflies 2, Ladybugs 2, all you guys over here. Sit in a circle." I point to the ground by my feet.

Dave gives me a nod and says something to the two boys closest to him. Caleb and Oliver come scampering back toward me.

"Did you see that?" Caleb asks, his eyes huge as he reaches us.

I shake my head. "I didn't see the whole thing." *Because I was busy flirting instead of keeping you guys safe,* I think.

"Liam threw the ball right into Maya's face!"

I could have guessed that from the look on Liam's face. He's still frozen in place on the field. "You boys sit here. I'm going to see if Liam is okay. The other counselors are good with Maya for right now."

The campers sit in a group, actually listening for a change as I make my way to the center of the field where most of the commotion is happening. Dave, Becca, and Vivien might be handling things, but they're not exactly *good* with things for now, at least not all of them. There's a lot of freaking out happening.

As I get closer, I can hear Vivien's animated voice talking about stitches and emergency rooms. Dave is practically hyperventilating, pacing back and forth.

Becca, however, is the picture of calm. She's focused solely on Maya and has managed to calm her down, too. The two are sitting cross-legged in the grass while Dave and Vivien pace around them.

I pass Lena, pausing to nod toward the seated campers. "Go ahead and sit with the other kids, okay? We'll get back to the game in a bit."

She scurries off without a word.

Liam looks to be on the verge of tears when I reach the spot between first and second base where he's standing, his chin quivering. I sling an arm around his shoulders as I stop next to him.

"I didn't mean to, honest," he says in a small voice.

"I know you didn't, bud." I ruffle his hair. "You're not in trouble. Accidents happen, and she's going to be fine. I'm going to go help calm things down, okay? Are you good to go sit with your buddies?"

He gives me a nod, and I let him go. I'm sure we'll have to talk more about this later; he strikes me as a sensitive kid who'll feel bad about hitting another camper, even by accident.

"How're you doing?" I crouch next to Becca, my hand on her shoulder as I size up the situation. Maya's nose is bleeding pretty profusely, the red fluid dripping onto the grass.

"We're fine," Becca says, her tone clipped.

I ignore the attitude and pull off my t-shirt. "Here you go. Hold this against your nose, okay?" I ball it up and pass it to Maya.

"I said we're fine," Becca says, glaring, like I took off my shirt just to show off my abs.

I mean, my abs are pretty nice, if I do say so myself. I work hard for my six-pack. And if she wants to look,

I'm not going to stop her. But this time I really did take my shirt off for altruistic reasons.

Maya needs something to absorb the bleeding, and it's not like Becca can take her shirt off.

I mean, I wouldn't complain if she did. I've seen her in a bathing suit, and it only has me itching to see more. She has the perfect round, soft body, her tits lush. I'd give anything to explore every inch of her with my fingers, my tongue, my—

"Are you going to do something or just pose?" Becca looks like she wants to murder me. Can she hear what I'm thinking?

I do my best to put thoughts of Becca's body out of my head and focus on the situation we have here. "Dave, Vivien, can you guys get the campers involved in something? I'm going to help Becca take Maya to the infirmary." I glance back at Becca, who still looks like she wants to incinerate me with her glare.

Unfortunately for her, I actually was paying attention during staff training. We're not supposed to be one-on-one with campers. So, she needs someone else to go with her to take Maya to the nurse. And lucky for her, I'm ready and willing to help. Plus, I want my shirt back.

But then I look at the cloth that Maya's clenching

to her nose, blood already seeping through. On second thought, maybe we'll just throw that in the trash.

"What's going on?" The camp nurse, a motherly fifty-something named Deb, holds the door open for us to enter the infirmary, her brows creased in concern.

"Bloody nose," Becca says, at the same time as I say, "Kickball injury."

Deb nods, glancing down at Maya. "I see. And who do we have here?"

The little girl pulls the bloodied shirt away from her face, grinning. "I'm Maya. I'm okay." A single drip of blood escapes from one nostril, rolling down her face.

As the shock of being hit in the face has worn off, she's perked up, even laughing at my jokes on the way to the infirmary.

At least someone thinks I'm funny.

"Well, glad to hear that, Maya. Let's come in here and I'll get you an ice pack, okay? You two, stay here." Deb ushers Maya into a back room and closes the door, effectively dismissing us.

I slide into a chair, while Becca crosses her arms over her chest and leans against a wall. I wait for her to say something, but all that fills the space are her sighs.

"Hey. She's going to be fine," I assure her. I'm not sure that's what's on Becca's mind, but I have to say something. "And she's going to come through this with a smile on her face. She's like my brother. He has Down Syndrome, too, remember? Maya reminds me of him."

Becca throws her hands in the air. "God, I can't believe this happened. We're off to such a bad start."

"Nah. It'll be a story the campers re-tell. I think they were having fun playing kickball, though. It worked out well to have you guys join us. Eight campers isn't exactly enough for a real game."

She narrows her eyes at me. "I feel like you planned this somehow."

I chuckle. "I wish I was good enough to have planned this. Nope, just a happy coincidence." I pat the seat next to me. "Sit, relax. It might be a bit."

Becca runs her hands over her face as she lowers herself into the chair, staring at the ground. "Thank you for helping get the campers under control."

I nudge her with my elbow. "Hey, that might be the first nice thing you've said to me."

This earns me the tiniest smile. "Don't get used to it."

I drum my fingers on my thigh. *Don't fuck this up, Miller.* "So. I'm sorry about last night." I reach over and give her thigh a light squeeze.

She looks at me. She doesn't respond, but her breath hitches, just enough for me to know she's affected by my touch.

"All better," Deb announces as she leads Maya back to the lobby, and I pull my hand back into my own lap. "Maya should take it easy for the next few hours, but she'll be fine. What activity do you have first today, honey?" she asks Maya, who's already starting to show signs of a black eye forming.

She thinks for a minute. "Canoeing is first after lunch."

Deb nods. "That should be just fine. Lunch and rest time should give you a little time to recover, and canoeing is a nice, gentle activity."

Becca laughs under her breath. "I'll make sure they don't do any canoe tipping today, okay? Maya, are you ready to head to lunch?" she asks.

I peer at the clock on the wall. Somehow the morning has flown by while I was busy showing reckless disregard for campers' safety. It's already 11:30. The younger kids will be lining up outside the dining hall for lunch already.

Becca focuses all of her attention on Maya while

we walk toward the dining hall, asking her questions about anything and everything, which keeps her from focusing on her injury.

Deb handed my shirt back to me before we left. I hold it balled-up in my fist, taking a cue from Becca to keep Maya's mind off the blood and, thus, off her injury. My shirt is completely covered with drying blood, and even a quick look makes it easy to see it's a lost cause.

I toss it in the first trash can we pass, glad to be rid of it.

"Don't you need a shirt to go to lunch?" Becca finally addresses me as we near the dining hall.

I look down at my bare chest, like I'm just now realizing I'm shirtless. "Huh. Look at that. Guess so."

She rolls her eyes.

Someday. Someday she's going to laugh at one of my jokes.

I switch gears. "Can you make sure there's a second counselor at my table? I'm going to run back to the cabin. To get a shirt," I clarify. "I might be a few minutes late."

Becca gives me a wave that looks, frankly, like a dismissal.

"Bye, Miller!" Maya says, waving with a large smile on her face.

"Bye, Maya. You were super brave today." I give her a high five, then detour onto a path through the woods to grab a shirt, my mind deep in thought.

I screwed up today. I get that, I really do. My job was to be watching the campers, and if I'd been out there on the field with my boys, I might have been able to block the ball, or yell a warning, or something.

I turn the corner, dodging the root that runs across the path as I try to figure out where to go next. The path to the cabin I've got. The path to winning Becca over? Not so much.

She doesn't seem to like the usual laid-back, joking guy that everyone else loves. Trying to be sincere and ask her questions about herself that night on the beach somehow crashed and burned. And now the only real interaction she's seen me have with the campers is where I got distracted and one of them got hurt.

I jog up the steps to the cabin and open the door. Maybe the problem is that Becca's only getting to see these glimpses of me in small doses. Maybe if I had more time to spend with her—a whole day, or even a few solid hours—I could show her I'm not whoever she's built up in her mind.

The more time I spend with her and pay attention to her, the more captivated I am by her.

At first, it was her looks. Her quiet confidence, her intelligence.

But there's so much more to her that I need to know. I'm just getting glimpses so far. But every peek, every layer I peel back shows me something else that's so uniquely Becca that I can't just walk away.

I pull a shirt over my head. This started as a silly bet, this whole camp thing, and I figured I'd be gone in a week. But now, I'm here for as long as it takes to win her over.

17

BECCA

Everything is fine.

It's been three days since the kickball disaster, and none of my other campers have gotten injured. Maya had a black eye, but it's already fading, and the nurse who spoke with Maya's parents said they're not upset, that these things happen.

They shouldn't happen, though. Especially under my watch.

It's also been three days since I've seen Miller besides in passing. We're at the dining hall at the same times for meals, but other than that, I've kept my distance.

And what do you know? No accidents.

There's a lesson in this somehow. Maybe it's that Miller being around leads to accidents. More likely, it's that I'm a hot mess when I'm around him, which frustrates me to no end.

During the kickball game, I should have been paying attention, focusing on my campers. Then Maya wouldn't have gotten hurt.

I nod to myself. No more getting distracted. Especially not by Miller.

"Do you all have your bathing suits if you need them?" Vivien asks, looking from camper to camper.

Their first activity periods start in a few minutes, which means they'll head out from the cabin to go to the classes they signed up for on their first day here, while Vivien and I go to our respective departments.

Murmurs of "yes" filter through the cabin from everyone but Bayley and Evie, who aren't taking any classes in swimming or boating so they don't need their suits.

"Towels, too?" I add, looking around the cabin.

Even though they've been doing the same routine for days, somehow at least one camper manages to forget something almost every day.

"Oh!" Mollie squeaks, her eyes going wide. I smile as she scurries out of the cabin to where the towels are hanging up to dry, Savannah following her.

I adjust the straps of my bathing suit, making sure the bottom edges keep my ladybug tattoo hidden as the campers come back inside, beach towels in hand. I grab my own towel from the laundry basket under my bed and tuck it into my backpack.

Boating has always been my favorite department. What could be better than hanging out on the beach the entire summer? Even when it rains, we always find ways to have fun. And while I could do without the rowboats, I absolutely live for sailing.

The camp bell rings to signal the end of rest hour, and the campers head off to their activities. As I head out of Ladybugs Cabin 2, other campers are streaming out of their respective cabins in a mass of excitement. I walk with Maya, who's taking canoeing first period.

"How do you like your classes so far?" I ask, stepping over a root.

Maya watches the uneven ground in front of us, walking carefully. "I like them a lot. Camp is so much fun."

"What's your favorite thing so far?"

She looks up at me for a second, a grin stretched wide across her face. "The goat class. It's so funny. Miller pretends like he hates Lucy. That's the goat."

I manage a smile. I'm not in the mood to talk about Miller, especially with Maya's black eye staring me in the face as a reminder of my failings. "How about canoeing? You liking that?"

Maya nods. "Yeah. I hope we tip canoes today. The counselor said maybe if it was hot we could."

I wave a hand in front of my face like a fan. "Well, you might be in luck. I'm already sweating."

Maya tells me all about her favorite things at camp as we make our way to the boathouse. When we get there, it turns out I was right: canoe tipping is indeed on the agenda for today.

Maya jumps up and down, the ends of her towel fluttering around her. "I'm so excited!"

I give her a quick hug before I step over to where the counselors are standing. "Have so much fun! I can't wait to hear all about it."

Each afternoon the kids get three activity periods in a row, moving between departments while the counselors stick with their assigned departments and teach classes. I have a rowing class—not my favorite—canoeing, and at the end of the day, sailing. The best class by far, the one I look forward to all day.

By late afternoon, the wind has sometimes picked up enough that we can really get a good clip going. Just fast enough to get the wind in your hair and feel the adrenaline zipping through you.

When the bell rings for third period to start, I look out at the lake, smiling as I see the darkening of the wind flowing over the surface of the water. It's a good day for sailing.

Three counselors are assigned to teach this class for third period. With twelve kids, it means we each get one boat to take out, and we divide up the campers, taking four in each boat. Most of the time we do the sailing ourselves, and the kids just ride along, maybe holding the rudder if they're feeling confident.

But sailing isn't something you learn in a few days, and most of them are just happy to be out on the lake and going fast.

Drew, the Boating department head, takes attendance after the campers arrive, checking off the kids one by one, and the sailing class splits into the same three groups as the other days.

I lead my group to the first boat. My crew is comprised of four thirteen-year-olds who have been remarkably fun these last couple of days.

"Do you guys remember how to pull the sail up?" I ask, looking around.

We went over this information both of the last two days. The goal of these classes isn't really to have them master anything, more just get an experience, but I always like seeing the look on the kids' faces when they realize they've acquired a new skill.

One of the boys points. "You pull on that rope."

"Yes! Good job, Jacob." I give him a high five. "Does anyone remember what the thing the rope is wrapped around is called?"

This group is on top of things. Between the four of them, they manage to recall the names for the cleat, jib, mainsail, and rudder, and it's only five minutes before we're all suited up in lifejackets and pushing out onto the lake.

I pull the rudder down into position and lower the keel as we get deeper, then steer us out into the open water. The wind is warm against my face, the sky a perfect blue.

I close my eyes, imagining. What if life could be like this every day?

Low stress, just enjoying the good things in life.

"Coming about," I say to warn the kids that the mast is about to sweep over their heads as we turn. As the mast swings, I switch sides of the boat, then direct the campers toward the front of the boat to switch the jib sheet, the smaller sail of the two. "Uncleat from your side, then pull it to your side. Good. And pull it through the cleat right there."

I love the smiles on their faces as they show off their new skill.

"Can we go any faster?" Abby, the camper next to me, asks.

At their age, it's understandable that they want a little thrill. I'm not the most thrill-seeking person to be honest, but I want them to have fun.

I pull the rudder to put us at a sharper angle to the wind, and we pick up speed.

"This is awesome!" one of them yells over the sound of the wind in my ears.

I turn again to slow us down, my pulse hammering in my ears.

Abby grins at me. "Wasn't that fun?"

That almost gave me a panic attack, but if they're enjoying themselves, that's what counts. Right? I take a deep breath to calm my racing heart.

"Can we do it again?" Tyler pipes up from next to Jacob.

"Give me a minute," I say. I take another breath to calm my nerves and look out at the mountains in the distance.

Being out here on the lake, where it's quiet and free? This is everything. I'm glad I made the decision to come up to camp this summer, because this is exactly what my soul needed. A chance to get away from it all.

And other than Miller, the summer so far has been perfect.

A small frown crosses my face, and I manage to school my features before any of the kids see it. What is it about him? There's something that just grates at me, gets under my skin somehow.

I think it's the way he looks at me. He holds eye contact way longer than most people. Usually, when you talk with someone, their eyes are all over the place, taking in the surroundings and focusing on you only part of the time. But when Miller talks to me, he's focused on me alone.

It makes the world shrink, makes me feel like I'm the only thing that matters in that moment.

Maybe it would be nice if it were someone else. Or if things in my life outside camp weren't such a mess, or if I were someone else entirely.

When he fixes me with his gaze, I want to tell him things, and that scares me.

Not to mention the way my body reacts when he's around. It must be because I haven't had sex in a while. Well, two years. But I've been busy, and my vibrator gets the job done, quick and efficient.

It's not like med school leaves a lot of time for dating anyway, even if I wanted to. Most of the people in my class—my old class, at least—who are in a relationship came into med school with it already firmly in place.

The rigor of classes and the stress has already caused a few divorces and breakups, in fact.

So I'm not looking for anything right now, and even if I was, it wouldn't be with Miller. Obviously. I'll just be happy with my vibrator until I'm established in my career. Or with nothing, like I'm doing in the cabin.

It's not laid out in the staff rules, but something tells me they'd frown on a counselor masturbating in a cabin full of ten-year-olds.

I force myself back into the moment, because sitting in a small boat with a bunch of young teenagers isn't the time to be thinking about the purple Jackrabbit in the bedside table back in my apartment in New York. "You guys ready?" I ask, looking around.

I'm hoping one of them will say something like *that was enough* or *you know, let's just take it slow for a bit*, but their excited expressions make it clear. This is happening.

A chorus of "yes" and "let's do it," blends together, confirming it. I smile. Their excitement is contagious. It's terrifying, sure, but I guess going this fast is also fun, once you push past the panic.

"Okay. Coming about." I switch sides again as the mainsail catches the wind, and the campers switch the jib without me having to remind them. "Hold on, guys. We're going to pick up some speed."

I take a deep breath as we start to pick up speed. I

pull the rudder and main sail in close to me, holding us steady as the boat starts to lean.

"Woo-hoo!" Tyler yells.

Abby leans her hand back. She's on the low side of the boat, her hand skimming the water as we lean even further over.

I pull in the sail some more, holding it tight against the wind. I lean back to give myself even more leverage. This is perfect, the spray in my braided hair as we skim across the waves. I feel powerful, free. In control.

I pull in even tighter as the preteens screech in delight. They're right. This is exhilarating, freeing. I let a laugh bubble up.

Then I feel it. A slight shift in the center of gravity that has my stomach dropping. No. No, no, no.

I let the sail go completely and push the rudder away from me, but it's too late.

We're too far to one side.

And all I can do is watch as the sail touches the water and the boat tips on its side, spilling us into Lake Winnipesaukee.

18

MILLER

"Can we play with Lucy today?" Oliver begs as we walk toward the Nature department for the first activity period.

We just barely survived the chipmunk invasion, and he wants to talk about more insane animals?

"I was kind of thinking about just getting Bonnie and Clyde out," I say.

The rabbits are manageable. You don't have to deal with them trying to kill you, unlike Lucy the goat, who seems to have an evil agenda. And they're not all that fast, so at the end of the day you just pick them up and deposit them in their cages.

You don't have to chase them around with a broom, either.

Picture this: Eight campers are nestled quietly on their beds, reading and listening to music or whatever. You have a belly full of chicken patties and potato chips and settle onto your own bed, ready for a nap.

And then you hear scratching. Then it comes again, from under your bed, where your remaining t-shirts that haven't been eaten by the goat are folded and where your snacks are safely stored.

You lean over to peer under there to see what the hell is making that noise. And a fucking *chipmunk* scurries out from where it's chewed a hole through your bag of Doritos.

You can imagine the reaction of said campers, who immediately deserted their beds and tried to chase the rodent around the cabin. Dave squealed like a little girl and pulled his legs onto his bed, where he stayed, completely useless. Two campers ran into one another head-on.

It took a good five minutes of me chasing the thing around the cabin with a broom to guide it out the door. Rest hour was pretty much over after that.

It turns out you're not supposed to keep food in the cabins unless it's in like a plastic container, because chipmunks and squirrels will come in and try to eat it, Dave explained to me after the fact.

Thanks. Information that might have been help-ful, oh, a week ago, when I stockpiled an entire pantry under there.

So I'm a little more soured on animals than usual as we head to the Nature barn. Bonnie and Clyde are all I can handle today.

Even with the rabbits, you have to latch the cages well. That was one of the first lessons Mary, the depart-ment head, taught me when I showed up here during staff training. Apparently, Bonnie and Clyde got their names when someone left the cages unlatched and both rabbits escaped from their crates and made a mess of the barn.

Barn is kind of a loose term, to be honest. Honestly, I expected worse.

It's a single house-shaped building, a little larger than our cabins, with the same peeling red paint and black roof.

Inside it's just one cozy room, with tattered posters of animals and plants on the weathered walls. Two worn armchairs sit at one end of the room, joined by a handful of folding chairs and a plaid sofa that has stuffing poking from holes in various places.

I can only imagine the holes were the result of one of Lucy's many bad deeds.

Lucy isn't supposed to go inside the barn, but Lucy does what Lucy wants.

Technically, only the rabbits live indoors. Lucy's pen is on the back side of the barn. Edison the sheep, Richard the Shetland pony, and Elsa the alpaca live out there, too.

I do not like any of them. And it's become obvious in the last few days that the feeling is mutual.

"Bonnie and Clyde are boring, and we played with them yesterday," Oliver argues with a pout.

"I'll think about it." That's about as close as I want to get to Lucy, or any of the other large animals, or animals in general, if I'm being honest.

Thinking. Not looking at or petting or, god forbid, taking out of their enclosures. The only bright spot in this whole Nature department nonsense is that cleaning their stalls—also known as shoveling poop— has somehow been branded as a "fun" camper activity, and thus isn't my problem.

When we reach the barn, I wince as I see Mary already leading Lucy out of her pen.

Oliver cheers and runs ahead. At least someone is excited about the goat.

To be clear, it's not that I don't like animals. I do —when they're the right kind of animals. Pets, mostly. I love dogs. Big dogs, small dogs, it doesn't matter.

Cats are cool, within reason. Goldfish? Absolutely. Even Bonnie and Clyde have some redeeming qualities.

But a goat isn't exactly on the *pet* spectrum. Goats, if Lucy is representative of her species, are evil, bordering on the spawn of Satan. Even if most goats aren't that bad, Lucy, specifically, just might be the Anti-Christ.

The goat makes eye contact with me—with her stupid, rectangle-shaped pupils—as Mary leads her to the group of waiting campers, who are waiting on the grass.

I swear Lucy smirks at my pained expression.

The second activity period today is a class entirely focused on goats. Goat, actually. Singular goat, which is one goat too many. I've accepted that Lucy and I need to be in the same space during that hour. But that one hour of her nipping at me, standing in my way, eating my shirts and doing her best to kill me in a variety of ways is enough.

I don't need a second hour of Lucy.

But even though the hour hasn't officially started, the kids in first period have formed a circle around Lucy and settled in.

"Miller," Mary calls.

I curse under my breath, quiet enough that the

kids don't hear it, and join their circle. This is my job. And if I get fired, I lose any shot I had with Becca.

Lucy spots me immediately as I join the circle and makes a beeline for me.

"Oh, no, you don't," I say, stepping back. "I like this shirt."

Yesterday Lucy grabbed a bite of my t-shirt, then took off, leaving me wearing a ripped crop top for the afternoon. The kids thought it was hilarious. And it was, but I need a few shirts. Between bloody noses and this goat, my supply is dwindling.

Lucy trots off the other direction. I breathe a sigh of relief.

We spend the entire class that way. The. Entire. Hour. Standing in a circle with the campers corralling Lucy, while she hops from person to person, nuzzling her head against them and letting them pet her.

Except for me. She tries to bite me or eat my shirt every time she comes near me. Sometimes both.

I swear, I must have been a goat-murdering peasant in a past life to deserve this type of treatment, because Lucy doesn't seem to focus her evildoing on anyone else.

I'm getting pretty close to being a goat-murdering non-peasant in this lifetime, to be honest.

The bell rings to end the activity period, and Mary waves as the campers scatter, headed to their next class.

Lucy attempts to scatter, too. She trots off toward the woods with a mouthful of grass.

"God da—darn it, Lucy," I mutter, catching myself as I jog past campers after Lucy.

The goat looks at me and hops off the other direction, like this is a game, as I try to chase her down.

Lucy pauses to grab another bite of grass, giving me the advantage. *I've got you now, goat.*

I grab her hindquarters and keep a hand on top of her as I walk around her to grab her collar. Lucy turns, evading me as I reach for her harness.

I move the other way. Two can play this game.

Lucy bleats as I walk behind her. Then, with no warning, she kicks me right in the stomach. I stumble backward, gasping for air as she runs off.

How is this my life? Chasing a goat who hates me and being assaulted by the stupid thing?

If it weren't for Becca, I swear, I'd quit right now. How much would I owe to the camper scholarship fund? I don't fucking care. I'd give my right nut to be able to never see Lucy again.

But Lucy and Becca are a package deal for now, so here we are.

I limp back toward the Nature barn, where the

second group of campers is gathering. They're standing in a circle around Lucy, who has brought herself back to the barn and is smirking at me. You didn't know goats could smirk? Me either, but this evil creature most certainly is.

"Why don't you walk Elsa?" Mary calls, correctly sensing that Lucy and I need a break from one another before this situation escalates further. "She needs to get a little exercise before the third period campers get here."

I'm not sure I like the alpaca any more than the goat, but at least she tends to be slower. Plus, she's confined safely to her pen, and I'll put a leash on her before I take her out. It'll be more controlled, at the very least.

We make it ten feet from the pen before Elsa sits down and refuses to move.

I tug on the leash. "Come on, Elsa."

Elsa has no intention of moving. I spend the next twenty minutes waiting for this very large, very stubborn animal to move. My only consolation is that the campers think this is hilarious.

At least someone is laughing.

I give Lucy a glare as I lock the pens for the night.

"I'm watching you, goat," I say, pointing at my eyes with two fingers and then at her. "No shenanigans tomorrow."

Lucy bleats at me through the chain-link fence, a clear *fuck you* in goat language.

Back in the barn, Mary and I take a few minutes to clean out the rabbits' cages and sweep out the inside of the barn together. The campers have down time between their last period and dinner, so there isn't a rush to get back. We close up the building as we head out, pulling the large door closed behind us.

Mary slides a phone from her pocket and taps at the screen, then laughs at whatever she's reading. "Oh my God. Did you hear about this?" She tilts the phone toward me.

I'm not sure how she gets to carry her phone when the rest of us aren't allowed to. Honestly, it seems like a lot of people choose to ignore this rule.

"Hear about what?" I close the lock with a *snick* and squint to read the small type in the text message displayed on her screen.

"You know Becca? She works in Boating?"

She's got my interest now. I do know Becca, in fact. "Yeah?" I glance back up at her.

"Jana sent me a text. Apparently, Becca tipped a

sailboat over last period," Mary says, laughing as she taps out a response. "All the way over. Turtled it."

"Turtle?" They have such weird names for things here. I wonder if this is a Camp Winnie thing or a real sailing thing.

"Yeah, like flipping a turtle over and it can't get back up. Or like a right-side-up turtle with its shell. I don't know why they call it that. But it means it went all the way over. It's really hard to flip those back right side up." Mary taps on her phone and holds up a picture.

The image on her small screen shows something that does look like a turtle, if turtles were white and really fucking big. Without the context, I'd have no idea that was supposed to be a sailboat. "Is she okay?" I ask.

I know nothing about sailing, but I'm pretty sure the boat is supposed to be the other way up. Picturing her tumbling out of that thing into Lake Winnipesaukee, my heart seizes.

Mary frowns, still staring at the phone. "Oh, I'm sure she's fine. This happens a few times a summer."

I don't answer. I'm deep in thought as we walk.

If Becca tipped a sailboat, she's probably feeling like crap, let alone turtling one. It might be a funny name, but she won't think it's as hilarious as everyone who wasn't involved.

"Are the campers okay?"

Mary nods and finally puts the phone away. "Yeah. It sounds like Drew had to go pick them up in the rescue boat. He's the Boating department head," she explains. I'm still trying to keep all the names straight. "They probably loved riding in the motorboat, honestly."

Mary's right. I can imagine campers getting a kick out of this whole situation. Becca, though? Not so much.

Becca still won't really talk to me, but I know she took it really hard when Maya got hurt. She takes herself too seriously. Even with the little I know about her, it's obvious to me that she's going to beat herself up for this.

"I'm going to cut over this way," I say to Mary, turning toward the Fireflies cabins as we near the Sports field. "See you tomorrow."

She gives me a wave as she continues the other direction.

I walk through the Fireflies cabins that are nestled together, sneaking a glance at Cabin 2. But I bypass my cabin and keep going until I'm between the Ladybugs cabins and the boating area. Just as I step out of the woods, I see her.

Becca is trudging from the beach, headed toward the cabins. Her gaze is on the ground, so she doesn't see me, but she's walking right toward me, too. Her shoulders are slumped. Just from her posture it's obvious that she's stuck in her head.

I lean against a tree and wait.

19

BECCA

Fuck. The cold lake water surrounds me as my panic rises.

This is not what's supposed to happen. I was supposed to keep the boat upright, obviously.

The top of the mast dips under the water, and my heart seizes. *No.* If the boat goes completely upside down, it's even harder to right. We call it turtling, because all you can see is the hull, looking like the shell of a turtle on the surface of the water.

"Oh my God, we're going to die!" Abby shrieks, her arms flailing.

"You're wearing a lifejacket," Tyler points out.

I ignore them as I do my best to swim toward the mast and keep it from pulling the boat all the way under. The mast doesn't seem that tall when the boat is upright, but it seems an insanely long distance away right now, and my usual quick strokes are hampered by the massive orange life vest around my neck.

The mast is a foot underwater as I finally reach it. I grab for the metal pole, but it slips through my fingers, the water-logged sail pulling it toward the bottom of the lake.

"Becca? Are you okay?" Jacob calls out.

I don't answer as I reach again for the mast.

My fingers brush the smooth metal, but I can't get a hold, and with the life jacket, I can't swim further down to bring it up. Even if I could, I know better than to grab onto a heavy, sinking object in the middle of a lake.

I move toward the boat, hoping I can grab the part of the mast that's closer to the surface, but it's too late. The weight of the mast pulls downward, the boat flipping from its side to upside down in slow motion.

Shit.

"Something is touching my foot!" Amelia shrieks, and Abby matches her pitch.

I swim toward them. Now that the boat has completely flipped over, there's no urgency. Now all we can do is wait for help to arrive.

I reach out and grab the thing that's touching her

foot, tossing it behind me. "It's just seaweed, you guys. You're fine. Just relax, and Drew will be out here with the rescue boat in a minute."

"Hey, we get to ride in the motorboat? Cool!" Jacob sees the bright side. He twists onto his back and kicks his feet, splashing the other campers.

Amelia and Abby let out identical shrieks at the water splashing them in the face.

"Hold it together, guys." Hell, I should take my own advice. Who turtles a sailboat, let alone this early in the summer? The whole thought of this summer camp thing being a good idea was obviously an illusion. The one thing I thought I was good at—being a camp counselor—and it's pretty obvious that I suck at this, too.

Med school is just one thing in a long list of stuff I can't do well. And the list just keeps on growing.

My eyes begin to burn with unshed tears, but I force myself to take a breath. "Let's play the alphabet game," I suggest. The little kids love this, so I cross my fingers that it works with the older ones.

"Cool beans," Abby says, the splashing and drowning and seaweed all but forgotten, and I love her for it. "I'm going on a picnic and I'm bringing apples."

Tyler seems to shrug, but I can't be sure with the

life jacket covering his shoulders. "Okay. I'm going on a picnic and I'm bringing apples and... bananas."

I keep stealing glances at the upside-down sailboat while we play the memory game, each of them reciting the items mentioned in alphabetical order and adding their own. Jacob contributes "dingleberries" as what he's bringing, which makes the entire game devolve into who can think of the raunchiest words, but for once I don't mind.

The rescue boat roars up just in time to drown out Tyler's suggestion of "turds" for T.

I send up a silent prayer of thanks. We guide the campers onto the boat one at a time, each of them marveling at sitting in the boat that's otherwise off-limits to campers.

Jackson hops into the water after the last camper is on board. "I'll help you get the boat back," he says.

We wave as Drew heads back toward shore with the campers, then Jackson turns back to me.

"How'd you manage to turtle it?"

I know I need the help, but I'm feeling shitty about myself, and I don't really want to talk about it. "I don't know. Strong gust of wind, I think. The kids wanted to go faster."

"You didn't cleat the mainsail, did you?" Jackson

asks, looking over his shoulder as he swims toward the boat.

Yeah, he thinks I'm an idiot, even though the kid is like four years younger than me, and I was on staff when he was a counselor-in-training. *Don't cleat the mainsail* is sailing 101. It's one of the first things they teach you, because if you do, it's easy to tip the boat.

"No," I answer. I leave out the rest of my thoughts.

The keel has slipped back from where it normally sticks out of the bottom of the boat and into its hold. The boat is designed that way so we can pull the keel up, out of the way, so it doesn't drag on the sand when we bring the boats into shore.

But out in the water, you need it to make sure the boat doesn't tip over, and when the boat is like this, the keel is the only way to get leverage to flip it back right-side up.

Jackson climbs on top of the overturned sailboat and does his best to work the keel out the slit in the hull where it's tucked itself.

"Do you need help?" I ask as I tread water, unsure of what else to do.

He shakes his head. "No, I think I-I've got it," he manages, as the keel comes out slightly.

It slips through his fingers and back into the hole with a thud as I wince.

If we can't get the keel out, it's going to be practically impossible to flip the boat back right-side up.

It takes another three tries before Jackson gets the keel to stay up enough to pull on. I push up on one side of the boat while he presses against the keel, using his body weight to bring it back into the water where it belongs and slowly—soooo slowly—the boat starts to flip.

The mast floats tentatively upward through the murky water toward me. Once it's within reach, I grasp the metal pole and pull as it rises to the top of the water. I breathe a sigh of relief when it breaks the surface. I push upward, helping it along as Jackson flips the boat all the way over to right side up. He falls into the water, but the boat is where it belongs.

We climb in one at a time as the mainsail drips lake water into the boat. Jackson sails us back to shore in silence. I help him pull the boat onto the sand and take down the sails, my face burning in embarrassment.

"It's no big deal," Drew says, joining us moments later. "I've tipped my fair share of sailboats."

"Same here," Jackson adds.

It should make me feel better, but it doesn't, not really. This is supposed to be the one thing I'm good at. Not just sailing but working at camp in general.

It's the entire reason I came here this summer. I

needed to be in a place where I could prove to myself that I'm not a complete fuckup. That I can do more than just disappoint my parents.

I always knew this summer would come to an end and I've have to go back to reality and the challenges I ran from. I was ready to face that, or at least acknowledge that it would be coming. What I'm not at all prepared to face is the reality that I suck at being a camp counselor, too.

I've never tipped a sailboat over, let alone turtled one, especially with campers on board.

I force myself to go through the motions of cleaning up the department: turning canoes upside down on their racks, hanging up oars and lifejackets that campers left on the sand, swimming the sail-less sailboats out to their buoys and tying them there for the night.

I double-check my bowline knot, then check it again. The last thing I need to be responsible for is the boat coming untied and drifting away in the middle of the night.

"Becca, you good?" Drew calls as he slides a lock onto the boathouse door.

I manage a smile. "Yeah. I'm okay. Just feeling silly about the whole thing."

He closes the lock with a click. "I get it. Seriously,

it's not a big deal. The campers are fine, and honestly, they probably loved getting a ride in the rescue boat. They were all smiles when I drove them in. And they'll love telling this story for years to come."

"I suppose. Glad they're okay." If I'd managed to be responsible, even indirectly, for hurting two campers in one week, I'm pretty sure Brett would fire me on the spot.

I can't bring myself to walk quickly back to the cabin, even knowing the campers are all congregating there. My feet feel like they're made of lead. Maybe they're just weighed down with the force of disappointing everyone.

"Becca!"

I stiffen at the sound of my name as I near M-Hall. I know that voice, and the *absolute* last thing I want to do right now is see Miller. He's already seen me fuck up once this week, even if that time we shared the blame.

I can just imagine the rumors if I let him get close.

Oh, Becca and Miller. That makes sense. The two screw-ups, the adults who can't hack it in real life who thought they could somehow make it work as counselors.

No. I need to distance myself from him. No one needs to associate us.

Especially me.

"Becca!" Miller's voice gets closer, too close to politely ignore and pretend I didn't hear him.

I turn around. "What, Miller?" I snap.

He's got his usual grin in place as he leans up against a tree. The smile is just slightly crooked and fits perfectly with his personality of joking around and playing pranks, but it's also strangely attractive, highlighting a row of perfect white teeth and offsetting his blue eyes.

"Just thought you might need a hug." He shrugs, like this is a totally normal thing to offer your nemesis.

Actually, maybe he doesn't consider me his nemesis. The hatred does seem to be mostly one-sided, which makes it even more freaking annoying.

Either way, no, I do not want a hug from Miller. I don't want to be anywhere near Miller. I want to curl into a ball in a closet and not come out for a very long time.

He tilts his head, his cocky grin fading into an expression that looks almost caring. "Hey. You okay?"

"Mmm-hmm." If I open my mouth, he's going to hear the tears in my voice. I need to get away.

"Becca?" Miller stops me with a hand on my arm and turns to face me. "I heard about the sailboat. Really, are you okay?"

I look at the ground, at M-Hall. Anywhere but at him.

He places two fingers under my chin and tips my face up until I have no choice but to look in his eyes. His face softens as he searches mine. "I'm proud of you, Becca."

A tear escapes and traces a path down my cheek. *Dammit.*

"You kept the campers safe even when unexpected shit happened. You're a good counselor, Becs."

I open my mouth, but nothing comes out.

"Hug?" He lets my chin go and opens his arms. Without thinking, I fall into them, and he holds me tight. Maybe it's a moment of weakness, but somehow, this is exactly what I need.

I lean into his strength, taking a deep breath. More tears leak out, dampening the front of Miller's shirt. This is brand-new to me. I fucked up, and he's not just pointing it out to make me feel bad. He's just... offering support.

"I'm proud of you," he says again, his voice rumbling through his chest.

20

MILLER

"You get the mail yet?" Dave asks, sliding into the seat at my table.

"No. I was going to grab it after lunch." I set the plates out for the campers, working my way around Dave. "Don't you have your own table to set up?"

He shrugs. "I'm sitting with Jackson today. He's setting it up."

Lucky bastard. They spread out the counselors, assigning us to tables so there's some kind of authority figure present; I use the term loosely when it comes to Dave and me. The way the numbers work out, there are some tables that have one counselor, and some with two. I've always been stuck alone, no matter how many times I try to swap the assignments to sit with Becca.

"Any idea what's for lunch?" I hand him the napkins to set out. If he's sitting at my table for now, he can help out.

"BLT, maybe?" He tosses a napkin on each plate, which I move into the appropriate spot. Was the guy raised in a barn? Napkin and fork on the left, spoon on the right. My mama raised me right.

"Nice. Anyway, I'll grab the mail on the way back. You expecting something?"

Dave wiggles his eyebrows. "Yeah. Weekend assignments, man. We get them on Fridays. The two-week campers go on overnight trips, camping and stuff. Some of the counselors have to go with them, and some stay here to help the one-week campers head home and then get a half day off."

"Cool. Well, if you get the mail, let me know so I don't have to stop at the office."

I focus on setting out cups. I'm not sure I'm particularly excited about the prospect of a weekend camping trip. I've never been camping, so I don't have anything against it, but I'm not sure I'm the guy you'd want in charge of an expedition like that.

If anything, I want to spend time at camp, if that's where Becca will be.

We're making progress. I can feel it. She let me hold her after the sailboat incident. Her leaning on me felt so good, literally and metaphorically. I want her to know she can lean on me any time. Because she has to trust me to let me in.

And we're *so* close to her opening up the tiniest bit. I can feel it.

The dining hall door bangs open, and the sound of hungry campers streaming in fills the room as Dave heads back to his table.

I rub my belly as I head to the office to pick up the mail, full of bacon and bread, which is the only part of BLTs that I actually like.

There's a stack of paper in the slot marked FF2—Fireflies 2—and I slide it out in one pile and sort it on the way back to the cabin. There are ten letters for the campers, which always amazes me since there are only eight of them.

I check the names, finding two for Noah, three for Ben, and one for most of the others.

Buried between the envelopes are two strips of paper, clearly cut from a larger list. I squint at them.

DAVE S: CABIN DUTY/OFF

MILLER Q: CHOCORUA/CO-COUNSELOR BECCA P.

I can't stop the grin from spreading across my face. I don't know what the fuck Chocorua is, or even how to pronounce it. But I know who Becca is. And this means she's stuck with me for the weekend.

I pull out the phone that I stuck in my back pocket before the activities period. Yeah, I know, no phones at camp. But it's not like I'm the only one breaking this rule. In fact, I think for most of the week I was the only one without a phone in my pocket. It has to be the most commonly ignored rule, after the one about keeping staff relationships secret from the campers. Everyone knows Jackson is hooking up with Lillian. The campers are the ones who told me about it.

CARD SHARKS

Things are looking up. I'm doing some kind of overnight with the girl.

Blake: That sounds promising. What kind of overnight?

Maddox: Like with campers? Or just you two?

With campers. It's some kind of camping thing, I think. Like in tents.

Cam: God, I'd pay money to see you sleeping outdoors in a tent. Are you bringing your scented candles along?

You'll be happy to know I've been surviving without them up here. Just me and the sweet smell of little boys' feet.

Blake: Well, let us know how it goes. Maybe find out what kind of camping before you go.

Blake: And don't let any campers fall off cliffs.

Dude, I may be new at this whole counselor thing, but I know you're not supposed to let them fall off cliffs. Becca's amazingly good at the whole counselor thing. Most of what I do here is just watching her and then copying, more or less.

Cam: So you're having fun?

Pretty much. Not last night when a kid woke me up at two in the morning because he had a nightmare. But otherwise.

Maddox: You think that's bad? Holly woke me up in the middle of the night two days ago and made me go to the store for mint ice cream and hot sauce. She ate them together.

I guess that mean's the pregnancy is still going well?

> Maddox: So far, yeah. She's into the second trimester.

> Cam: Man, I can't wait to see you as a dad.

> How's Addie?

> Cam: Busy busting my balls as usual. Love her to death. Going to nail down some wedding plans once Blake gets back.

> Back from where?

> Blake: I'm in Colorado with my brother. Middle of nowhere.

> Nice. Talk soon.

> Cam: Good luck.

We get more information that evening, passed out at dinner to each of us assigned to trips. It's a single page, which for someone going camping for the first time seems woefully insufficient.

There's a list of the campers that will be coming along: three of the two-week campers from my cabin, and four girls from Becca's cabin. A packing list, which includes mostly items I don't have. And some information about Chocorua, which is apparently a mountain that we'll be hiking.

Brett knocks on the cabin door as I'm reading through the list while the campers brush their teeth and clog toilets in the bathrooms. "Hey, how's it going?"

I look up from the paper. "Hey. Good. What's up?"

"Everything okay?" Dave looks mildly alarmed at the sight of the camp director.

"Yeah, everything's fine. Just stopping by to say hi."

Dave nods, then excuses himself to head to the bathroom to supervise.

Brett chuckles as Dave heads toward the communal bathroom. He sits on Dave's bed. "I usually only come by the cabins when someone's in trouble. He probably thinks I'm going to fire you."

I snort. "You won't fire me. You want the payout for the camper scholarship fund."

"True story. You're sticking it out so far, though. Need anything for the trip this weekend? I wasn't sure if you had all the backpacking gear."

I rub a hand over my chin. "Yeah. I have, like, none of this stuff."

"Want me to see if Dave will go instead?" Brett smirks.

"Fuck no," I say, too quickly, as Brett's smirk grows.

"Thought so." He stands. "We have a bunch of wilderness gear for anyone to use. Backpacks, water bottles, all of it. I'll have someone show you where it is after breakfast tomorrow."

"We have to *carry* all of this?" I stare in disbelief at the musty-smelling item Jason is holding out.

"Um, yes. Were you planning to drive your car up the side of the mountain?" The wilderness coordinator looks like he's judging me, and frankly, I don't need that.

"I mean, obviously not. I just figured we'd hike and then settle at a campsite or something." The thing he's calling a *backpack* not only smells weird, but it's massive and somehow attached to a metal frame.

I take it, and Jason turns around to search through a pile of equipment for something else.

"You will. The campsite is a good three miles from the parking lot." He holds out another canvas-covered item, this one a garish shade of orange. "And you sleep in tents. That you also bring with you."

He loads me up with not only the backpack and

the tent, which is apparently contained in the orange sack, but also a sleeping bag that doesn't smell much better than the rest of the gear, four water bottles, a cooking stove that he shows me how to assemble, a canister of fuel for the stove, and a bottle of iodine pills.

"To purify your water," he explains. "But there isn't a water source where you'll be camping, so you'll need to carry a bunch in."

I'm really, really not sure about any of this. But then again, it's a chance to hang out with Becca, so I'm taking it.

Maybe she knows how to use this stove.

"Who's ready to go hiking?" Becca asks the gathered campers the next morning.

They cheer in response.

"Okay, let's make sure everyone has their gear before we go. Yes, Liam?" she asks, nodding at my camper's raised hand.

"I brought my green shoes," he announces.

Bayley raises her hand. "I have a flashlight. It has different colors if you push a button."

Becca hold her hand up. "Good, thank you both.

Now, no talking for a minute, just listening ears. If I say something and you *don't* have it, raise your hand. Silently, remember? We can run and grab it now, but once we get in the van, we just have what we're carrying. Okay?"

She looks from camper to camper, then to me before she lists off items. Somehow, I actually have everything on her list, thanks to Jason.

We stow the kids' backpacks in the back of the massive van, stacking and fitting them together so everything fits.

Becca slams the back door of the van. "You want to drive?"

I may not have any clue about camping, but I know how to drive, even a massive vehicle like this. "Sure. You going to join me in the front?" Maybe we're starting off well.

She shakes her head. "I'll supervise in the back. It's a big van, and I don't trust them."

I hate missing out on one-on-one time, but she has a point.

With Becca's presence keeping them sane, the kids hold it together for the thirty-minute drive to the parking lot by the trail head.

I pull the van off the main road and onto a dirt path marked by a small wooden sign. There are two other cars in the parking lot. A large sign stands to one side, where the path begins. I park the van in the large open space. I don't trust myself to park this monstrosity between the Prius and the Subaru, both of which look like they belong to people who fit the idea of *outdoorsy kids* much better than I do.

The kids pile out of the van. We help them struggle into their backpacks one by one. Mine easily weighs four times what one of theirs does. I stagger a step backwards when I heft it onto my shoulders.

Becca swings her backpack onto her back with practiced ease. Hers is dark purple and doesn't have the metal frame that mine does. She leads the way to the trail head.

"Okay, guys. Here's the deal. I'm going to be the leader, so no one goes ahead of me. Miller is going to be in the back."

I give a small noise of protest. Becca pointedly ignores it.

"We're going to take it slow and steady, okay? Lots of breaks. No one falls back behind Miller. If you lose sight of the people in front of you, just wait for the people behind you."

Okay, one of us in front and one at the back makes sense when she explains it that way. I'm still disappointed that I don't get to hike next to her, but maybe

I can do a better job and stay focused enough that no one gets hurt.

"We're off!" Becca announces, starting the trek into the forest.

I count the campers as they file past me, following Becca. By the time the last camper passes me and I take up the rear, Becca is so far ahead that I can't see her.

The backpack makes every step heavy, and I struggle to keep my balance as we get started, but after a few hundred yards I hit my stride. I smile to myself. Becca may be yards ahead of me and too far away to talk to while we hike.

But we do have all weekend together.

21

BECCA

One night. That's all.

Plus, several hours today and more tomorrow, but there's a time limit. I won't be stuck here with Miller forever.

Honestly, it's not entirely that I don't want to be around him. He's growing on me, in a weird way. My initial impressions of him—too easygoing, takes nothing seriously—are definitely true, but there's more to it.

That's just the surface. Once you get deeper, he's different. More sensitive, observant, sweet. The way he let me lean on him after the sailboat incident was just what I needed in that moment.

At this point, my objection to him is more that around him, I seem to be a hot mess.

I don't need this weekend to add any more incidents to the tipped sailboat and Maya's black eye.

Thinking of Maya makes me smile. She left after her one week at camp, and the way all the girls clamored to hug her, some even tearing up that she was leaving, made my heart swell.

I'm not sure they'll appreciate it until they're older, but they all learned so much from one another this past week. I had to blink back tears when I said goodbye to Maya, too. She's going to be one I'll remember for a long time. She promised to write to Vivien and me while we're at camp the rest of the summer, and I can't wait to get a letter from her.

I send up a silent prayer to the camping gods that we can get through this weekend without anyone else getting injured.

The start of the trail is flat and easy. The path is shaded by a mass of trees and soft from layers of pine needles and fallen leaves, and the air smells even more strongly of pine here than back at camp. I take a deep breath in through my nose. Pine is my favorite scent, because it reminds me of camp. But this place might even have Camp Winnie beat.

We walk along at a reasonable pace, and I do my best to keep track of time so we can stop every ten or fifteen minutes for water. After a mile, the kids are the ones stopping us for breaks.

"Can we stop for a snack?" Lena asks from her spot right behind me.

I check my watch. It's been three minutes since our last break. "Let's give it a couple more minutes."

One minute goes by before Bayley asks for trail mix.

I pause on the side of the trail and pull out the baggie that holds the nut mixture. The kids hold their hands cupped out and I pour some out for each of them.

"Need some trail mix?" I ask Miller as I reach him.

"Nah. I'll eat the nuts they don't want."

Sure enough, the kids eat the chocolate chips and then hand Miller the peanuts and almonds and raisins. So basically, we stopped to feed them chocolate. Great.

"Okay, let's get moving again," I say, returning to my position at the front.

"I'm thirsty."

I refrain from rolling my eyes as I unclip Ben's water bottle from the outside of his pack and hand it to him. He takes two sips, then hands it back. It seems light for having just started, but maybe he's sharing it with one of the other kids.

"Do you have another water bottle you want me to

clip on the outside?" I ask him. We may as well dig through his backpack while we're stopped.

He shakes his head and wipes his mouth with the back of his hand. "I just brought one."

"No problem. You can borrow some water from a friend if you need." I take the bottle from his outstretched hand and clip it to his pack.

His little eyebrows are knit together when I turn around. "I think we all brought just one."

Oh, no. No, no, no. I told my girls to bring their three. We don't have a water source once we get higher up. I look at the four of them, but they look guilty, too.

Dammit. I say one thing and they do the opposite. Is this how my parents felt when I was a teenager?

"We didn't want to carry too many waters. They're heavy," Mollie admits, with as much of a shrug as she can manage with the heavy pack on her shoulders.

I look at Miller. He's ignoring us, play fighting with Liam. Clearly, Miller doesn't seem to grasp the gravity of this situation.

Less than a mile into this hike, and things are already falling apart.

The campers eat more chocolate chips while I conference with Miller, who decided to only bring two water bottles himself.

"We can just refill them, right?" he asks with an easy smile.

Oh, if only it were that easy. I grit my teeth, reminding myself that there are campers standing near us. I'll have to yell at him later.

"Down here, sure. But up where we're supposed to camp tonight, there isn't water available. We'll end up dehydrated." I consider the options, tapping a finger against my lips. We could turn around and head back to camp, but I'd hate to do that to the kids.

"If there's water down here, why don't we just camp down here?"

I'm about to tell Miller that we can't just stay anywhere, but something stops me. He has a point, actually. Every part of the rule follower inside me is screaming that we need to follow the map we were given, camp at the spot we're supposed to be at—but why?

Wouldn't it make more sense to keep the campers safe, even if it's going a little off-book?

I chew on my lip while I look over my shoulder to make sure no one has choked on a peanut while we've been conferencing. The kids are chomping away, unconcerned with the fact that they're consuming massive amounts of sodium without enough water to drink.

Finally, I give in, "Okay. Let's look at the map and find a place."

Miller pulls the trail map out of the pocket on the front of my backpack and hands it to me. I look it over for a minute. The stream runs close to the trail at about the one-and-a-half-mile mark from the trailhead, and there's a tiny figure on the map that indicates camping is allowed in that area.

"Let's detour to this side trail and camp here." I point at the spot I found. "We're probably almost there already."

"Sweet," he says, popping a peanut into his mouth.

We get moving again. It's less than half a mile to where we're headed, and with the frequent stops for trail mix and water, we reach the site in an hour, with most of the water bottles empty.

As I take in the site and the campers, I realize stopping here was definitely the best option. It would have taken us at least three hours at this rate to reach the campsite we initially planned to stay at, and we would have had no water for the last two hours, not to mention all night.

Miller and I help the campers fill their water

bottles from the stream and drop in iodine pills to purify. As soon as my watch beeps to indicate the required time to purify the water, the kids begin gulping from their bottles.

Yeah, this was definitely the best choice.

"Why don't you guys start setting up the tents?" Miller asks. He looks at me, lowering his voice. "I just don't want them to drink so much they puke. Or pee their pants."

There are three tents in total: one each in Miller's and my backpacks, and then one that's been distributed among the campers in pieces. We gather the parts, and it looks like all of them are there. Finally, one thing on this trip that's gone right.

After the kids leaving water bottles behind, I was expecting to be missing a rain fly or the poles to set it up.

I find three relatively flat spots to set them up and point them out to the campers. "Okay, girls, let's set this one up together, then the other girls' tent. Three in one, and two in the other tent. Miller will help the boys." I start to pull items out of the canvas bag and lay them out.

"Hey, Becca?" Miller calls.

I straighten and turn to look at him. He's sitting on the ground, his back reclined against a pine tree, looking like he has no intention of helping to set up a tent. I wonder if it makes me a bitch to hope he gets sap in his hair.

"Come here, I have a question for you. Kids, start setting up while Becca and I talk." He motions with his hand again for me to come towards him.

"What's up?" I ask as I get close. My heart beats a little faster at the thought that I messed something up. It's not at the lines that form at the corner of his eyes when he smiles. It's not. "Are we missing something?"

He shakes his head and motions to the ground next to him. "Let them do it," he murmurs, so softly I think I'm mishearing him at first.

"Huh?"

He takes my hand and tugs until I sit on the ground next to him. "Let them do it. Alone, without us."

Now I know he's crazy. "Uh, they don't know how to set up a tent."

He shrugs, a grin spreading across his face. "So they'll learn. We have extra time to kill, right?"

"I guess." I'm not sure this is a great plan. What if they mess it up?

He sits on a boulder and motions for me to sit next to him. "Here's the thing. If we help them set up the tents, the tents will be set up."

"I think that's the point."

Miller shakes his head. Even with a grin on his face, this is as serious as I've seen him, so I listen. "But if we make them do it themselves, the tents will also be set up. And they'll feel accomplished. And be closer with one another."

"I—" He has a point, I realize. They might make mistakes. But the end goal of this weekend isn't getting tents put up. It's making friends. Making memories.

"The quickest way to bring people together is a common goal. And maybe a common enemy, which is what we can be, the mean counselors making them do this themselves while we sit in the hammock."

"How come you're not helping?" Liam asks.

It's taken a solid fifteen minutes for them to realize we never came back to help, which was long enough for Miller to get out the double hammock he somehow crammed into his pack. He strung it up between two large trees, and now the two of us are sharing it while the campers do all the work.

Miller drops an arm over his face. "You guys can do it."

I peer at him from where I'm lying in the

hammock, my head by his feet. He looks the picture of a guy who just doesn't care. If I didn't know better, I'd think he truly just didn't feel like helping.

Until Liam walks back toward the tent he's working on, and Miller lifts his arm to wink at me.

I watch the kids as they struggle, but when Mollie finally gets the poles in the tent correctly, the proud smile that stretches across her face has me convinced. Miller was right.

This time.

I follow his lead and act disinterested, while still trying to keep a close eye on the campers. I don't think I'm pulling it off as effectively as Miller, but the campers barely look in our direction. Getting all three tents set up takes them longer than it would have taken me, but they seem to be having fun once they get the basic idea of what to do.

"It's working," I murmur in amazement as one tent stands up. Four campers give one another high fives.

"I'm not as dumb as I look," Miller says, flashing me another wink. Does he know how sexy he looks when he does that?

My cheeks heat. "I never said you were dumb."

"Just thought it, right?" he teases.

Maybe. Or at least thought he was inexperienced.

How did he end up working at camp, anyway? This isn't exactly a common summer gig for people once they hit their early twenties, and both of us are well past that.

"How come you're working at camp?" I ask finally, curiosity getting the best of me.

"Honestly? No idea, really," he says, shifting his body and making the hammock sway. "Brett's an old high school friend. We played lacrosse together. I was looking for something different to do, he needed help... here we are."

"Different from what?"

He nudges my arm with his knee. "Ah, I knew you'd be interested eventually."

I try to shrug, but my arms are trapped against the fabric of the hammock. "Not interested. Just making small talk."

Maybe you're interested, a tiny voice inside me points out. I choose to ignore her.

"Well, to answer your question, I've been playing poker professionally since college. And it's fun, but I'm almost thirty, you know?"

I raise a brow at him. "So, you thought you'd go to summer camp?"

He laughs, throwing his head back. I'm realizing that *this* is Miller. He expresses his feelings fully, out in the open. Pretty much the opposite of what I do, keeping my emotions bottled up. "Kind of. I thought I'd make some changes, maybe find something different to do with my life. Settle down at some point, all that. And this was the first different thing that popped up."

It makes sense, in kind of a weird way. "So you signed on for the summer without having any clue what you were getting into?"

"Nah." Miller shakes his head, looking over at the campers and then back to me. "I honestly didn't think I'd last more than a few days. Brett bet me that I couldn't hack it, and I can't turn down a bet."

I snort with laughter, then cover my mouth with my hand. "This is all a bet."

"Yeah. If I bail out, I have to donate my salary to the camper scholarship fund. So it's more for fun than anything, and it helps Brett out either way." He closes his eyes, his wide grin fading to a smaller smile. "I like your laugh. You should do it more."

"I laugh plenty," I protest, but his words are turning over in my head. For all his laid-back, devil-may-care attitude, he might just be a good guy at his core.

"Nah. You giggle, but you don't usually make that cute little snort. I like it."

This is getting dangerously close to flirting. Our bodies are close, our sides pressed together in the hammock. My stomach flips as I focus on the spots where our bodies are touching.

Suddenly, every point of contact feels like it's on fire.

I suck in a breath and look over toward the campers, needing a minute. I'm surprised to realize all three tents have been erected. One is facing the wrong way, and one has the rain fly on upside down, but they did an admirable job.

I shift my gaze to the right to find seven campers walking toward us, Lena and Noah leading the way.

"We want our own tents," Lena announces.

"What?" I ask, trying to figure out her angle. There are three tents. Three boys plus Miller in one. Five girls —four campers and me—split between the other two, three in one tent and two in the other. How else is she planning to divide things up?

"The boys are going to sleep in one, and all the girls want to sleep together. You guys take a counselor tent for the two of you."

22

MILLER

Becca may play her cards close to the vest when it comes to a lot of things, but when it comes to her emotions, she's an open book. I watch them play out across her face as she tries to figure out a tactful way to get out of spending the night in close proximity to me.

Her initial confusion gives way to protest as she opens her mouth. "I'm not sure that's a good idea, guys," she says. She looks at me to back her up.

This seems like exactly the type of thing I'd try to plan, but this time, it's just good luck. Who am I to fight fate?

"It could work," I say.

Becca's eyes shoot daggers at me. "It could *not* work."

Lena uncrosses and recrosses her arms, looking between the two of us. "If we split up the girls, someone's going to be left out. Do you want someone left out?"

Oh, she's good. She's very good.

"Well, no..." Becca trails off. I can't tell if she's cracking under the pressure, if she just hates confrontation, or if she, like me, is intrigued at spending the night close to me. I can only hope it's the latter.

And the outcome will be the same. Becca and me in one tent, alone.

"Tell you what, guys," I say, clapping my hands together. "Let's do this. My campers in one tent. Becca's campers in the other tent. Becca and I will take the last tent, but *if* there is any noise—I'm talking like a *peep*—after we tell you to go to bed, we'll make everyone get up and switch to the original plan."

"Deal!" Noah says, jumping up and down.

Lena gives a serious nod.

"Also, you have to gather wood. Don't go anywhere that you can't see me from where you are. If you guys bring back enough, we'll have a campfire."

They squeal with delight and run off. I mentally pat myself on the back. I may not have a lot of experience with kids, but I remember a former teacher using a tactic like this. I'm feeling pretty proud until I turn to Becca.

She looks like she wants to murder me. "I can't share a tent with you."

"You can sleep in the hammock if you really want. Probably pretty buggy out here, though," I say with a casual shrug. "Plus, look at it this way. I got them to gather the firewood, and I've guaranteed that they'll shut up and go to bed. What more do you want?"

She sets her mouth in a thin line. I get the sense that what she wants is to be far away from me.

I give her a playful nudge, my arm to her leg. "But seriously, Becs. I'll behave. I promise. This is good for the kids to bond. Really. I'm not trying to be shady."

The last thing I want to do is come off as a sleaze or force her into something that she truly doesn't want. But from the hardened nipples I can see through the thin fabric of her t-shirt, she's not entirely opposed to the idea of one-on-one time with me.

Becca sighs, then shifts on the hammock. "We'll figure it out." She climbs out of the hammock, sending it twisting and me scrambling to grab on and balance it to avoid being dumped on the ground.

"Anyone want to go exploring?" I ask. The campers have finished moving their sleeping bags into the tents, and we still have a couple of hours until it would be a reasonable time for dinner.

All seven of them jump at the idea. Becca is less enthusiastic, but she joins the group as we head back out to the trail.

"I figured we'd hike up part of the way that we were going to go," I say, pointing. "Get a little of that even if we're camping down here. And it should be faster since we don't have our backpacks."

We left the huge backpacks inside the tents and are walking with just a few water bottles held in our hands. It's amazing how much lighter I feel after taking it off, practically ready to sprint up this trail. I'd imagine the campers feel the same way.

Becca brings along a smaller backpack that she apparently had stowed inside the bigger backpack, carrying some water and a first aid kit.

Chocorua's key feature, I learned from searching the internet yesterday during rest hour, is that its peak is above the tree line. So, once you get above a certain point, there are no more trees—just rock. We make it to the tree line and keep going. Without the foliage in the way, we can see for miles.

Everything looks so small from up here. The lakes are tiny dark patches amid forest or surrounded by thin lines of road. The other mountain peaks stand out against the blue sky.

At least, over us it's blue. It's darker off in the distance.

"Whoa! Cool!" Liam exclaims, pointing. "Did you see that?"

I follow his finger to the mountain range we were viewing. "What?"

He doesn't have to answer, because then I see it too. A lightning bolt hits the top of the mountain. The sky behind it isn't just dark; it's practically black. It jolts through me like I was struck, rather than just a spectator.

"I think there's a storm rolling in," Becca says, her brows knitted together. "We should head back down. It could be dangerous if we get stuck up here in a storm."

The clouds look like they're moving quickly. We're not quite to the tree line when it races over us. The sky above us darkens, blocking out the sun until it's as dark as late evening, even though it's closer to three in the afternoon. A crack of thunder rents the air, followed by fat raindrops pelting down.

"Stay together," I order. The campers link hands. Becca takes up the rear this time, and I lead us down as quickly as possible.

My heart pounds in my chest, and I force myself to keep my fear hidden from the campers. *Fuck, don't let us get hit by lightning.* Had I known the storm was coming, I never would have suggested leaving the campsite.

The campers, for their part, are having the time of their lives, almost certainly because they have no idea how much danger we're in.

Through the fog, I can almost see Becca. Her face is pinched with worry. I mentally kick myself again. Every time I try to prove to her that I'm not just a guy who likes to screw around, I mess something up.

"Great job, guys," I say, raising my voice over the wind. "Keep it going." I keep repeating lines like this, over and over.

Becca hasn't said anything since we started hiking back.

I slip on a wet rock and catch myself before I fall. "Careful of the rocks," I say, looking back.

Is Becca okay?

The fog is less dense when we get below tree line, and I can see her face more clearly. She's not just worried; she's terrified.

"Almost there," I say, loud enough for the group to hear, but I'm talking to Becca. I'm going to get us back safely if it's the last thing I do.

It seems to take twice as long to get back as it did to hike up, even though we're going downhill. We make it to the tents just as the rain starts to let up, all of us wet and a little cold but safe. I let out a sigh of relief.

"Go into your tents and change," I order, pointing. It's a good thing we had them put all of the backpacks in the tents before we left, and that we fixed the upside-down tarp thing on top of the tent that Becca called a rain fly.

All of our stuff—other than the wood that's stacked in a clearing between the tents—is clean and dry.

I motion toward our tent. "Come on. You can change first if you want."

Becca doesn't make a move.

I step closer to her. "Becca?"

She's trembling.

There's a time to give a girl space. I get it. Thanks, Holly. But this isn't it. She's not just worried about campers.

I take her hand and lead her toward the tent. "In you go," I say, crawling in behind her.

Becca sits cross-legged on the floor between our

two sleeping bags. She blinks, like she suddenly remembers where she is. "Sorry. I was a little—sorry. I'm good now."

"You're still shaking," I point out. "Come here." Without waiting for her reply, I scoot around until I'm sitting next to her. I put my arm around her shoulders and draw her into me.

I wait for the protest, for her to push me away, but it doesn't come.

She leans on me and slowly, the shaking stops.

"How are you doing?" I ask when her breathing evens out.

"Um," she stammers. "I'm okay. Sorry."

"You don't have to be sorry. You did a great job getting those kids down the mountain." I pull her closer.

"Fuck," she whispers.

I crack a smile. "I think that's the first time I've ever heard you swear."

This earns me a small smile. "I don't swear at camp. You're not supposed to, either." The smile fades. "I just... the idea that one of the campers might get really hurt. I was on the verge of a panic attack back there." She shakes her head. "It's just... why am I such a fuck-up when you're around?"

Why is she *what*? I shake my head. "What are you talking about, Becs? You're a great counselor." She really is. I've seen her with the kids. She has infinite patience, is a great teacher. Any kid would be lucky to have her as their counselor.

"I know," she says with a small shrug against my chest. "I used to be, at least. But this summer... I came back here because this is what I know. What I'm good at. Before this summer, I'd never turtled a sailboat, or gotten campers stuck in a thunderstorm, or had a camper get a black eye. It's like the one year I need this, need to do something right, everything falls apart."

The rain has eased to a gentle patter on the walls of the tent.

"Why?" I ask, because I have a lot of questions that start this way.

Why does she think she's not good enough? Why does she need to prove to herself that she's good at something? And why does she think things are falling apart?

She shrugs again under my arm. "We should get back to the campers."

"The campers are fine, Becca. I promise."

She nods. "I failed," she says, so softly I think I mishear her.

"You failed? No, you didn't, Becs. You got them safely back to camp. Everything is fine."

Becca finally looks up at me. Her eyes shine bright with tears. "I failed a class at school. I have to repeat the year. That's why I needed to come up here. To prove that I'm not bad at everything."

My heart twists at the sight of the tear that squeezes from a corner of her eye and traces a trail down her cheek. I have to force myself not to wipe it away with my hand. "Fuck, Becs. You're great at a lot of things. I've only known you for two weeks and I can see that already. Who cares about school?"

Jesus, how can she think she's anything less than perfect?

"My parents," she sighs, looking down. "My dad's a surgeon. He always wanted me to follow in his foot-steps. I think *I* always wanted to follow in his foot-steps. It's just... harder than I thought it would be. And I hate the idea of disappointing him."

Suddenly, it all makes sense. The reason she didn't want to talk about what she does when she's not at camp. How upset she was after some of the minor inci-dents this week. She's viewing everything as a reflection on her.

I'm still not quite sure I understand the reason she's so upset now, though. Everyone is fine. We got caught in the storm, but it wasn't something we could control.

No one messed up, least of all her. And we all got back here safely.

"Becca?" I ask after a moment of quiet.

She sniffles in response. "God, you must think I'm so pathetic."

Does she really not see it? "That's the last thing I think about you, Becs. You're amazing. Why do you think I've been trying so hard to spend time with you and get to know you?"

She scrunches up her face in confusion. Pieces of hair have fallen out of her usually tight braid, and with the wet strands stuck to her face from the rain, she looks like an adorably confused puppy, one of those long-haired types.

Maybe I'll just keep that thought to myself.

"I thought you just liked annoying me."

I hold back my laughter. I do, but only because she's fun to tease. "Well, maybe, but that's not all I like. But why were you so upset with the storm? There wasn't anything we could have done to avoid that. Was it just the thought of the campers getting hurt? We're all fine."

"Oh." She pushes a strand of hair back from her face to join the braid in the back. "It was mostly being terrified that we wouldn't get back with everyone okay. But also, I'm, um, scared of thunderstorms."

This time, I can't hold back my smile. "Aww, Becs," I say, pulling her in again. "That's fucking adorable. You're this hardcore, tough-as-nails chick who's super smart and on top of everything. And you're scared of thunder."

She stiffens, but this time I see it for what it is. It isn't me, at least this time. She's scared of not being perfect, or at least of people finding out she isn't perfect.

I let her go and pull her backpack across the tent toward us.

"I like that about you. It makes you human. And for the record, I'm sorry," I add.

She stops digging in her backpack and looks at me. "For what?"

"I should have noticed. I should have been there for you. The campers were all having a great time, and you were freaking out. I'm sorry I didn't see it."

She pulls a dry shirt out of the backpack and balls it up in her fist. "It's okay. But, um, thank you." Her cheeks are stained pink.

"Are you good now? Do you need a hug?"

"I'm good now." She looks at the exit to the tent,

where the rain has stopped as suddenly as it started, then back at me.

Right. "I'll let you get changed. Then can you show me how to work this insane stove thing we brought with us?"

23

BECCA

The campfire is a bust with the wet logs, so it's a good thing the stove works. We have pasta along with some sort of shelf-stable sausage that, if you ask me, looks suspicious, but the kids seem to love it. The entire dinner process takes so long that by the time we clean the dishes, they're already yawning.

Miller reiterates the warning about going *right to sleep* as he zips the boys' tent closed for the night.

I peek my head into the girls' tent. They're lined up in their sleeping bags, heads all against one wall of the tent. "Are you sure you guys are okay to sleep in here without me?"

Lena scoffs. "Of course. And some of us would

have had to sleep without a counselor anyway, remember? There are two of you and three tents."

She makes a good point, and it makes me feel a little better that I'm not completely abandoning them. "Well, sweet dreams, ladies. Remember, right to sleep. See you in the morning."

I zip their tent closed and stand upright to stretch. The sun seemed to set quicker than usual here in the woods, or maybe it's later than I realized. I let out a yawn and head for my tent.

Our tent, I guess.

I thought I'd be more weirded out by the idea of sharing a tent with Miller, that the tension would grow between us all day like it did when I first met him. When the campers first brought it up, I was one hundred percent opposed to the idea.

But Miller's been so sweet today, shocking me. He took charge when we were stuck in the storm and got us down the mountain safely, even with me freaking out. And he didn't laugh when I told him about med school.

He didn't even bat an eye, come to think of it.

I wonder if maybe, just *maybe,* I misjudged him.

Miller is just ducking into the tent when I reach it. He holds the flap open for me, like some kind of backwoods gentleman, and I crawl inside and sit cross-legged on my sleeping bag.

"How are you feeling?" Miller asks as he zips the flap closed.

The campers accidentally positioned this one with the door facing the woods, rather than facing the other tents. We left it where it was, since it seemed easier than moving things around, but now that we're turning in for the night, it feels somehow more private, even though we're only separated from the campers by a couple of sheets of thin nylon.

I take inventory, rolling my shoulders. There's a twinge of soreness, but nothing that truly hurts. "Not too bad. Maybe a little tender from where I was carrying my pack, and I'm still kind of cold, but I'm okay. How about you?"

Miller takes his shoes off and slips into his sleeping bag fully clothed. I'm confused for a minute, but then he starts to toss clothing—his pants, a shirt, socks—out of the sleeping bag, and I realize he's changing inside it. For someone who's shown me his bare chest on multiple occasions, it seems overly modest.

"Don't want me to see your man chest?" I tease. I take my own shoes off and climb into the sleeping bag to follow suit.

He grins. "Hey, if you want to see it, just ask." He pulls the covers down slightly to show off his pecs.

I groan. "I was joking. Put those away." Because honestly? They're hot, even more so in this confined space.

The muscles ripple as he laughs, and I find myself wondering what it would be like to run a finger along the ridges of those muscles. To have him hold me close with nothing between us.

A shiver runs through me as I imagine the warmth of his hard body.

I turn away from him as I slip off my pants inside the sleeping bag and pull my bra off from under my t-shirt. I won't be sleeping topless, thank you very much, but as my nipples rub against the cotton of my shirt, it feels more exposed than if I were completely bare.

I snuggle deeper into my sleeping bag, pulling it to my chin. Inside the thick fabric, I feel like I have an extra layer of protection, somehow. Like I can talk to Miller and tease him, and it'll all be okay.

"What are you in school for?" he asks. He lays on his side, the top of his torso still very much visible from this angle.

I wait for the dread to kick in, the way it usually does when someone asks about med school, but it doesn't come. Maybe I'm just distracted by those pecs.

And the very top of those defined abs. His entire body is strong and defined, the muscles of the arm that's propping his head up tensed.

"Um. Medical school. Second year."

"Ah. Right. Following in your dad's footsteps."

He remembered.

I roll onto my side, facing Miller. The sleeping bag dips, almost exposing the top of my t-shirt, and I pull it higher. "You seem different. Like, the last few times we've talked. You were one way when I first met you, and I didn't like you at all. But you're different now."

I'm not sure I'm making any sense, but Miller nods.

"It's all me, I guess." He rubs his chin as he thinks for a minute. "Most people seem to like the outgoing, funny guy, so that's what I do most of the time. I realized that when I was maybe ten or eleven, and since then I just give the people what they want."

I chew on my bottom lip. I'm so far down in this sleeping bag that I could probably nibble on the fabric, too. "So, is this just showing me what you think I want?"

He shakes his head and blows out a breath. "Not at all. Honestly? There's something about you, Becs. It makes me feel like I can be myself around you."

What happened when he was a kid that made him

feel like he couldn't be himself? It seems too invasive to ask, but then he keeps talking, and I don't have to wonder.

"My brother had some health problems when he was little. Still does, but not as dramatic. And I realized people seemed sad when they saw me, like they felt bad for me or something. I didn't want their pity, so I found ways to make them laugh instead."

My heart clenches at the thought of a ten-year-old Miller having to put on a brave face. "Is your brother... okay now?"

He nods. "He is. He's pretty independent with his own job and all, but he lives with my mom. Eventually, I'm sure he'll come live with me, so that's part of the reason I feel like I need to find something other than playing poker to do with my life." He shrugs, an easy smile on his face. "Sorry to dump on you."

I'm quiet as I think to myself. Miller's need to make everything a joke, how he seems to take nothing seriously, is hitting in a different way. He's not some flippant, arrogant guy. He's a man trying to make people happy.

I pull my chin out of the sleeping bag. "You're not dumping anything on me. Thank you for telling me."

Miller leans on his elbow, resting his head on his

hand. "Right back at you, Becs. I think I like you more the more I get to know you."

My cheeks heat. Normally, I'd want to hide at this point. Miller saying he likes me? Yeah, that'll make me blush every time. But I don't feel the need to run or to keep it from him.

I clear my throat. "Um. Thank you?"

He chuckles and scratches his jaw. "You're welcome. Any chance you're starting to like me, too? Or do you still hate me?"

"I never hated you. More just... disliked. You annoyed me at first. And then whenever I was around you, I turned into this person who got distracted. Made mistakes." The truth comes spilling out of me. He's so open and honest in this moment that it's hard not to do the same.

"And you didn't want anyone to figure out you're not perfect," he says softly, startling me with his blunt accuracy. That's exactly what I've been worried about, isn't it?

"Well... when you put it like that, it seems silly," I say with a nervous laugh.

"Maybe. But you know what? I always knew you weren't perfect," Miller says, his face growing serious. "I liked you not in spite of the fact that you weren't perfect, but *because* of your imperfections. They make you who you are, Becs."

I squirm and do my best to change the subject as I roll to my side, propping myself up to face him. "Why do you call me that? Becs? No one else calls me that. No one outside of camp even calls me Becca. I'm Rebecca everywhere else in my life." I like the nickname when he says it.

"It suits you. More than Rebecca or even Becca, if you ask me." Somehow, he's gotten closer as we've talked. His breath tickles my face. "At least, it suits who you are when you're with me. And I like that girl."

"I think I do, too," I whisper. Even though I'm the furthest thing from perfect around him.

Miller reaches over and tucks a stray hair behind my ear. "You should. She's pretty awesome." His fingers trace my jawline.

I turn my face into his hand, so he's cupping my cheek.

He leans forward, his face only inches from mine. "Can I kiss you?"

I blink in surprise as I nod. I never imagined Miller would be the kind of guy to ask. He's the kind of guy who takes what he wants.

"Because if I start kissing you, I don't think I can stop." There's the alpha male.

"I know," I whisper, and that's all it takes.

In one smooth motion, I'm on my back and Miller is leaning down over me, his hands on either side of my head. He bends down and captures my lips with his. It's soft at first, sweet. Then firmer, more demanding as he parts my lips with his tongue and explores my mouth. The varying pressures are dizzying.

His body molds closer to mine, pushing me into the ground beneath me. My legs part inside the sleeping bag as his thigh presses between them, and he kisses me harder.

I gasp for breath when he finally pulls back. My head is spinning, my pulse thrumming through me. There's an ache between my legs as I look up at him. A need I haven't felt in so long.

"Too much?" he asks, smiling as he runs a finger along my cheek.

I reach a hand up and trace my lips. They're swollen from our kiss. More than just a kiss, actually. It seemed like the start of something... more. "No. Not enough."

Even in the dimly lit tent, I can see his eyes darken just before he presses his lips to mine again. He rests some of his body weight against me when his hand comes to my jaw again. His fingers skim along the hammering pulse in my neck.

I moan into his mouth. I've kissed boys before, but *damn*. This feels more intimate than having sex, and we're both fully clothed with sleeping bags between us. Our voices have been low, making sure the campers can't hear us, but if we keep going, I'm not going to be able to stay quiet.

"Miller," I whisper when he stops kissing me for a minute. I'm not really sure what I'm asking. To stop? To keep going? To unzip my sleeping back and fuck me into oblivion right here in the woods, a few feet from the campers?

He gives me a peck on the lips. "I'm going to kiss you a lot more, Becs. But if I don't stop now, I won't be able to. And... campers."

I bury my face against his chest as I laugh. "God, I'm such a bad counselor when I'm around you. What the hell were we thinking?"

He grips my chin and tilts my face up toward his. "That I couldn't lie here next to you and not take my shot, Becs. I've been dreaming about this since I met you. Maybe even before that, when you shot me down in those first texts."

I flush at the reminder. "Yeah. Sorry I was kind of a bitch. I was... going through things."

He lies back and pulls me toward him, so my head

rests in the cradle of his shoulder. "Was that when you found out about the school stuff?" he asks gently.

"Yeah." I snuggle into him. It's warm and comfortable and safe. Everything I've been missing.

He presses a kiss to my forehead. "Well, that's understandable, I guess. You get these texts from some random person you've never met, and you weren't exactly in a mood to talk to anyone. Even a dashing stranger that was mysteriously captivating over text."

I snort. "Sure. Dashing and mysteriously captivating with a line about what color underwear I was wearing."

He continues as if I hadn't spoken, "And even though you hadn't seen his face, you knew in your soul that you'd be making out with that mysterious stranger with a rock digging into your back, just two weeks later."

This time, his quirky jokes make me smile instead of sigh. "I don't have a rock in my back. You can move if it's not comfortable."

He pulls me tighter. "This is the most comfortable I've ever been, Becs. I don't want to move a muscle."

We stay curled together just like that as we drift off to blissful sleep. I usually toss and turn all night when I'm camping, the hard forest floor a stark change from the mattress I'm used to, but I fall into the deepest sleep I've had in a while.

I don't even wake up early, when the sun rises, the way I usually do when I sleep outside.

When I wake, it's with a start, and Miller sits up at the same moment. We look at each other, eyes wide, as the sound of campers screaming fills the air.

24

MILLER

The campers aren't just yelling. They're yelling a name.

"Bayley!"

I exchange a glance with Becca, who's already climbing out of her sleeping bag, her brows pinched with worry as she pulls her pants all the way up. I'm too worried about what's happening out there to even enjoy the glimpse of her round ass, covered by a pair of deep blue boy short underwear.

"I'm coming!" she calls, pulling her shoes on. She leaves the laces undone in her rush to get to the campers.

I slip a shirt and pants on and quickly follow her out of the tent.

The campers are frantic, six of them standing throughout our campsite calling Bayley's name.

Liam is the closest to me. "What's going on?" I ask, breathless from running.

He looks up at me, his little face lined with worry. "We can't find Bayley. When the girls woke up, she wasn't in the tent."

My stomach drops. This is potentially a huge problem. We're not at camp, where there's a finite number of places a camper could have gone. We're in the middle of the woods, and not even at the campsite we'd planned to stay at, where the camp director thinks we are. There are any number of places she could be or things that could have happened to her.

Besides the possibility of bears or mountain lions or other predators, there's always the even worse possibility of a human predator.

"Bayley's missing," Becca says breathlessly, coming over to me.

"I heard." I place my hands on Becca's shoulders, pressing down gently. "Take a breath, and then we're going to figure this out."

She does, exhaling a long breath.

"Again."

Her shoulders rise and fall beneath my palms. The tension is still there, but she finally looks me in the eye and nods, and I drop my hands and step back.

"I'm good. I'll go look for her. I took a class on search and rescue, and I can bring the map so I can find my way back. Can you stay here with the campers and figure out breakfast?" She glances anxiously toward the woods.

"Of course. And Becca?" I wait until her gaze comes back to meet mine. "We've got this. It's going to be okay," I assure her.

"Are you two going to kiss?" Liam asks, his little eyes sharp as he looks between Becca and me.

Becca startles and takes a step back.

I just smile. "No. She's going to find your friend. Now, who wants oatmeal?"

It takes close to an hour, but I manage to get the stove set up and boil water. Yes, I know the joke about people who are such bad cooks that they can't boil water, but camp stoves are a whole different beast. I pour the boiling water over the instant oatmeal in each of the campers' cups.

"What if we can't find her?" Lena asks, blowing on the steaming cup in her hands with a worried look.

Savannah's eyes go wide. "You think we won't find her?"

"We'll find her," I say firmly. "We will." She's a kid. How far could she have gotten?

The campers are occupied for the moment while they eat their breakfast. I wish I'd had the foresight to bring along some coffee, even if it was the instant kind. I could use a shot of caffeine right now.

If I were a kid, where would I go? I look around the campsite. The clearing is only large enough for the tents and some space to sit on the makeshift seats the kids have made out of logs and rocks. She must have gone into the woods, obviously.

Maybe more important is the *why*. What made her leave? Did she get up to use the bathroom and got lost coming back? Did someone say or do something that made her run off, or need time alone?

My money is on the second option. If she just went to pee in the woods, she wouldn't have gone far. I'm willing to bet she wanted time and space alone. That's the only reason she'd go so far that she couldn't be seen.

I'm about to take a bite of my own oatmeal when the sound of approaching footsteps makes me pause. "Becca?" I call. "Bayley?"

There's no answer, but Becca appears a few

seconds later, out of breath. "I can't find her," she says, frantic. "And now it's getting cloudy. Can you help me?"

I look around at the six remaining campers. There's not one right option here. Should I go out on my own to look and leave Becca with the campers? Leave the campers alone while I go with Becca?

I look back at Becca. Her eyes are frantic as she looks around us, like she might have somehow missed Bayley sitting next to one of the trees right next to the tent.

"Okay. Here's what we're going to do." I raise my voice so the campers can hear me. "Kids, come here."

They hop off their rocks and logs and trot over to us.

"Should we all go look?" Mollie asks, her voice tinged with concern.

"No!" Becca exclaims. "I mean, no, Mollie. We don't need anyone else getting lost. I need you to all stay in one spot."

I reach over and squeeze her hand, then let it go before the campers get any big ideas. "Becca's right. She and I are going to go find Bayley. But we need you guys to be extra helpful for us. So, here's the thing. If we're not here, you all still need to be following rules and behaving, right?"

They all nod, their faces serious. At least they understand the gravity of the situation.

"When I say go, I want you all to head into your tents and zip them up." I hold up my hand as Noah turns to the tent and takes a step toward it. "Not yet. When I say go."

Noah turns back. "Sorry."

I give him a smile. "It's okay, bud. Just want everyone to get all the instructions, right?" I make sure all six campers have their gaze fixed on me before I continue. "So, here's the deal. When I say go, you'll all go to your tents and zip them up, then hang out in there. You can play games, talk, relax. But you may *not* leave the tent. Does anyone need to go to the bathroom before you go to your tent?"

Six shaking heads are my answer.

"Okay, good. So, no leaving the tents, even to go to the bathroom. We won't be gone that long. While we're gone, Lena is in charge."

Lena puffs up, a proud smile on her face.

"Which means you need to *listen* to her. Because if anyone does something they shouldn't, not only will you be in trouble, but Lena will be, too."

Her smile fades slightly.

"With great power comes great responsibility,

Lena. I trust you. Make good choices." I nod at her. "Any questions?" I turn to the others, raising a brow.

"What if you can't find her?" Mason asks.

Becca stiffens beside me.

"We will, buddy. And if we can't, we'll move on to Plan B. There's always a backup plan." I don't know what the backup plan is, honestly. I hope to God Becca has one. "Okay. Go."

Becca and I stand there and watch as the campers scurry off into their tents and zip them up.

I turn to her and put my hands on her shoulders. "Take a breath. We're going to figure this out. We're going to find her. Got it?"

She nods, but the lines of worry between her eyebrows don't ease at all.

"Good. Now, let's go find our girl."

I reach for her hand. Her fingers are small as they slide across my palm, and I give them a squeeze.

"We can do this. Now, which way should we go?"

She looks around. "I went the other direction, mostly. So maybe... straight and to the right? And we can adjust from there?" Becca tries.

I nod, trusting her sense of direction, and we set

off hand in hand. I keep my eyes open for any kind of sign Bayley has come this way—footprints, a scrap of fabric or trash, a noise.

Becca starts to chew on her lower lip after we've been walking for a few minutes.

"So, what are you going to do after the summer? You said you had to repeat the year, right?" I ask, trying to distract her from her nerves as my gaze sweeps over the landscape.

She thinks for a minute before taking an unsteady breath. "Yeah. I guess I'll just redo the year. That's the only way I can keep going and eventually be a doctor."

"That's really impressive."

She scans the forest in front of us. "Funny."

I pause and look at her. "I'm not joking, Becs. I think it's really fucking impressive that you failed and you're getting back on the horse. That's what makes people great, right? Not the lack of failing, but the ability to keep trying when you do fail."

The fact that she's willing to go back and try again makes me really proud of her.

"I... didn't really think of it that way, I guess." Becca lets out a sigh. "My whole life has been focused on winning, on getting top grades, on never failing. This experience just seemed like a... stumbling block, I guess. Another strike against me."

I shake my head. "This is a chance to do it again and come back better. I have faith in you."

We keep walking for another five minutes without any sign of Bayley. I look up at the sky, giving Becca's hand a squeeze when I realize there are dark clouds rolling in. Not a good sign.

She follows my gaze. A shiver runs through her. "Miller, it looks like it's going to storm again."

I squeeze her hand again. "We need to find Bayley and then get back to the campers. They'll be fine in their tents for now. Are you okay?"

She takes a shaky breath, then visibly swallows. "I'll be okay until the thunder starts. So I'm good for now. Let's go this direction and then turn back toward camp so we can cover another section."

We turn to the right and keep walking. I have to shorten my stride to keep pace with Becca. I've got a good foot of height on her, and my legs are a lot longer.

"So, what would you do if you didn't play poker for a living?" Becca asks after a while.

"Are you going to think it's silly if I say I want to be a teacher?" I took a few education classes in college, enough for a minor, but never got a teaching certificate. It's something I've wanted to do for a while.

She smiles up at me. "Not at all. I think you'd be

really good at it, actually. What would you teach? High school?"

I laugh, thinking of Addie. "Oh, hell no. My buddy's girlfriend is a high school math teacher, and her students are nothing but drama. I'd teach special ed."

"Why special ed? Is it because of your brother?"

The interest started because of Jordan, but it's grown into more than that. "Kind of. Growing up with Jordan definitely shaped who I am. But I really like seeing who people are below the surface. And with kids who have disabilities, a lot of time people never look below the surface. There are a lot of people I've met who don't see Jordan at all beyond his Down Syndrome. So... that's why.

"I mean, teaching is cool and all. But it's also that I want to be someone in their lives that can see them for who they are."

Becca's eyes are shiny. "That's really... that's beautiful, Miller."

I wink at her. "And I hear a teacher's salary is pretty sweet. So I'd be in it for the money, too, of course."

She throws her head back as she laughs at my sarcasm, the sound filling the space around us. "God, you're insane."

I grin at her. "Yeah. You like it."

Becca opens her mouth, but she doesn't say anything. She freezes.

"You okay?" I look back at her from where I am, a few feet in front of her.

"Shh. I think I hear something." She closes her eyes to listen, and I do, too.

The wind whistles through the trees, and the dried leaves on the ground rustle. I hold my breath, but there's nothing besides the normal forest sounds. I let my breath out in a sigh. "Never mind. I thought there was something there, but maybe I was hearing things."

Just as I'm about to start walking again, I see something that makes hope rise in my chest.

"Look," I say to Becca, pointing.

The ground is soft from the rain yesterday, and even though most of the forest floor is covered in dead leaves, it's still visible. Footprints.

25

MILLER

"There!" Becca points, whispering just loudly enough that I can hear her over the sound of our footsteps on the wet ground.

I follow the path of her pointed finger, and I see it, too. Bayley is slumped against a tree, her eyes closed. We run to her together, and I crouch down beside the small body.

"Bayley?" I tap her shoulder.

"Is she okay?" Becca asks, kneeling next to me. "Bayley?"

Bayley's eyes crack open. A rush of relief goes through me. "Are you okay, kiddo? You scared us."

She blinks a few times, then focuses on Becca.

"Becca? You found me!" She reaches her arms out, and Becca folds her into a hug.

"Of course we found you, Bay. We've been looking for a while. What happened?"

Bayley draws in a shaky breath, looking between the two of us. Her lower lip trembles. "I feel silly now."

I shake my head dramatically. "Hey, no feeling silly. We were scared because we were worried about you. We're not mad, and we've all done silly things."

She swallows as she sits up a little straighter. "I just wanted some time to think. We stayed up in the tent talking and we were having fun. We were talking about all of the activities we want to do next week at camp. I want to do the goat class. Mollie said it's really funny."

"I hate that goat," I say without thinking. It kind of pops out by accident—God knows it's the truth— but it earns me a smile.

Bayley even giggles for a few seconds before she sobers again and continues to talk. "But then Mollie and Savannah and Lena were all talking about what they were going to say to their parents when they wrote to them when we got back. And..."

After a minute, Becca prompts her softly. "And what, Bayley?"

The girl sniffles, and I realize she has tears welling in her eyes. "And it made me think about my parents."

Becca and I exchange a questioning glance.

"Are you missing your parents?" I ask gently. Homesickness is one thing, but leaving the tent in the middle of the night?

Bayley shakes her head, wiping a hand beneath her nose. "I mean, I am. But it made me sad because my parents sent me to camp so they could... could pack things." She meets my eyes, and a tear runs down her cheek. "My daddy is moving out cause they're getting divorced."

Her words hit me right in the heart. Suddenly I'm a kid again, not much older than my campers, hearing that speech. *Your mom and I love you kids very much, but...*

I twist so I'm sitting on the ground next to Bayley. "That sucks. I'm really sorry."

Becca gives me a sharp look from where she's crouched in front of us. Maybe *sucks* is one of those words you're not supposed to use in front of campers. But honestly? This is a situation that calls for it. Trust me, I know.

"My parents got divorced when I was eleven," I tell Bayley softly. "I was really sad for a long time."

Bayley's eyes widen as I speak, worry creasing her forehead. "They said it's not my fault. But then they sent me away to camp."

I reach an arm out, and she snuggles into my side. Jesus, she's freezing. How long has she been out here? I look at Becca, trying to communicate silently. We need to get Bayley back to the campsite, then back to camp as soon as we can.

I give Bayley's shoulder a gentle squeeze. "I bet they sent you to camp because they thought you'd have fun here, and being around people who are getting divorced isn't very much fun."

She nods, looking thoughtful. "My mom and dad fight all the time."

"That can be scary to hear, too, huh?" Jordan was too little to understand what was happening back then, but I knew. I remember the fear that froze in my chest every time they started yelling at one another.

Becca stands from where she's been crouched down and takes a few steps back, giving Bayley and me some space.

"I don't like hearing them fight, so maybe you're right about that. And camp is fun," Bayley admits.

I squeeze her shoulder comfortingly. "And next week is going to be a lot of fun, too. Maybe even more fun than last week. *Especially* if you hang out with the goat." I wink at her.

Bayley giggles, the smile brightening her entire face.

"How long have you been out here?" I ask her.

She shivers against me, like she's finally realizing how cold she is. "All night."

Becca's leaning against a tree a few feet away, but she must be able to hear us still, because her eyes go wide, and she stands up straighter.

"Can you tell me what happened?" I ask.

Bayley shifts on the ground next to me. "We were talking in the tent, like I said. And I just wanted to be alone to think. So, after the other girls fell asleep, I snuck out and walked for a little bit. But then it was dark, and I couldn't find my way back, so I sat down here. I must have fallen asleep." She shrugs.

I don't miss Becca's sharp intake of breath. I nearly gasp, too. What if a bear or mountain lion or *something* had found her before we did? What if she'd taken a wrong turn and fallen? Jesus, this could have turned out so badly.

I force my voice to stay level. None of those things happened. Bayley is safe.

"Well, I'm glad we found you. Next time, you need to tell us if you're leaving the tent, okay? We need to know where you are. Or one of us would have walked with you."

She nods, wiping another tear off her cheek. "I didn't know your parents got divorced. I didn't want to talk to the girls about it because it seems like their parents are so happy and they wouldn't understand."

"I get it." I give her a small side hug. "I'm happy to talk about it whenever you want, okay? There are a lot of other people who've gone through it, too, that you can talk to. And you know what?" I lean down with a conspiratorial whisper. "My parents are both happier now. They were making one another sad."

My mom is happier, at least. We haven't heard from my dad in years, but Bayley doesn't need to know all of that right now.

This earns me another smile that warms my heart. "I don't want my mom and dad to be sad."

"Exactly. Now, should we head back? Everyone else is worried about you." I stand and hold a hand out.

Bayley takes it and rises to her feet. "Are you going to tell them about my parents?"

"Absolutely not." I look at Becca, who dips her chin in a small nod. "And Becca won't, either. That's your stuff. Thank you for sharing with us. But neither of us will ever break your confidence about this. What would you like us to tell them?"

Bayley thinks as we start to walk. "Can you just tell them I went to the woods to go to the bathroom and got lost?"

I laugh. "If sneaking out to pee is less embarrassing,

then you've got it. That's our story and we're sticking to it."

We can't be more than a five-minute walk from the campsite, but when I look up, the clouds have gotten even darker. I take Becca's hand and squeeze it.

"Can you walk a little faster, Bay? It looks like it's going to rain," Becca says nervously.

Bayley nods and increases her speed a little. We trek together in silence, keeping our eyes on the ground to avoid tripping. The first raindrops start to fall just as the tents come into view through the trees.

"Go, go, go!" Becca cries, laughing.

We run the last few feet to the campsite. I go to the boys' tent while Becca and Bayley head to the other.

I unzip the flap and stick my head in. "Good news, boys. We found Bayley. She just got lost, but everything is fine. It's starting to rain again, so we're going to hang out in our tents until it passes, then pack up and head back to camp, okay?"

All three boys have big smiles on their faces.

"I'm so glad you found her!" Liam says.

Ben nods eagerly. "I like her. We put up the tent together and she was so much fun. Now we're like best friends."

See? Told you they'd bond if they did the tents themselves.

"Yeah. She's super cool," Noah adds.

"I'll let her know. While it rains, why don't you guys make sure everything is packed up in your backpacks so we can head back as soon as it stops?" I wait for them to agree before I zip the flap back up and head to my tent.

Voices drift over from where Becca and Bayley are sitting in the girls' tent.

"We were so worried about you!"

"Are you okay? Are you still going to be at camp this week?"

"Do you want me to carry your backpack on the way back?"

I can't help but snort at that last one. It sounded like Lena. Her heart's in the right place, but how is she planning to carry two massive frame backpacks down the mountain?

The chatter continues for a few more minutes before the zipper on my tent slides open and Becca slips inside.

"It seems like she's okay," she remarks, scooting in to sit next to me. "A little shaken up and chilly from spending the night outside, but she's going to be fine."

I reach and arm out and pull Becca into my side in a mirror image of the way I was sitting with Bayley under the tree. "And how are *you* doing?"

She shrugs. "Okay, I guess. I was kind of freaking out."

"You don't say," I tease, giving her arm a squeeze. "You? Freaking out? Never."

She gives me a good-natured shove. "Shut up. Plus, you aren't the one who's going to have to call her parents."

"True. But I will if you need me to."

She's silent for a minute, looking at the tent wall. "I didn't know about your parents. I'm sorry."

"It was a long time ago. But I get where Bayley's coming from. I was pretty torn up about it for a while after it happened."

Becca twists to look at me. "But they're happier now?"

"Oh. Um." I drop my voice low, so Bayley can't hear us. "My mom is. My dad actually left us. I haven't heard from him in years. I didn't think Bayley needed to hear all of that, though."

"Oh. Shit, I'm sorry," Becca says with a frown.

I give her a grin, trying to lighten the mood. "My mom more than makes up for it. She's as cool as two parents any day. You should meet her. You'd like her."

Becca is silent for a minute. "Parents are weird, huh?"

Slight change of topic, but I'll take it. "I mean, sure. Why?"

"Like, we love them, and they love us, but the things they do and the way they raise us makes us into who we are."

I nod. "True. I swear a lot because of my mom. Lori Quinlan swears like a sailor."

Becca giggles. "I want to meet her someday. My parents are more... serious, I guess." She frowns. "I can't tell them about failing my second year of school. They don't even know I failed one class, let alone two."

"Why?" I can't imagine keeping anything from my mom. She's the one I go to for advice, the one I lean on when things get tough. I've always known we had a unique relationship, but it's such a part of who I am that I can't imagine what I'd do if I couldn't talk to her about things.

"They'd be so disappointed. My dad got himself from an Indian immigrant kid who couldn't speak English all the way to being a cardiothoracic surgeon. And I can't even hack it with all the help they've given me along the way." Her shoulders slump.

"And then what? What would happen if they were disappointed in you?" I push.

She thinks for a minute. "I... I don't know. I just hate disappointing them."

"Would they stop loving you?" I tilt my head.

She pauses. "I... no. I don't think so."

"Or supporting you?" I prod.

Becca shoves me. "Jesus, you're like a goddamn shrink."

I grin. "Hey, I took a few psych classes back in college. Maybe I'm like half a shrink. Or half a therapist or something."

She snorts. "Yeah. That's what the world needs. Miller Quinlan, therapist."

"My patients would leave laughing," I say innocently. "And pulling pranks makes everyone happy, so I'd consider that a good therapeutic option."

Becca's body shakes with laughter before she relaxes against me. "You're different than I thought you were," she admits.

"So you said." And I don't know which god or higher power to thank for the fact that she realized that, but if I find out, I'll be on my knees thanking them every fucking day for the rest of my life.

Becca sits up, away from me, and looks me in the eye. She bites her lip. "So, um. What are we going to tell people when we get back to camp?"

26

BECCA

"She did *what*?" Brett's voice gets louder and somehow deeper, if that's even possible.

Jesus, he's scary, especially sitting here in his office. He's behind a large desk, arms crossed over his chest, while we're sitting in front of it, like kids who've been called into the principal's office and are being asked to fess up to their crimes.

"She, uh, snuck out of the tent. She was upset about her parents and wanted time to herself," I say, trying to gauge how much to tell Brett.

"They're getting divorced. The other girls were talking about their parents, and she was upset. Understandably, right?" Miller takes over. "Everyone was asleep. No one knew she was missing until we all woke up."

I notice that he conveniently leaves out the part where he and I took a tent to ourselves and left the campers sleeping in tents by themselves. Also the part where we left them alone while we went to look for Bayley.

"Jesus, fuck. This is a disaster. Is she okay?" Brett pinches the bridge of his nose.

I nod. "She's fine. She was shaken up, but Miller, uh, talked to her and helped her calm down. I think she's looking forward to another week at camp." *Please don't fire us.*

"And here I thought you two would make a good pair," Brett mutters, dropping his arms with a sigh. "Best laid plans and all that. Okay. Miller, go help Jason with putting all the backpacks away and hanging out the tents. They all need to dry out. Becca, let's call Bayley's parents together."

Miller gives me a sympathetic look before he ducks out.

Brett pulls the phone to the center of his desk. He taps on a computer keyboard, then stares at the screen while he dials a number. He puts the call on speakerphone.

My stomach clenches as the phone rings. The sound seems to echo in the small office.

"Hello?" a woman's voice answers.

Brett speaks first. "Hello, is this Ms. Kingston? Bayley's mom?"

The woman hesitantly responds, "Yes, this is she."

"This is Brett Morton, the director here at Camp Winnie. Everything is fine, and I'm here with Becca Patel, Bayley's counselor. We just have a little update for you."

A little update seems to be putting it mildly.

Brett looks at me and nods. I force my fists to unclench and clear my throat. "Hi, Ms. Kingston, this is Becca. I'm Bayley's counselor, and I was one of the leaders for her overnight trip this weekend. We went backpacking on Mount Chocorua."

"Okay." Bayley's mother sounds understandably concerned. "And?"

I swallow hard. "She was a little upset the night we stayed out there, camping. Some of the girls were talking about their parents."

There's a brief silence. Then, "Oh. I, um, Bayley's dad and I are getting divorced. That's probably why."

Brett nods at me to keep going.

"Yes, she mentioned that. So I guess she wanted to be alone for a bit and think. She snuck out of the tent after everyone went to sleep."

"What?" Mrs. Kingston exclaims, her voice

through the speaker phone echoing around Brett's small office. "What in the world was she thinking?"

"I'm not sure. But, um, she ended up getting lost. We didn't know she wasn't in the tent until the morning when everyone woke up. My co-counselor and I found her, and she's fine, but she did spend the night sleeping in the woods."

There's no answer for a minute, and I start to worry.

Is she in her car already, on her way here to skin me alive for not watching out for her daughter? Texting a killer-for-hire to do the dirty work for her?

"Ms. Kingston?" *Please don't be hiring an assassin.*

"She's that upset about the divorce?" Her voice cracks.

I swallow against the lump that rises in my throat. Maybe we're all worried about disappointing someone. Unable to speak, I look at Brett.

He clears his throat and takes over. "It sounds like she was upset enough to want some alone time. Regardless, she's fine now. We do have a policy that says campers aren't allowed to call their parents, and this is largely to decrease homesickness. But I think in this situation it might be helpful if she could speak with you, and maybe with her dad as well."

The woman sniffles. "Yes, of course."

Brett nods to me, and I stand as he keeps speaking. "Becca will go get Bayley now. Hold on a minute."

Bayley is seated on a picnic table outside the office, twisting her small fingers together in front of her. I wave at her from the doorway. "Come on in. Your mom wants to talk to you."

She heads in, and I take her spot at the picnic table.

Bayley's talk with her mother must have gone well. She has a smile on her face as we walk back to our cabin, and it doesn't fade as she meets the two new campers that replaced Maya and Helena, as we hear about the overnight that Emma and Olivia went on while we were hiking, as we go to swim screen and dinner and orientation, even as we get ready for bed.

I give each of the girls a high five as they tuck themselves into bed.

Vivien and I head to the picnic table outside the cabin. "Do you want to go to the dining hall tonight?" I ask. "You've spent more time supervising the cabin than I have."

She taps a finger against her lips. "In a little, maybe. I want to hear more about your overnight. I need all the gossip, girl. You guys came back and then you disappeared into Brett's office. What happened on your trip?"

I sink onto the bench next to her. "It was... interesting. We camped at a different spot than we planned, got stuck in a thunderstorm, and then Bayley got lost. It was kind of a disaster." I sigh, twisting my fingers together. "I'm just glad we're home in one piece."

"And?" she prods.

"And what? You need more screwups than that?"

Vivien narrows her eyes. "No, doofus. I want to hear about you and Miller."

Oh. Right.

My cheeks heat at the thought of our night in the tent. "Uh. Well, the campers wanted to have tents to themselves, so they didn't have to break up the girls. So, uh, Miller and I shared one."

"One what?" Vivien's forehead wrinkles in confusion.

I chew on my thumbnail. "Um, a tent."

Her mouth falls open. "*And*? Then what? You two spent the night together?"

"We talked. He's... not as much of an asshole as I thought he was."

"Oh my God, you're the worst at girl talk. Did you kiss? Cuddle? Bang? Are you together now? We need answers."

I frown as I think. "Well, we kissed, but... I don't know the rest. I don't know if we're together or a couple or what. He wasn't like touchy-feely when we got back, but you know, campers. God, this rule about keeping things from the campers makes it really hard to know when someone likes you."

Vivien rolls her eyes. "Everyone on camp knows that Miller likes you, Becca. It's not some big secret. Even some of the campers have picked up on it. The question is if *you* like *him*."

Yes. "I don't know."

"Why?" Vivien presses. "You guys kissed. You slept in the same tent. That's a lot of time to spend with someone and not know if you like him."

"I just... need to think, I guess. I like him, I just don't know the rest of it. Like, are we even together? Maybe he just wanted to prove he could get me to kiss him or something. Maybe it was all a prank." Now that I haven't seen Miller in a few hours, doubt is creeping in.

Would he go that far? Get a girl to fall for him just to prove he can?

"Go." Vivien gives me a shove. "That settles it. You go to the dining hall, find your man, and fucking talk to him. You guys are the oldest people on staff besides

Brett. If you can't figure your shit out, there's no hope for the rest of us."

I grab my phone from the cabin before I head to the dining hall. Vivien is right. Of course, she's right. Why is it so hard to talk to guys about this stuff?

"Hey there," a voice says as I walk past M-Hall, nearing the dining hall.

I turn around to find Dave a few yards behind me. My stomach sinks. If Dave is here, Miller is back at the cabin.

"I hear you're my co-counselor-in-law," he says, looping his arm through my elbow.

"Huh?" I'm not sure that's even a thing, and if it is, I have no idea what it means.

He laughs, pulling me in tighter to his side for a brotherly hug. "You're with Miller, right? And he's my co-counselor. Hence, co-counselor-in-law."

I groan. "That's not a thing, Dave." But that means Miller said something to him. My heart leaps at the idea of Miller telling people about us.

Because it means maybe there is an *us*.

"Well, it should be." Dave says with a shrug.

We reach the dining hall door, and Dave releases my arm as I pull my phone out of the pocket of my jeans and hold it up. "I'm going to check my phone real quick. I'll see you in there," I say.

But as I head down to the beach, I slide my phone back into my pocket without looking at it. Because what I really need is time alone, time to think.

I wander down to the beach, reliving the last week. How has Miller changed so much in my eyes?

It seems like forever ago that I was standing right here, hoping to avoid him by spending time walking along the beach. Now, there's a pit in my stomach, because I won't get to see him tonight.

My phone vibrates in my pocket, and my heart leaps, hoping it's him.

God, I'm turning into one of those girls, aren't I? The kind who gets excited about a text because it might be from the guy they're thinking about.

But I'm so hopeful that the message is from him that I don't even care. I pull the phone out so fast I almost drop it into the sand. A smile spreads across my face when I see the name.

MILLER

Hey. Hope you're getting to spend some time away from the campers. Dave bugged me until I caved and sent him away, so sorry I'm not there. I wish you could come over here.

> Too bad I'm not allowed to hang out by the boys' cabins at night. Tomorrow is my night off, but maybe the next night?

> Your night off is mine now. I have plans for us.

> Yeah?

> Yeah. Meet me at the swing after dinner.

> What are we doing? What should I wear?

I stare at the phone, waiting for an answer, but there are no three little dots indicating that Miller is typing an answer. After three minutes of waiting, I force myself to put my phone in my pocket. Maybe a camper woke up and needed him or something. That's the reason one of the counselors has to stay within view of the cabin, after all.

But even after I walk the length of the beach, all the way to the very end of the Boating department and back to the dining hall, there's still no answer.

And despite how much I wish he'd text me back right now, I can't tamp down my joy.

I have a date tomorrow.

With Miller.

27

MILLER

Not even the goat can ruin my day.

Lucy fixes me with her evil stare, but I just give her a smirk. She can't get to me.

Because I'm seeing Becca tonight. I have no idea what we're going to do, or where we're going to go, but honestly, I'm happy just to spend time with her.

Each counselor gets a night off once a week, and last week, I spent mine driving to McDonald's to get a Big Mac with Jackson. We get to leave camp, or at least have time off from campers, from the time dinner ends until curfew. Which I still think is stupid, but the days are so busy that by the 10:00 p.m. curfew I'm ready to drop into bed.

As I wait by the barn for Mary to show up with the key, I rub my hand over my chin, thinking about what to do tonight. I want to show Becca a good time, prove to her again that I'm a good guy.

And fuck, if I can touch her, kiss her, I'd die happy.

Mary walks up just as I start imagining what Becca's luscious breasts feel like. They'd be more than a handful, for sure. I wonder if they're sensitive.

"How was your weekend trip?" Mary asks, snapping me back to reality.

Do not get a boner in front of the campers. "It was good. Interesting, but good."

Mary smirks, confirming that the camp gossip mill is working overtime. She pulls a key from her pocket and inserts it into the padlock that holds the barn door closed. I help her pull the door open as the first campers show up for the day.

I herd the campers into a group, sitting them on a patch of grass while Mary pulls out the attendance sheet. She goes through the list, checking off each camper to make sure we haven't missed anyone, then shoves it in her back pocket and claps her hands twice.

"Okay, welcome to Nature!"

The campers cheer. I clap along with them,

because why not? Despite the goat, this place is growing on me.

"You're here because you signed up for the big animals class! That means we're going to spend extra time with our animals that live out here." She motions to the pens that hold Lucy along with the pony, alpaca, and sheep. "They're a lot of fun but a lot of work, too! And we're going to learn all about them this week."

Mary goes through the safety rules for the department. Wear closed-toed shoes, don't get animals out without permission, don't touch animals without permission, don't feed animals without permission.

Mostly, make sure you have permission before you do things with the animals. You'd think we wouldn't have to say it so many times.

Wait. Scratch that. Now that I've spent a week living with pre-teens, I've realized something. You do, indeed, have to say things like this many times. Because they'll find a loophole.

"Can we go in the pens with the animals if we don't let them out?" a boy sitting in the front of the group asks.

See?

Mary shakes her head firmly. "No. Anything with the animals is off-limits unless you're with a counselor."

The camper looks disappointed, his dreams of crawling into the sheep's little house dashed for the time being.

"Any other questions?" Mary asks, looking at the group. When no one else raises a hand, she claps hers together again. "Alright. Now, who do you want to meet first?"

I breathe a sigh of relief when they choose the sheep. Edison is the most chill of all the animals and seems to be the one who hates me the least.

The day goes by smoothly, especially for a Monday, and my prayers of avoiding Lucy are answered for today when she blessedly stays in her pen through all three classes.

Once the barn is swept and the animals are all fed, Mary locks the barn and holds something out to me. "Here."

I take it automatically, then look at the key in my hand with furrowed brows. "Why do I need your key?"

Mary points to the padlock she just snapped shut. "Tomorrow is my day off, so I won't be here. You'll have to open the department. Guard that with your life. The last thing I need is for campers to get a hold of it. Remember how one of them wanted to go play in the pens with the animals? You lose the key, we'll end up finding him sleeping in one of their shelters."

I slide the key into my pocket next to my phone. "Will do, boss. Have a good day off."

I finger the key as I walk back to my cabin, a plan starting to form in my mind.

After dinner I pat my pocket, making sure I didn't lose the key yet, as I make my way the few steps from the dining hall to the beach. I slide my sandals off and hold them in one hand, the sand warm beneath my toes.

The sun is starting to dip lower in the sky, orange light reflecting off the glistening waves of the lake, but nature's beauty pales in comparison to what's waiting on the swing for me.

Becca's hair is down instead of in her usual braid. She's twisting a lock of it around her finger, her knees hugged to her chest as she stares out at the water.

For a moment I stop in my tracks, taking her in. God, she's stunning.

I want nothing more than to run up to her, sweep her into my arms, and carry her off to my bed, but there are campers spilling out of the dining hall, on their way to their evening program, so I settle for a wave. "Hey, Becs," I call to her.

Becca looks up at me, a smile warming her face.

"Hey," she says. She hops off the swing and walks toward me. "You never told me what you had planned for tonight, so I'm just wearing my usual camp clothes. I can stop by the cabin to change, though."

I shake my head, resisting the urge to pull her into my arms and hold her close, because campers. "No need." I drop my voice low enough that only she can hear. "Let's get out of here. I need to get you away from these campers."

We make small talk as we wander past the throngs of kids. It's torture not being able to hold her hand, put an arm around her shoulder, kiss her. And it's not like we're hiding anything, if you ask me.

The tension between us is so thick that it radiates off us in waves. How could anyone look at the two of us together and not see it?

We walk across the Sports field, which has somehow quadrupled in size. It's in plain view of the campers, and it feels like an hour for us to cross it and finally be hidden in the woods that separates the sports area from the Nature barn.

I look back to make sure we're hidden from view, and as soon as I'm sure, my control snaps.

"Come here," I say roughly. I pull Becca into my chest, spinning her around and then backing her up until she's pressed against a tree. I set one hand on the trunk behind her head while the other pins her in place at her hip.

Becca's breath hitches when my thumb traces a pattern over her hip, and her tongue darts out to wet her perfect lips.

"I've wanted to do this since the first time I saw you," I say, and then my lips are on hers.

Our mouths fit together just like they did that night in the tent, both of us pressing back against the other like we can't get close enough. I use my tongue to trace along her lips, and when she opens them, I slip inside, swallowing her moan.

Our tongues tangle together in a dance that feels like we've been doing it for years. It's perfect, it's everything, and yet somehow, it's not enough.

Becca's breathing hard when I lift my head to look into her eyes. Her pupils are so dilated there's just a faint rim of brown surrounding the black. Her pulse hammers in her neck as I trace a finger over it.

I take a deep breath. "Okay. That's all I wanted. Have a good night," I deadpan.

Becca giggles, fucking giggles, and it's the best thing I've ever heard. She throws her arms around my shoulders. "Nice try."

I grin, pulling her in tight with my arms around her waist. "I knew you'd get my humor eventually. Let's go."

She slides her hand into mine and follows me as I lead her through the woods. "Where are we going?"

I don't look back. "You'll see."

To my surprise, she doesn't argue, and I'm hoping that finally, *finally*, she trusts me. I keep a tight grip on her hand as we emerge from between the trees and the Nature barn comes into view. It looks different, somehow, without all of the campers crowding around it. Even the pens are silent, the animals asleep for the evening.

Becca gives me a questioning look until I reach into my pocket and hold up the key. "Look what I have."

Her brow pinches together. "Where did you get that?"

"Mary." I slide the key into the padlock and turn it until the lock pops open. "Her day off is tomorrow, so she gave it to me to open things up."

I pull the door open, and Becca walks inside. "You'd think after so many years as a camper and counselor I'd have been everywhere at camp, but this is one of the few places that's still brand-new to me." She looks around the space in wonder.

I close the door behind us, making sure we won't have any unexpected guests.

When I turn back to her, Becca is engrossed in a poster that lists flowers that are native to the area. Yarrow, aster, butterfly weed, honeysuckle. I've spent some time studying it myself.

I step up behind her and splay my hand over her stomach, pulling her into me, her back to my front. Her breath hitches slightly, but then she tenses her muscles, sucking her belly in until it's practically flat.

"Don't," I say. My lips brush the shell of her ear, and she tilts her head to the side, subtly giving me permission. I trace kisses down the soft skin of her neck. "Relax. I like you just the way you are."

Her pulse hammers in her neck. I scrape my teeth lightly along her skin.

"Relax," I say again, and this time she does, letting out a breath, and her stomach rounds beneath my hand into that perfect softness.

I nip at her jaw.

"Perfect," I whisper. "You're so fucking perfect."

She moans, just barely loud enough to hear. I've been hard all day, thinking of this moment, but she makes that noise and somehow, I'm even harder.

"Fuck," I grind out. I need to touch her, hold her, kiss her.

I'm painfully aware that we're still at camp, that we're in the Nature barn of all places, and God knows this isn't going to be where I finally get to fuck her for the first time. For that she deserves a five-star hotel, 1,000-thread count Egyptian cotton sheets.

But I need to touch her.

I tug her toward the couch and sit. "Come here."

Becca follows me and plops down, close enough that our shoulders are almost touching. I hold my arm out, and she settles against my shoulder.

"Talk to me," I say. "It's been forever since I saw you."

She snorts, an adorable little sound if I've ever heard one. "I saw you yesterday."

"That was a long time ago. How are your campers?"

Becca tilts her head. "You really want to talk?"

I shrug and shift us on the couch so she's resting against one side, her legs on my lap, then pull her sneakers off one by one, dropping them to the floor as I rub her sock-covered feet. "I want to do whatever you want, babe. If all you want to talk, that's what we'll do."

She bites her lip as I massage her foot and lets out a groan as I find a tight muscle. "God, that feels good."

She tips her head back, closing her eyes. But as I switch feet, starting to massage the other one, she looks up at me and pulls her feet away. She tucks them underneath her as she moves closer to me. "I don't want to just talk," she whispers.

28

BECCA

My entire body is on fire. Every touch of Miller's hands ignites a new flame that courses heat through me, settling between my legs.

His strong arms surround me as he moves me exactly where he wants me, maneuvering our bodies until I'm on my back on the couch and he's positioned over me. His hand skims my side while his lips caress mine.

I gasp as he bites down on my lower lip, just enough for a hint of pain to blossom before his tongue soothes the area.

Miller's hand reaches the hem of my yellow Camp Winnie t-shirt, and I wish yet again that I was wearing something... prettier, maybe. Sexier.

But my thoughts about my wardrobe vanish as his fingers slip beneath the fabric and trace a line along my abdomen.

All of my thoughts vanish, honestly. The few times I've hooked up with a guy it's been awkward, both of us fumbling while all I can think of is what I should be doing with my hands or feet or elbows.

This is the farthest thing from awkward. Our bodies know one another. It's like a dance we've done thousands of times before as his fingers find the sensitive patch of skin just above my hipbone, the place where my waist dips inward at my side. His other hand cups my jaw, fingers skimming my hairline as he kisses me slow and long and languid.

We're both fully clothed and haven't done more than kiss, but somehow it feels a million times more intimate and erotic than a makeout session on an old couch should be.

Miller's hips pin me to the sofa, his erection pressing between my legs. I lift my hips, needing more friction, and I'm rewarded with a groan.

"Fuck, Becs," he says, his jaw tight. He slides his arm around my back, and then suddenly he's lifting me off the couch and to my feet, twirling me around until my back is pressed up against the wall.

He holds me in place with one hand on my hip, the other pressed to the wall next to my head, and brings his lips to mine, harsh and demanding.

His thumb draws circles on my hip, fire blazing outward in a spiral from his touch.

When he slips his hand beneath the waistband of my shorts, my breath comes in short pants, and I'm fairly certain I'm about to spontaneously combust.

My head falls back against the wall as his fingers explore, slowly moving toward my center. So, so slowly.

I moan and push my hips toward him, needing more, but my movement only makes him stop.

Miller smiles against my mouth. "Patience, Becs."

I have no idea how he's holding back. His erection is obvious against his pants, and yet he's the one taking this at a snail's pace.

When he finally slides my underwear to the side, he groans. "Fuck, Becs. You're so wet."

He traces a line along my slit, and all words escape me. The world shrinks down to encompass just the two of us, just this moment.

Just the blaze of pleasure that's building between my legs.

And right as I'm about to start begging, he slips a

finger inside me, and I gasp. Then he adds another, pressing his thumb to my clit, and I'm a complete goner. I have no shame, my hips moving wantonly against him, fucking his hand.

My body tightens, the sensations overtaking me as my vision goes black and I see stars. The only sound is the rushing of blood in my ears, until his voice breaks through.

"Come for me, Becs. Come on my fingers."

And I shatter, clenching around him, every muscle taut as I fall over the cliff.

I barely remember making it back to the couch, but as I finally come back to reality after the most mind-blowing orgasm of my life, I find myself curled against him on the worn cushions.

"That was beautiful, Becs," he says, gently running a finger along my cheek.

I reach out, tentative, needing to do something for him too, but he shakes his head as he covers my hand with his.

"Tonight is about you." Miller presses a kiss to my forehead, then takes my hand and pulls me to stand. "You ready?"

I'm not sure what else he has planned that could top that climax, but I follow him nonetheless as he leads me out of the barn, walking past two rabbits in a cage who look like they're scarred from what they just witnessed.

Miller locks the barn and slides the key into his pocket, then takes my hand again and guides me toward the woods, back toward the Sports field and the cabins. The sun is below the horizon now, but there's still enough light to see.

This twilight is my second favorite time of day, after the magic of the pre-sunrise morning. There's an almost ethereal glow to the world as the day slips away. I breathe in the pine-scented air as we step onto the dirt path.

It has to be at least 8:30 p.m. if the sun is going down, which means campers are safely tucked in their beds. We don't need to worry about being caught together.

The trees open up to the Sports field, broad and empty. We're halfway across the grass when Miller stops and points upward. "Look."

I follow his finger to see the moon already shining bright. It's a thin crescent tonight, its white light stark against the darkening sky.

"Come here," Miller beckons, and I follow

without question as he sits on the grass and lies back. "You can see a ton of stars from here. Look."

When I first peel my eyes away from the moon, all I see is darkness, but as my eyes adjust and the last bits of light slip away, the stars shine brighter. I try to count them.

"Look at that!" I gasp, as something grabs my attention. Miller follows my direction as I point out the shooting star.

"Make a wish." I can hear the smile in his voice as I squeeze my eyes closed, wishing this moment could last forever.

Okay, not forever. I didn't think I was that sexual of a woman, but being this close to Miller is highlighting some needs I didn't realize were quite so pressing.

But this closeness, this intimacy, sitting here together in comfortable silence? This is what I want.

I open my eyes to find Miller propped on one elbow, looking down at me. "What did you wish for?" he asks. He brushes a piece of hair back from my face.

I mime zipping my lips and throwing away the key. "It's a secret."

He gently pinches my jaw between two fingers and runs his thumb over my lips. "I'll bet I can kiss it out of you."

I smile. "You're welcome to try."

It's well past curfew when we sneak back to our cabins.

Miller breaks the no-boys-in-the-girls-area rule to walk me back to my cabin, where Vivien is reading a book by the light of a flashlight at the picnic table.

She smirks as we walk up hand in hand. "Have a nice night, kids?"

Miller raises my hand and brushes his lips across my knuckles. "It was a very nice night." He leans in, still holding my hand as his lips graze my ear. "I can't wait to see you again," he whispers, so softly only I can hear it. "Have a good night, babe."

I wait until he disappears between the trees, heading back to the Fireflies cabins, before I sink down on the bench next to Vivien with a sigh.

"Details," she says, nudging me with her elbow. "All the details."

We tiptoe into the cabin, doing our best not to wake any campers. I grab my phone from the charger and slip it into my pocket as I head to the bathroom to brush my teeth. I left it in my cabin this morning, turned off so the battery wouldn't drain.

I'm sure there are a slew of emails in my inbox, the usual spam that never stops showing up no matter how many times I unsubscribe.

I power the phone on and set it on the counter next to me while I squeeze a line of toothpaste onto my brush and stick it in my mouth. As the screen comes to life, there are a couple notifications.

One text message from my mom—I cringe—and a voicemail from a number in upstate New York that I don't recognize.

The voicemail is probably spam, or a robo-call of some type. Who leaves voicemails these days?

I check the text message first.

MOM

Just wanted to check in on you. We miss you. Hope everything is going well at school.

Miller's words from our camping trip come back to me. My parents might be disappointed in me for failing my classes, but they'd still love me. Maybe I should talk to them.

I type out a quick reply to my mom and then

check my voicemail, my finger ready to delete whatever nonsense this is.

But I blink as the sound comes through, trying to make sense of it. My heart beats a little faster.

It's not spam.

I listen to it again, my stomach doing somersaults as I wonder if I'm understanding correctly.

After a third listen, I pull the phone away from my ear to look at the time. It's far too late to call anyone back tonight, so it'll have to wait for tomorrow. I tuck the phone in my pocket and head back toward the cabin, my heart beating a little faster as I replay the message in my mind.

***

9 a.m. is a reasonable hour to call people back. It's also really, *really* far away when the campers wake you up at 6:30.

With the early wake-up, I manage to get a shower in before breakfast. My hair is still wet when we walk the campers to the dining hall, but at least it smells nice.

Miller is seated at the opposite end of the space from where my table is. He makes eye contact and waves. I smile back, but my mind is still on the voice-mail from last night.

"How come you're not eating?" Lena asks, grabbing a slice of bacon off her plate and bringing it to her mouth.

I focus on the campers seated around my table, all of them hanging on Lena's words. "Sorry. Was just distracted, thinking about some things. I'm going to grab more French toast."

I head to the buffet, more for a break from the campers and their questions than for more food, but since I'm here I load a few more slices onto my plate along with a generous helping of syrup. My phone in my pocket bumps against my backside as I slide into my seat, reminding me of the phone call I need to make. My stomach flips again.

I finally have my chance after breakfast. Vivien and I usher the girls through the woods back to our cabin.

They have a half-hour designated for cabin clean-up, and even though some of them have only been here less than a day, this place is a disaster. There are clothes all over the floor and somehow two pinecones in one corner.

How are little girls this messy?

I sit on my bed after tidying my part of the cabin.

My knee bounces up and down as I stare at my watch. 8:57.

"Dude, you okay?" Vivien gives me a strange look. She folds a t-shirt and tucks it into the cabinet next to her bed.

"Yeah." I glance down at my watch again. "I just have to make a call. I was going to wait until nine."

Vivien folds a pair of shorts and looks at her own watch. "It's 8:58. I think you'll be okay to call whoever you need to talk to. I can keep an eye on the girls until you get back. How long do you need?"

How long *do* I need? I have no idea, honestly. Five minutes? An hour? "Um, not really sure. Maybe ten minutes? If it's longer, I can ask if I can call them back at rest hour."

Vivien shoves her empty laundry basket back under her bed and reaches for the broom. "Okay. It's 8:59 now, anyway. Go ahead."

I give her a grateful smile and unplug my phone from the charger. I look around as I step out of the cabin. Where will I have service and privacy? Everyone is doing the same cabin clean-up.

I finally settle on walking toward the beach. Ladybugs 2 is close enough to the beach that we can see the lake through the trees, so I don't go too far. I slide my flip-flops off when I reach the sand and curl my toes while I dial the number.

"Hello?"

My stomach twists. "Hi. It's, um, Becca. Rebecca Patel. I'm returning a call?"

29

MILLER

"Hey, have you seen Becca?" I try for a casual tone as I reach for another piece of garlic bread to dip in my spaghetti sauce, but I'm not sure I nail it. Because I'm, to use a Becca term, freaking out here.

After last night, I thought we were on a new page with our relationship. That there *was* a relationship. I don't do stuff like that with just anyone. But she looked distracted when I waved to her at breakfast. She didn't answer a text I sent her during cabin clean-up time. And now it's lunchtime, and she's nowhere to be seen.

"Uh, I think she had to leave," Jackson admits. He twirls spaghetti on his fork, puts it in his mouth and chews before continuing. "Jana is moving into the cabin with Vivien for the week."

My stomach bottoms out. I do my best to school my features, because the campers don't need to know that I'm about to lose my shit. "Like, left camp? For a few days or what?"

Jackson shrugs, the picture of casualness and lack of concern. "Don't know. I don't think Brett is planning on her coming back, but you never know. Why?"

I take a deep breath and let it go, then force myself to take a sip of my water. "Just wondering. We're friends, so I was worried when I didn't see her at lunch."

Lies. All lies. We're more than friends, and I'm pretty sure that damn near everyone at camp knows I've liked her since the minute I saw her.

So why would she just leave without saying anything?

"Do you like her?" Noah asks from beside me. The red juice has given him a pale pink mustache above his upper lip.

I nudge him with my elbow. "I like her as a friend. Go away."

Jackson raises his eyebrows. "As a friend. Got it."

I pile spaghetti onto my garlic bread and add

another slice, turning it into a spaghetti sandwich, and bite into it. How could she just *leave*? And why?

Rest hour is perfectly timed after lunch. I let Dave know that I'll be back soon and detour to the office.

"Can I help you?" Lois asks politely from the front desk.

I walk past her, straight into Brett's office, without knocking.

"Where did she go?" I ask without preamble.

Brett looks up from his computer. "Hey, Miller. How's it going?"

"Shitty. Where is she?"

Brett looks supremely amused. "Who is it you're looking for?"

I want to reach across the desk and strangle him by the collar of his stupid golf shirt. "Becca, you asshole. Did she leave? Did you fire her? What did you do?"

He holds his hand up. "Whoa, there. I didn't *do* anything. But why do you care?"

I glare at him.

"Did something happen between you two?" A smile plays on Brett's lips, making it clear he knows every detail of what happens at his camp.

I slam my hands on his desk. "She finally gave me a fucking chance, that's all. And now she's gone? What the fuck happened?"

"I *knew* you liked her," Brett says, smiling triumphantly. "If you two geniuses hadn't lost a camper, I'd say that overnight was a resounding success."

I don't want to be reminded of that right now. "Seriously, Brett. Where is she?"

Brett straightens in his chair. "She had to leave camp. That's all I can tell you."

"Did you fire her?"

He shakes his head. "It was her choice to leave, and her reasons. If you want to know more, you'll have to reach out to her."

Damn right I'm going to reach out to her.

I grab my phone as soon as I get back to the cabin. Being detached from technology has its advantages, but it also means there are piles of emails and texts to go through every time you actually pick up the phone.

I pull up Becca's number and start a new text.

What do I say? *Where did you go? What happened? I thought we were on the fast track to falling in love and now you left without saying a word?*

None of those seem like good options, to be honest.

At a loss, I finally pull up the group message with the guys while I think.

CARD SHARKS

Hey, how is everyone?

Cam: Generally good, Addie is in a mood. How are things at camp?

Maddox: Ooh, Hurricane Addie. Good luck with that, man.

Blake: Still single, still loving it. How's the girl you were obsessed with?

Uh, things were looking up. We went on a camping trip this weekend. I kissed her.

Maddox: *party emoji* Admirable work! And?

Cam: Did she kiss you back?

Yeah, she kissed me back. And we talked a ton. I thought we were heading the right direction. We spent time together last night, too.

Blake: That sounds promising. Why do you say you thought you were headed the right direction? What happened?

Um, no idea. I haven't seen her in two days and then today I found out she left camp.

Cam: You drove her away?

I'm really fucking hoping that's not what happened. But I don't know why she left.

Maddox: Did you text her? You have her number, right?

Yeah, I've had her number since before the summer started. I think my texts to her before we met are what made her hate me to start with, honestly.

Blake: Yeah, you can come across like a jackass over text if people don't know you.

Thanks for the heads up.

Cam: So, have you texted her yet?

No. I don't know what to say. I'm afraid of fucking everything up again. Fuck, I think I'm falling for this girl.

Maddox: It's been a week, dude.

When you know, you know. And how many times did you meet up with Holly before you knew she was the one?

Blake: He has a point.

Maddox: Send her a text. Tell her you're missing her and hope she's doing well. THAT'S ALL.

Cam: Agree with Maddox. Under no circumstances should you profess your love for her over text.

Blake: Oh, how the mighty have fallen. I'll think of you all fondly while I'm living the single life in Vegas.

Yeah, as soon as you meet the right girl, all that's going to go out the window, man. I didn't believe it either.

Maddox: Good luck.

Any input from Holly?

Maddox: She's at work. Want me to add her to the chat?

Cam: Dudes only.

Blake: Agree with Cam.

Fine. Just wanted a woman's perspective. Talk soon.

I stare at the blank text to Becca, typing a few words and then deleting them over and over. I finally settle on Maddox's suggestion—*Hey, I miss you. Hope things are going well*—but before I can send it, the bell rings.

"Time for activity periods!" Dave announces.

The campers bounce off their beds and pull on shoes and bathing suits as they head off to their first classes.

"You okay?" Dave asks as we head out, closing the cabin door behind us. "You seem like you're in a funk."

I run my hand over my face. "Yeah. Kind of. Did you know Becca left camp?"

Dave frowns. "Like, *left* left? I figured she was gone for a few days, but I guess it makes sense that Jana took over her spot in the cabin if she's gone for good. She get fired over you guys losing a camper? How come you're still here?"

I shrug and step over a root. "No idea. Brett won't tell me. I don't think he would have fired her over that and not me, would he? It seems a little excessive."

Dave pauses at the fork in the trail. "You think she left cause of you?"

Fuck. "That's what I'm afraid of. I mean, we kissed and talked. That was it." As far as Dave needs to know. "You think that would have scared her off?"

He shrugs. "No idea. I'm not exactly a guru when it comes to the ladies." He looks down the path toward the Sports field. "I've got to get going. Let me know if you hear from her, okay?"

I wave as I turn the opposite direction, toward the Nature barn. I'm feeling like a rebel with my phone in my pocket, but I don't think Mary will care. We're the only two counselors in the Nature department, and she always has her phone on her.

Some days in Nature, we go on outings, like hikes up the hill to the ridge behind the Bumblebees cabins to look out on the lake. Some days we do scavenger hunts, looking for various nature-type things around camp.

And some days we just sit in a big fucking circle playing with the animals.

First period we only have to deal with the rabbits, which is fine with me. Bonnie and Clyde have grown on me, their little noses twitching in joy when I give them treats.

"What happens to them at the end of the

summer?" I whisper to Mary, as she lowers Clyde into the circle in front of me.

She shrugs. "They go back to the animal shelter, I think. Sometimes they get adopted by one of the counselors. Why, you want to take them home?"

"Uh, no," I say, too quickly. I don't need rabbit turds all over my apartment. I'm pretty sure there's a clause against pets in my lease.

She laughs and heads back to the barn to grab Bonnie.

The campers love these days, when they just get to watch rabbits hop around. Sometimes the rabbits jump into their laps and they get to pet them, which really makes their day. I usually like these days, too. Low mental bandwidth needed.

Today, however, I desperately need something to distract me. I wish we were hiking up Winnie Ridge, or on an expedition looking for anthills by M-Hall. Anything to keep me from ruminating on Becca and why she left and what to say to her.

"Miller, can we get Lucy out?" The camper next to me tugs on my sleeve.

"No," I say, a little more sharply than I intended. "Sorry. No, we're not getting Lucy out. There are only about ten minutes left of class. But tomorrow we'll play with Lucy, okay?" I hate that I'm promising anything to do with this damn goat.

Somehow, I manage to make it through all three activity periods without losing my cool.

"You doing okay?" Mary asks as she sweeps the barn.

I shake my head. The campers are gone, so there's no need to put on a front now. "I'm kind of freaking out. I thought I was starting something with this girl, and she left camp. I'm not sure what to do."

Mary looks thoughtful. "I don't know the whole story. I don't know that anyone does, even though everyone knows Becca is the one who left. Have you talked to her?"

I shake my head. "What do I say? I don't know if she left camp because of me, or for some totally unrelated reason."

Mary purses her lips. "Well, you know what they say."

I don't. I wait for her to elaborate, but she doesn't. "What? What do they say?"

She laughs. "Lots of things, actually. 'Go for what you want'. 'You don't know unless you ask'. Also, my personal favorite, 'When you assume, you make an ass of you and me'."

I consider. "You may have a point there."

We walk out of the barn together and Mary clicks the lock closed on the door. "Just make sure you know what you want before you ask her for something. Okay?"

I nod, standing still as Mary walks away. With a sigh, I pull out my phone.

BECCA

> Missing you since you left camp.
> How are you doing?

I stare at the phone as I walk slowly back to my cabin, waiting for a response.

30

BECCA

This is my chance. I can't afford to get distracted.

I force myself to re-read the words on the page. *ACE inhibitors, angiotensin receptor blockers...* How does anyone remember which is which? I write out the drug names on a flashcard and their mechanism of action on the back.

I always knew I'd have to redo pharmacology after failing it last fall. But after my grade on the pathology final, I figured it would be during this coming fall, with the rest of the incoming second years.

I didn't anticipate having to squeeze this class's redo into these six weeks, a single test at the end deciding my fate.

The conversation plays in my head again. *Reviewed*

the final... questions thrown out and grades adjusted... pass. When the dean told me they'd updated my grade to a pass for pathology, and that I could start my third year with the second rotation if I passed a pharmacology make-up by August, I thought he was joking.

And I knew I had to grab this chance.

I realize I'm underlining so hard I'm indenting the page and force myself to ease up.

I can do this. Failing and coming back to try again makes me stronger. That's what Miller said. Right?

Miller. I wonder what he's up to right now.

My stomach bottoms out when I think of him, because now I'm not only the crazy lady who was mean to him for the first two weeks of the summer, but now I'm the girl who ghosted him and left camp after we finally started... something.

I pull out my phone and look at his text message again, like I've been doing almost once an hour since I got it a few days ago.

MILLER

Missing you since you left camp.
How are you doing?

How do I even answer that? *Doing well, how are you?* would be the polite response. *Stressed as fuck and missing camp and missing you* would be more accurate. *Second-guessing all my life choices, wondering if medicine is the right fit and panicking and also pretty sure you've moved on to someone less neurotic* might be the full truth.

I can't bring myself to type out that level of honesty, though, and I don't know what else to say. So all I've managed to text back is, *I had to leave. I'm sorry. I'll tell you more when I can.*

I turn the page to read about beta blockers. How many types of blood pressure medicine do we need? I write them down on four new flashcards. Atenolol, propranolol, metoprolol, labetalol. At least their names are vaguely consistent. I add a star to the vague differences as I write them out.

I finally talked to my parents and owned up to failing this class. Somehow it felt easier to tell them I'd failed one class rather than that I was planning to repeat the entire year.

And you know what? Miller was right, again.

They weren't mad, they didn't cut me off. My dad grumbled a comment about "stupid drug names" and how "no one needs to know that shit."

I almost dropped the phone. I'd never heard my dad swear.

I focus on my book again, trying to memorize the

nuances of the different types of medications. Ten more minutes before I take a break.

My watch beeps to signal it's time for a break just as I move on to calcium channel blockers—you guessed it, more blood pressure medicine—and I stand up and stretch. The library is quieter than normal in the summer. During the school year, there are tons of first- and second-year students in here studying, and the stress emanates off them in waves.

But this year's first year class hasn't started yet, and the rising second years have the summer off. So it's just me, as far as I've seen.

I glance down at my open book, scrunching my brows. I'm going to need a coffee to keep on focusing. There are only so many drug names you can memorize per gram of caffeine in your body, and I've hit my limit.

I type out a text message to Vivien while I wait in line at the cafe next door to the library.

VIVIEN

> How are things at camp?

She's the only one I've really been in contact with since I left. We talked on the phone last night after her campers were asleep. She told me about everything I missed—Lena leading a grilled cheese eating contest,

Bayley opening up about her parents some more, Mollie talking nonstop about the goat.

It made my heart clench a little to think that I should have been there for that.

I felt guilty when I talked to Brett about what to do, that morning after I made the phone call. I wondered if I could abandon my campers to head back to school.

But Brett, being Brett, was unconditionally supportive.

"You have to do what's right for you, Becca," he said as we sat in his office that morning, less than an hour after the phone call that changed everything. "Camp will always be here for you. And we can cover your cabin. One of the department heads can fill in for a week if needed. But what happens if you don't take this chance?"

"I'd have to repeat the entire year," I muttered, grimly looking at my hands.

"And pay the tuition again?" Brett pressed.

I nodded, unable to meet his gaze, thinking he was about to guilt trip me for caring about money over the kids.

But when I finally looked up, his expression was gentle. "So, it seems like a no-brainer," Brett said, shrugging his shoulders like it was the easiest decision of his life. "Go back to school, Becca. We'll miss you. But this is your future."

So, I did. And here I am, holed up in the library while fueling myself with enough caffeine to make myself actually vibrate.

My phone buzzes in my pocket as I step up to the counter. I order my usual—Americano, black, with an extra shot—and pull my phone out.

Good. Missing you. The campers this week are… special. All eight-year-olds. One of them peed the bed last night.

That's the part I don't miss.

Yeah, lugging a pee-soaked sleeping bag to the laundry room at six in the morning isn't exactly the high point of being a camp counselor.

Are they at least fun?

Oh, they're actually a blast. The littlest ones always are once you can look past the pee accidents and the late-night crying when they're homesick. Want to hear a joke one of them told me?

Um, yes. Did she make it up herself?

Pretty sure.

What do you call a bat that is single?

Uhh…

A BATchelor.

I slide my phone in my pocket as the barista passes me my drink and look around the small cafe, considering whether I have time to sit and enjoy my drink or if I should get back to studying right away.

My mind wanders to my mornings on the swing back at camp. I miss that sense of freedom and being relaxed. I wonder if there's a way to find some kind of feeling like that while I'm in school. Maybe I should try yoga.

I take a sip of the too-hot coffee. It jolts me back to reality with its bitter taste. No, there's no time for yoga or meditation or any of that other new-age nonsense.

If I have time for that, I have time to study more.

At the end of six straight hours in the library, I'm the proud owner of over two hundred flash cards, each with the name of a medication on the front and how it works, what class it belongs to, and what it's used for on the back of the card.

I'm feeling moderately accomplished, but making the cards is only the first step. Now, I have to memorize all of it.

That's step two, which we'll start on after dinner.

My only real downtime today is my dinner time. I let myself watch part of *When Harry Met Sally* while I eat my macaroni and cheese. Nothing but gourmet here.

I consider licking the bowl once the pasta is gone but realize I'm supposed to be an adult, so I eat an apple instead, to balance my diet out. I've always thought it was funny how med students have the worst diets ever while learning to take care of people. I wonder if it stays this way once we move on to residency and then to being a full-fledged doctor.

I turn the iPad off and rinse my dishes in the sink, then settle on the couch with my zillion flashcards. Okay, time to memorize.

I jolt awake when the flashcards hit the ground. How did I fall asleep? I pick up the mess of three-by-five index cards, sorting them back into a pile. The last one I remember looking at was *Atenolol*, which was right at the top of the pile.

I stretch my arms over my head. It's too late for

more caffeine if it's after dinner. I peek at my watch. It's only 9 p.m.? How am I so tired?

Maybe those weeks of 10 p.m. curfew forced me into early-bedtime mode.

I pull out my phone. 9 p.m. means campers are going to bed. It's weird how my brain still hasn't adjusted from the camp schedule. Every time I look at the time, I think about what's going on up there. What would I be doing if I were still at Camp Winnie?

Right now, I'd be sneaking out of the cabin with Vivien to sit at the picnic table. One of us would be headed to hang out with the other staff at the dining hall.

Miller might be calling his mom. At the very least, he's probably looking at his phone. I stare at his text again, the one I still don't know how to answer. It's been way too long for a polite response, hasn't it? It's been a week. We're into ghosting territory at this point.

I chew on my lower lip while I think. I miss him. Or do I just miss camp?

I'm still not sure what Miller and I were starting, if we were starting something at all, or what would have happened if I'd stayed.

Either way, I'm here now, in upstate New York and back at school. He's still in New Hampshire, and he'll be heading back to Philadelphia in a few weeks.

There's really not a future there for us, even if I once thought that might be a possibility.

Plus, I need to focus on school.

But I still owe him an explanation. I don't have to start a relationship or anything. We can be friends. Who text. I text Vivien, and I don't want to sleep with her.

MILLER

Sorry for the radio silence. Long story, but they recalculated, and I didn't fail pathology, so I just have to retake pharmacology so I can start my third year just a couple months late. So that's what I'm doing. Sorry I had to leave camp early, but I couldn't pass this chance up.

I read it for a third time, nodding. Nothing about feelings. Just facts so hopefully Miller realizes me leaving camp had nothing to do with him.

My finger hovers while my stomach flips. Why does this make me so nervous?

I steel myself. If I can handle med school, I can handle sending one little text. I take a deep breath and hit *Send*.

31

MILLER

Becca

I'm proud of you for going back.

You're not mad? I feel bad that I left camp. Is Brett pissed?

Not at all. No one is mad. Brett won't tell anyone why you left, though. He says it's your business. Want me to tell people it's for a school thing? I won't say anything else about failing classes or anything. Not that you should be ashamed AT ALL.

You can tell them it's for school. And yeah, I know, but... I just don't want everyone to know. You know?

Of course. I miss you, though. In case you were wondering.

A loud noise has me looking up from where I'm lying in my bed, texting Becca during rest hour. I don't see it until I stand up: One of the campers has somehow managed to fall from his top bunk. I toss my phone on the bed, flipping back into counselor mode. I'll have to text Becca later.

"You okay there, buddy?" I ask, holding a hand out to help him up.

Maverick looks up at me, tears welling in his big blue eyes. "I fell off."

"I see that."

He takes my hand and climbs to his feet. I watch as he eyes the top bunk with trepidation. "What if I fall off again?"

"I think you'll be okay, but if you want to switch, you can ask one of the other guys." I look around the cabin. Most of the boys have headphones on, listening to something on their tablets. They're only allowed electronics during rest hour, and they take full advantage.

"I can switch," Patrick pipes up. The boy has the bunk right below Maverick's this week. He looked disappointed that all of the top bunks were taken when he got here, so maybe this could work out in everyone's favor.

Maverick nods vigorously, confirming it.

I help the two boys to switch their sleeping bags, then wait while they climb into their newly appointed beds. "You both happy now?"

"Yes."

"Yep."

"Alright." I pat the bedframe once and head back to my own spot.

My phone buzzes in my pocket as I'm walking to the Nature barn for yet another showdown with Lucy. It's been three days since I've talked to Becca, giving her space to get her studying done. I pull the phone out, hoping it's her.

BECCA

Pharmacology is the devil.

I can only imagine. Just think, you could be here, dealing with a kid who wakes up crying with homesickness every morning at 3 a.m. instead of memorizing shit.

crying laughing emoji Yeah, I guess things could be worse. You leading any overnights this weekend?

Nope, I'm on cabin duty. After our overnight, I don't think Brett will let me lead one ever again.

It wasn't our fault a camper wandered away.

Not entirely.

I breathe a sigh of relief when the last camper leaves, his father weighed down with the kid's duffel bag while the child carries the treasure box he made in woodshop.

This has been the most challenging week so far. Besides Maverick falling out of bed, this week has seen campers fighting with one another, two who tried to sneak out at night, and zero who would listen to me and Dave. It made for a rough few days.

I pull out my phone, needing to talk to Becca. She always cheers me up.

BECCA

What color underwear are you wearing?

Uh, that wasn't funny the first time you asked me.

Sure, it was. I'm wearing boxers with little yellow smiley faces all over them.

Information I didn't need to know.

I, on the other hand, have a burning desire to know about yours.

If something is burning you should probably get that checked out.

Why do you think I'm texting a future doctor?

eyeroll emoji How's the goat?

Evil as fuck. She bit my shirt today. I'm down to four t-shirts.

You could just go topless. She'd have nothing to bite.

A few flaws in that plan. One, I only like to take my shirt off to impress you, and you're not here. Two, she'd probably bite my nipple.

> One, it's not that impressive. Two, your nipples are decorative. You don't need both of them.

> I'm kind of attached to them either way.

Today is Becca's final for her make-up class. I'm sure she's freaking out, but for some reason, I am too. This is important to her, so it's important to me. I'm re-reading the text I sent her earlier, wishing her luck, when a new text message pops up.

BECCA

> I did it. I passed.

> Yessss! I knew you would, babe.

> Thanks. How are things at camp?

> Honestly didn't think I'd stick it out this long after the first day or so. I only made it through the first week because I was sticking around to win you over, and then it… kind of grew on me.

> Sticking around to annoy me, you mean.

> Same thing. It worked, didn't it?

No comment.

Any chance you're going to make it back up here before the end of the summer? There's one week left...

I wish I could I start my clinical rotations on Monday.

Bummed I won't see you. But I can't wait to hear about you kicking ass with those, too.

Six Weeks Later

"So, the goats really ate most of your shirts?" Blake asks with amusement, picking up two beers from the bar top.

"Goat. Singular. And she was the devil incarnate." I hand the bartender a credit card to start a tab and pick up the other two beers and a soda to carry them to the table, where the rest of our group is seated. "I would have been shirtless for the last week without Becca sending me new t-shirts."

He nods. "Yeah, she has great taste. Between the *Mama's Boy* one and *I Love Goats* one, she absolutely nailed it. When do we get to meet her?" Blake sets the bottles on our table.

"The girl?" Maddox asks, reaching for a lager. "I

want to meet her, too. The woman who can manage to put up with Miller. She's a legend."

"To be fair, she's not exactly *putting up* with me," I point out. "She hated me for two weeks, we had a good weekend, and then she left camp. It's been all phone calls and texts since then."

"I've gotten texts from you. I'd say if she hasn't blocked your number yet, she's putting up with you," Cam teases, grabbing his soda and taking a sip. "Anyway, less about you and your drama. Lawton, man, it's good to have you back." He raises his glass toward the guy sitting next to Blake, the two of them practically identical with their blue eyes and dark hair, although Lawton's square jaw and ramrod posture give him away as a cop.

"Hey, I'm moving out to the middle of nowhere to take a job. I figured the least I could do was spend some time with my old poker buddies before I disappear forever." Lawton tips his beer back.

Blake's younger brother was part of our poker group for a few years, but since he gave up traveling for tournaments and enrolled in the police academy, we haven't seen him much.

"Where are you moving again?" Maddox asks. "Lonesome Heights?"

"High Lonesome," Lawton corrects him. "Small town in the Colorado mountains. You guys should come visit once I get settled out there with Kristina."

"We could road trip," Cam suggests.

Blake snorts. "The four of us plus all your girls crammed into an RV? Yeah, hard pass."

Becca would be a great road trip companion, wouldn't she? I can just imagine her making lists of all the shit to pack and planning out our route, then freaking out when we get lost.

A smile plays on my lips. I could talk to her for hours while we drive across the middle of nowhere.

"Addie is awesome," Cam protests.

"You love Holly," Maddox says at the same time.

Blake holds up a finger. "I tolerate them because you love them, but I don't need any women in my life. I'll stick with my bachelor lifestyle, thank you very much."

Lawton rolls his eyes. "Yeah, keep telling yourself that. I said that before I met Kristina, too. And now look at us. We're moving in together when we get up there."

"You going to marry her?" I ask, vaguely interested.

They met almost three years ago, about a year after Lawton stopped playing poker with us to head to the police academy, and moving across the country together suggests a commitment, at least in my mind.

Lawton shrugs and leans back against the cracked vinyl booth. "Maybe someday. I don't want to rock the boat right now. Maybe once we're settled in High Lonesome and things are good with my job."

"What's she going to do up there?" Blake asks.

He shrugs a shoulder. "Not sure yet. We're going to check out options once we get up there." Lawton brings his beer to his lips.

"Well, good luck, man." I lift my drink toward him.

Lawton grins and mirrors my motion with his own glass. "Thanks, Miller. And to put the pressure back on you, when are you seeing your girl again? Are you going to go visit her?"

I frown, thinking. Maybe I could go up there one of these weekends. I've wondered before how far her school is from my mom's house. I set my glass on the table and pull my phone out.

"Dude, I didn't mean you should plan a trip right now," Lawton says, laughing, and the others join in.

I ignore them. I'm used to my friends having fun at my expense, and it doesn't bother me. If anything, I love being the butt of their jokes. I pull up my Maps app and type things in.

Becca goes to Syracuse, which is... just about two hours from my mom's place in Elmira. Probably less, the way I drive. Maybe I can convince her to let me visit sometime when I go up to visit Mom and Jordan.

"Raise." I toss more chips in the pot and reach for my beer.

Maddox calls my raise, adding his own chips. "So, what was the bet you made with that camp director? Did you win by sticking it out the whole summer?"

I study my cards as Blake flips over the turn card. "The bet was that I wouldn't last as a camp counselor. If I couldn't stick it out, I said I'd donate my salary to the camper scholarship fund. It covers the cost of camp for some kids whose families can't afford to pay."

"But you stuck it out," Cam points out, a carrot stick in his mouth from the snacks we doled out. "Shocking all of us, honestly. We had a side bet going about how long you'd be gone. I think the outside bet was one week, so we all lost."

I nod as I take another handful of Doritos. "Glad you all had so much faith in me. Honestly, before I got there, I probably would have placed my bet on me making it a few days. But yeah, technically I won the bet with the camp director, I guess. The place just kind of grew on me, you know? But I ended up donating a bunch to the fund anyway. Cause... I don't know. It's a good cause."

Blake grunts. "You should donate to me. I'm a good cause. These post-doc programs don't pay shit."

I laugh as I raise the bet again. "Yeah, you won a shitload of money in Atlantic City last week. You're no one's charity case. Plus, isn't it just a one-year thing? And you get a real job next year?"

He scowls and turns over the final community card. The added eight gives me a straight. Not too terrible. "This is a real job. At least as real as being a camp counselor. Probably more so."

He's got me there. I grin as we turn over the cards and my straight beats Maddox's three of a kind. I sweep the chips toward myself and pile them up as Blake hands the deck to Cam to deal the next round.

"So, does this mean you're back for good now, Miller? Done finding yourself or whatever the fuck you were doing over the summer?" Cam asks as he shuffles.

I open my mouth to answer but then close it again, trying to understand my own mind. I spent the summer at camp because I felt like something was missing, like I needed something different in my life. Did I find it?

I want to say I'm back and ready to get back to normal. That was the goal, after all, when I first started looking for something different. Do something to shake things up and then get back to my groove of winning poker games and building up a nice little nest egg. But even winning hands is only a short-term high now.

I'm happy for a minute, then I go back to feeling... empty. Like something is missing.

My fingers brush against the phone in my pocket. They itch to text Becca, see what she's up to. She started her clinical rotations, and I'm dying to know how it's going.

"You in for this round, Miller?" Maddox nudges me.

I realize they're all waiting for me to put up a blind. It rotates which player has to put in their chips before even seeing their pocket cards, and it's my turn. I force my mind back into the game and push two stacked chips toward the center.

Cam deals out two cards to each of us. I look at mine: a king and a queen. A decent deal, but all I see is a man and a woman. Me and Becca.

This is why poker players aren't supposed to fall in love. It screws up your concentration.

But even as I'm thinking it, I know it's not true. Look at Maddox and Cam. They're blissfully happy, and their poker games have never been stronger. Since getting married, Maddox has won two major tournaments and a handful of smaller ones. And since getting together with Addie, Cam has been on a roll too, winning plenty of games.

It's just me that sucks, apparently. But then again, it's not like I'm happily settled down with my girl. Yet...

"Hey, you want to come over this weekend?" Cam asks as he turns over the flop, the first three of the five community cards. "Addie still wants you to meet Annika. You remember her teacher friend?"

"I think I'm busy," I say, pushing chips into the pot. "And I don't need to be set up."

Maddox laughs. "Also, Annika would eat him alive, Cam. Who thought the two of them together would be a good idea? You?"

Cam shrugs. "Addie just wants someone to double date with who isn't her brother."

"Yeah, understandable." Maddox nods. He folds, placing his cards on the table. "It's still weird to see you two together." His lips twist into a grimace.

The next community card gives me nothing, and I eye my pocket cards again before I fold with a sigh. "I still feel like there's something missing."

Blake raises again. "Yeah? I think it's your dignity. Either go after the girl or hook up with someone new. You know which I'd vote for."

We *all* know what Blake would vote for. He hasn't had a real relationship since I've known him. It was cute when he was in his early thirties, but he's thirty-seven now. It's time for him to settle down. God knows we can't tell him that, though.

"I'm going to call it a day," I say, standing and stretching.

I walk the ten blocks home from Cam's apartment in the early fall heat. The humidity hits different in the city than at camp, by the lake. The smells are more sewer-forward than the piney smell of the woods.

A pang of longing hits me. Maybe this is what Becca meant when she talked about missing camp those years she wasn't there.

I pull my phone out as I wait at a crosswalk. A text won't mess up her day, will it? I'm trying to respect how busy she is, not bother her, but I suppose she can just ignore it if she wants to.

Thinking of you. Hope your rotation is going well.

Yeah, I have no dignity left. I ended up sending her flowers—again—because I couldn't *not* send her something. I was passing a florist and the sunflowers made me think of her. Everything makes me think of Becca these days.

I never believed in the whole *absence makes the heart grow fonder* thing before, but it seems to be the case for me.

I thought sending her something and texting her would help to clear my mind, but it did absolutely nothing. If anything, she's now front and center of all my thoughts.

And things are becoming clearer.

When I headed up to camp, I figured it was a one-time break from the poker world to clear my mind, but as happy as I am to be back with my friends, something is still lacking.

But now I know exactly what's missing. It's Becca.

Becca is who I'm thinking of as I head to the shower. I step into the glass-enclosed space and take a breath of steam. One kiss, and she's entrenched herself in my mind.

I'm already hard, thinking of her soft body, her

smile, her prickly demeanor when something bothers her.

And once again, it doesn't help at all with clearing my mind when it's her that I picture as I stroke myself to a quick, fast climax.

32

BECCA

MILLER

Thank you for the flowers.

You're welcome. I saw them and thought of you, so I had to send you a bouquet. How's the rotation going?

Um... it's rough. I thought I'd love obstetrics, delivering babies and all that. But I don't think it's for me.

Too much vagina?

I was at a delivery today and there was so much blood. I almost passed out.

Are doctors allowed to do that?

It's generally frowned upon to pass out when you're supposed to be the one catching the baby. The doctors who pass out at blood tend to choose outpatient specialties. And psychiatry.

Makes sense.

What are your thoughts on your specialty now?

No idea, honestly. I start pediatrics next week. I figure I'm good with kids, so maybe that?

You're great with kids, Becs.

This month will be better. Kids are fun, and I like being around them.

I smile at the artwork on the wall as I walk into the children's wing. I hadn't realized until yesterday that I'd be starting on the inpatient service, but I'm not going to let it get me down. Kids are kids, right?

I knock on the door of the workroom, where several people in scrubs are tapping away at computers. One of them turns around at the knock.

"Hi. I'm Rebecca Patel, the new med student?" I cringe at the question in my voice.

Ironically, I'm less anxious on clinical rotations than I ever was during our pre-clinical blocks. I'm not sure if it's because this is what I went to med school for —taking care of patients and helping people—or if it's just that having a defined role to play within a team eases my social anxiety.

Either way, it's easier, and I'm doing a much better job. Despite hating OB and almost passing out in the OR once, I earned Honors on the rotation.

The woman stands from her chair and holds her hand out to me, pushing her thick-rimmed glasses up on her nose with her other hand. "Welcome! I'm Grace Langley, the senior resident on the team."

I shake her hand with a polite smile. "Nice to meet you."

She motions to a chair next to hers. "Sit. Now, what rotations have you done so far?"

Everyone else is on their third rotation, while I'm just on my second. I spent the first block redoing my pharmacology class. "Just OB."

"Oh, perfect!" Grace doesn't question it. "You saw the babies being born, and now you get to see what happens when they grow up. Let's start you with one patient to follow. How about Matthew? He's the sweetest little guy."

She pulls his chart up on the computer in front of me and leaves me to read through his history. Matthew Powell, age three. Trisomy 21—Down Syndrome. And he has leukemia.

My stomach bottoms out when I read that line in his chart. How is it fair that little kids get cancer?

I scroll through more of the notes. He's here getting chemotherapy. I re-learned enough of the medicines in my pharmacology studying that I recognize the names of most of the drugs he's getting.

The notes in the computer don't seem to do him justice. I can't picture him by the words on the screen.

"Is it okay if I go meet him?" I ask Grace as she taps away at her keyboard.

"Absolutely. We'll start rounds at nine, so just be back here by then."

I check my watch. It's 8:40. I follow room numbers until I find Matthew's room—215—and knock on the door.

I manage to hold in my tears until I get to my car. This is not how I pictured this rotation going. Not at all.

Matthew *is* the sweetest little kid. It absolutely gutted me to see him bald from the chemotherapy, hooked up to an IV.

And the rest of the patients weren't much better. Every child there was sick, in pain, unhappy. This isn't what childhood should be like.

I hold on to my steering wheel while I let the tears course down my face. It's not like I didn't know this is how it was going to be. I've seen just about every medical TV show out there. What I didn't realize was how hard it would hit me. How hard it would be to let it go when I walk out of the hospital.

And the one person I want to talk to about this is Miller. I know he'd be there for me, let me talk it out and be nothing but supportive.

But I don't want that to be all our relationship is— me dumping on him. I want to be able to be there for him, too.

I pull myself together for the short drive home and wipe my tears on my sleeve. I'll text Miller about dinner once I figure out what I'm going to make. Even if I can't unleash all my sorrows on him, it'll make me feel better to talk to him.

Macaroni and cheese. Again. It's cheap and it's quick, so it's a staple around here. I stir the noodles in the pot, feeling proud of myself for the step up from the microwave instant stuff. It's the little things, right?

I squeeze the pre-made sauce onto the cooked noodles. Maybe one of these days I'll graduate to the real thing, making the sauce with butter and milk, but if you ask me, this kind is better. I carry my bowl to the table along with a glass of wine.

My phone vibrates just as I set it on the table next to me. I flinch at the sound. My parents called to check in on the first day of my last rotation, and they're creatures of habit.

I've been dreading their call, because they like details. They want to know what types of patients I saw, what interesting diseases, all of that. And I can't get Matthew and his sweet face out of my head.

I take a sip of wine for strength and turn the phone over to see a text. Not from my parents, but from Miller.

MILLER

How was day one? Everything you hoped for?

Not exactly.

The sound of an incoming FaceTime call startles

me, nearly making me drop my spoon. I'm not ready to talk to Miller, to explain why I'm a total wreck, so I let it ring until the call disconnects.

But as soon as I shove another bite of pasta into my mouth, the phone rings again with another video call.

I swallow my mouthful and swipe to answer it. He's not going to give up. But instead of dread, the realization makes me feel... safe, somehow. Cared for.

Miller's face fills the screen of my phone. "Hey. Tell me about it," he says, his forehead wrinkled with concern.

I shrug, scooping more mac and cheese onto my spoon. "It's... it just wasn't what I was expecting. Some of the kids are so sick. It's hard to watch. I didn't think it would hit me this hard, and then the fact that I'm taking it tough makes it worse. Like, how can I think about how hard it is for me, when they're the ones with the illness? I just want to make them all better." My voice catches at the end. I take a sip of wine to cover it up.

Miller doesn't miss a thing. "Want to talk about it? Maybe telling me about your day will make it better." His blue eyes shine on the screen as he gives me that easy grin. My heart melts the tiniest bit, the way it always does when I talk to Miller.

I don't regret leaving camp early, because it gave

me this shot at moving forward in my career. But if I could go back and do everything over again, I would. Because I regret pushing him away for so long.

I take a deep breath. "I can't tell you all the details, obviously. But I have a patient I'm taking care of, a little guy who's only three. And he's just been dealt such a shitty hand in life already." How do I explain this without stepping over the line of doctor-patient confidentiality? "He... well, he's like Maya. And Jordan."

Miller nods, understanding completely without my having to spell it out.

My voice cracks. "And he has cancer. It's just... it's so unfair. Why do things like that happen to sweet kids? How can I watch him go through that and still be *me* at the end of it? And what does it say about me that all I can think about is how it's affecting me? God, I'm such a bitch." The words pour out along with a fresh set of tears.

Miller waits until I take a breath and gather myself. "Um. It says you're human, babe."

I shake my head, wiping my cheek with the back of one hand. "Doctors aren't supposed to be human. Remember?"

He laughs, the sound a refreshing change from the pity in most people's voices when they're talking to someone who's crying in front of them. "Oh, Becs. You know that isn't true. And feeling like this shows you're a great doctor. If you saw kids sick and in pain and didn't feel anything, that's when I'd be worried."

I manage a small smile and sniffle. "Thanks. And I appreciate your support. I just... it's hard to understand. And I know I can't tell you too much more."

"I know," he says, then hesitates. "I... okay, I don't tell a lot of people this, but I feel like it might help you to know this."

My brow furrows. "Okay?"

He swallows, his Adam's apple bobbing. "So, you know Jordan has Down Syndrome, obviously. But I don't usually talk about when he was sick."

I lift the glass of wine to my lips, focused on the image of Miller on the screen in front of me.

"When Jordan was two and a half, he got diagnosed with leukemia. You didn't say it, but I'm imagining that's what your little guy has, too. Kids with Down Syndrome are at higher risk for it."

He doesn't wait for an answer, knowing I can't go into details about my patient.

"I was nine and it was tough, obviously, having a brother who was sick and going through all that. My dad left not too long after, and now I wonder if that's what broke their marriage. But my point is..." He looks at something off camera, then back at me. "Jordan made it through. He's healthy and happy and honestly, so many of the kids with that particular illness are. They get to grow up, thanks to people like you."

The tears are flowing freely now. I wipe the back of my hand across my cheek.

Miller waits for me to catch my breath. "One of my most vivid memories from back then was the day Jordan got diagnosed. The doctor came in and was explaining everything, and then she said the word *cancer*, and everything just... stopped. And my mom cried, of course, but so did the doctor who was telling us. She cared. And maybe she went home and cried in her macaroni and wine, too. I don't know. But she was an amazing doctor. She cared, and she fixed my brother."

"Miller," I say, my voice cracking. A tear squeezes from the corner of my eye and makes its way down my cheek.

He gives me a crooked grin across the video call. "So, if you hate pediatrics in the hospital, that's fine. You'll find something you love. But don't beat yourself up for caring."

"You're such an asshole," I manage. "Why do you always say the right thing?"

"Years of practice, babe." He looks serious all of a

sudden. "You know, you asked me why I like to screw around and don't take anything seriously?"

I nod. "Yeah. I hated it at first."

"It started back then. Everyone just looked at us with... pity, I guess. Like it was hard for them to be around us. It made them sad. So, I was goofy and told jokes to make them not sad. And it stuck."

I feel tears welling up again. "Mill—"

He cuts me off. "Oh no, you don't. No look of pity. Need I remind you of the boxers up the flagpole? All those times the goat ate my shirts?"

I giggle through my tears.

"We all grow up, Becs. Jordan got better and grew up. He's doing amazing now. And I am, too. And so are you, even if you don't know it yet." Miller pushes his hair back from his face. "You should come up and meet Jordan. See what happens when people like you do what you do."

I furrow my brows in confusion. "Up where?"

"Up to my mom's house. She doesn't live too far away from you. Maybe we can make something happen. When do you get time off?"

33

MILLER

BECCA

How was day two?

Better, sort of. Matthew really liked the pictures I showed him of the goat.

That's my girl.

And I'm glad someone likes that damn goat.

I sent a baby home today! They were just here for a fever, and it turned out they had a cold, but their parents were so happy. I feel like I fixed someone.

> You're my favorite doctor, Becs.

Not a doctor yet.

> Semantics.

> How's your buddy? Still holding strong?

Yeah, he's in the middle of his chemo. I wish I could introduce his family to you and Jordan. Show them there's life on the other side.

The updates are getting more positive as Becca settles into the outpatient side of her rotation, and mine are, too. At Becca's suggestion, I looked into volunteering for the Special Olympics, and I've been helping with their events for the last couple of weeks. It's made me more certain that I want to become a special ed teacher one of these days, but it's giving me something to look forward to.

I felt bad at first, spending so much time telling Becca about all the people I was meeting and working with, but she lights up when I talk about it, too.

BECCA

> You working over Thanksgiving?

No, they deem us med students "nonessential workers," so we get a few days off. Why?

Want to come to my mom's house for Thanksgiving? She's a mediocre cook at best, but she's dynamite with a corkscrew. And you can meet Jordan. I've told him so much about you, and he's begging to meet you.

> It wouldn't be imposing? I don't want to intrude on your family gathering.

Having you there would make it better.

November

"Any updates on the girl?" Mom asks from the other side of the kitchen. She twists the handle of the can opener, the main step in her preparation of the cranberry sauce.

"I mean, other than the fact that she's coming to visit for Thanksgiving? Not really." I hand her a dish to hold the can-shaped gel. "How come you don't do, like, real cranberry sauce? Maddox's mom does all sorts of shit from scratch."

She scoffs, pushing her short blonde hair out of her face with the edge of her hand. "Go to Judy's house if you want her cranberry sauce so bad."

I snicker. Mom knows I like the weird cranberry gel, just like I enjoy the mashed potatoes from a box. Her cooking may not be fancy, but I love it. Almost as much as I love giving her shit about her lack of cooking skills.

"Did you check on the wine supply? We have an extra person, so we might need extra. Maybe you should run to the store to pick up a few extra bottles." Mom takes a sip from the glass she's been nursing since 11 a.m., leaving another lipstick remnant on the rim.

I give her a look of disbelief. "You bought a case. I think we're good for a month."

Mom shrugs. "Well, you've never brought home a lady friend before. I want to make sure we present ourselves well."

"As alcoholics?" I ask, snagging a cube of bread.

She rolls her eyes. "As whatever. Now, get out of my kitchen. The stuffing is the one thing that doesn't come from a box. I can't fuck this up." Mom focuses on chopping up celery to add to the bread that Jordan and I cut into cubes last night.

As kids, the one job she gave us was to take the stale bread and cut it into pieces for the stuffing. We've grown up, but our kitchen responsibilities haven't graduated beyond that one task. If I'm being honest, it's probably for good reason.

Or many good reasons, like the fact that Jordan and I cut up most of the bread and then started chucking pieces of it at one another. I spy a cube of bread under the table and pick it up to throw away.

"When is Becca coming?" Jordan asks, joining us in the kitchen and nabbing his own piece of bread.

Mom smacks his hand. "Both of you boys, get out of my kitchen. I hate you both."

Jordan and I laugh as we head to the living room together. Walking through the hallway, I look at the pictures on the wall: framed candid shots of Jordan and I at all different ages. My favorite thing about coming home might be the house itself. It's a reflection of Mom, all cozy and comfortable. Nothing fancy or brand-new.

"She's coming, right?" he asks again as we settle on our favorite couch. He's been excited to meet Becca since I told him about her.

I nod and toss a worn throw pillow to the carpet to make more space. "She promised she'll be here by one or so. God, I'm starving. Think we can get Mom to serve dinner any earlier this year?" I glance back at the kitchen.

"Nah. Mom won't do that." Jordan is right. Thanksgiving dinner has been at 4 p.m. on the dot ever since we were little.

"Want to play Mario Kart?" I ask him, nodding toward the gaming system. If we're not allowed in the kitchen, we may as well amuse ourselves until Becca gets here.

Jordan frowns, his brows pulling together. It's not an expression I'm used to seeing on his face, especially when we're talking about Nintendo games. "What if she doesn't like me?"

"Aww." I sling my arm around his shoulders. "Then I don't like her. Bros before hoes, right?"

"Mom says you shouldn't say that," he points out.

"Anyway. I know she'll love you, and if she doesn't, you're my family, Jordan. Becca's just a..." Girlfriend seems too generic for what we have. I search for another word, something that could describe the connection we have.

"I think you like her." Jordan raises his eyebrows at me. "When you talk about her, you get a mushy look on your face."

I pick the pillow up off the floor and chuck it towards him.

Jordan has beaten me in four square rounds of Mario Kart, and now he's disparaging my favorite driver, Princess Peach. Who, for the record, is the best character.

"Why would you choose a girl? Girls are bad drivers," he says, laughing as he tosses out a bomb.

"Dude. That's sexist." I avoid his obstacles on the screen. I'm almost caught up to—

Ding dong.

She's here.

My heartrate picks up, my excitement rising in my chest at the thought of seeing Becca in person after so long.

"Good game," I say, abandoning Princess Peach and hopping off the couch in a flurry. "You're on your own."

Jordan ignores me and keeps playing, maneuvering Yoshi across the finish line as I head for the front hallway. As excited as he is to meet Becca, he won't stop in the middle of a game.

I won't say I'm unhappy about the fact that I get to greet her, to spend a few minutes alone with her before Mom and Jordan descend on her.

I pull the door open, and there she is, right there

on my mom's doorstep. The same package of curves and sass and wit that I've missed for the last few months. Her dark hair is down around her shoulders, cascading in smooth waves. She's wearing leggings and an oversized sweater and God, she looks sexy as fuck as the sweater slips the tiniest bit off one shoulder.

"Get over here," I say. I pull her into a hug and hold her tight, soaking in the feel of her curves against my body. How long has it been since I had her in my arms? Too fucking long, that's for sure.

"Hi, Miller," she murmurs against my chest. "I brought wine."

I finally release her and take the bottle she's holding out to the side, protecting it from our embrace. "Cabernet. Awesome. My mom will love you."

Becca raises an eyebrow while her lips quirk to the side. "I thought you said she'd love me no matter what."

"Lies. She only likes people who bring alcohol. We were almost running low. Only a case or two left for the four of us." I carry the wine into the kitchen, Becca trailing behind me. "I've got more booze," I announce, holding up the bottle as Mom looks up from where she's using her hands to mix the stuffing ingredients together.

"And me," Becca adds. "Almost as important, right?" She gives me a gentle shove.

"Becca!" Mom cries, blowing past me and the wine to wrap her arms around Becca, a few pieces of stuffing falling to the floor. The two of them embrace, and for what's probably the first time in my life, I'm jealous of my mom. Because she has Becca in her arms, and Becca is relaxing against her, hugging her back.

After a few seconds too many, I clear my throat. "You two need a room?"

Becca looks at me with a smirk on her face. "We might. You have a spare one we can use?"

"I like her," my mom announces with a grin.

Yeah, that's cause you're wearing off on her already, Mom.

And that makes two of us. Now that she's in front of me, it's even stronger. I want to take her in my arms and never let her go.

Mom gives me a not-so-gentle push. "Miller, go play with Jordan. Becca and I will finish making dinner." With that, she waves me out the kitchen.

What?

I don't like this plan.

In fact, I object wholeheartedly to this plan. Becca is here to see me. *Me.* Not Lori Quinlan and her jellied cranberry sauce and whatever gossip Mom is planning to share. She loves bringing up embarrassing stories from when I was little.

I open my mouth to protest.

"Have fun," Becca says, dismissing me before I can get a word out.

I slink back to the family room, shoulders low, where Jordan is busy beating the computer as Luigi. He glances at me as I slump onto the sofa.

"I'll play you the next round."

"What did you guys talk about?" I whisper to Becca as we sit at the table.

I double check that my prank is set. Each place setting is as perfect as my mom laid it out, with one key exception. I hold in my chuckles. It's all about the timing.

She sits next to me and fills her glass with crimson wine, then reaches over and fills mine. "You, mostly."

"Really?" My eyes widen at this admission. Not that I'm surprised. I figured they'd just gossip about me.

Becca grins as she hands the bottle off to Mom. "Maybe. What did you do while Lori and I slaved away to make this epic meal?"

I look at the spread. Jellied cranberry sauce, microwaved butternut squash soup, frozen green beans. "You outdid yourselves. And Jordan and I played Mario Kart."

Becca's eyes go wide in excitement. "Oh, I forgot you guys like to play that! I love that game. Can I play after dinner?"

Jordan studies her, considering. "What player do you want?"

Becca shrugs. "I like Princess Peach, but really, any of them that can beat you."

Jordan looks at her with admiration. My mother practically flutters her eyelashes at Becca.

And suddenly I'm the least popular person in my own family. But looking over at Becca, I don't mind at all.

My mom looks down at her place setting, her brow creasing as she tries to figure out what's changed.

I press my lips into a thin line to hold back my amusement, waiting for her to work it out herself.

It only takes a few seconds before realization snaps into her features, and she points at me as I roar with laughter. "What happened to all the spoons?"

True to their plans, Becca and Jordan settle into the family room after we finish the pumpkin pie—thank you, Marie Callendar's—and buckle down for a serious matchup.

I just refill my glass of wine every few times one of them wins and they start again, agreeing on "nine out of seventeen" or something equally ridiculous. At this rate, they're going to be here all night and I'm just going to be drunk.

"What do you do when you're not a camp counselor?" Jordan asks, his gaze focused on the game.

Becca's character crashes on screen. "I go to med school. I'm going to be a doctor someday."

"That's cool." Jordan's hands work the controller. "What kind of doctor?"

"No idea," Becca says with a shrug. "What do you think I should do?"

Jordan thinks for a minute while he keeps playing. "You could do what my doctor does. He gets to keep seeing kids even when they grow up."

He might be on to something. Becca has mentioned she doesn't want to work in a hospital a few times now. Jordan's doctor was mine, too, when I was growing up, and he still sees my mom. Dr. Chen. He does family medicine and has a specialty clinic where he sees a lot of patients with Down Syndrome, which is how we wound up in his office in the first place.

As they finish round eighteen—tied at nine wins each—Becca checks her watch and lets out a gasp. "Oh! It's 10:30. I think it's time to take a break."

Jordan shuts down the game and starts to put the controllers away.

"You weren't planning on heading back to your place tonight, were you?" I ask. I hope she's not leaving so soon. Between my mom and brother, they've commandeered all of her time since she's gotten here. We haven't really even had a chance to talk.

And talking is at the very bottom of the list of things I want to do with Becca.

Becca shakes her head as she stands from where she was sitting cross-legged on the floor next to Jordan. "I mean, I don't want to assume that I can just stay here. I don't want to impose. It's not a problem to find a hotel if you want. I just don't feel like I can drive all the way home after those glasses of wine."

My mom steps into the family room from where she was clearly eavesdropping in the hallway. "You're more than welcome to stay here tonight, Becca. I figured you might want to, so I put an extra toothbrush and some supplies in the bathroom."

"Oh. Thank you, Lori," Becca says. She looks back to me. "Miller, you sure that's okay?"

"You can stay with Miller. He has a queen-size bed," Mom pipes up, perhaps a bit too eagerly.

"Mom!" There were many times when I was a teenager that I wanted to murder my mom. And if not murder, then at least tie up and put in the shed out back temporarily, so she couldn't embarrass me in front of girls.

I thought we'd gotten past that point, but apparently not.

She smiles and shrugs unabashedly. "Anything you need is in the bathroom. Holler if you need me." She breezes out of the living room and up the stairs to her bedroom in one swift movement.

I roll my eyes. "Thanks, Mom."

Becca shrugs, smiling, and turns toward the stairs.

I catch her hand before she can get too far in the wrong direction. "This way. Jordan and I shared a room as kids, but it's his room now. I get the guest room."

"Not upstairs?"

I shake my head. "Basement. More privacy that way."

34

BECCA

I chew on my lower lip, trying to read Miller's expression. Spending the night with him is exactly what I want to do, and if we share a bed, we're definitely going to need our privacy. I want to finish what we started in the tent.

But it's been months, and all of our banter has been just... friendly. Maybe Miller is just being nice. Maybe he's thinking we can cuddle as friends, or something.

I shrug, trying to look casual. "I don't mind sharing. If that's okay with you."

"Sure. It's cool. Follow me." Miller motions for me to follow him as he guides me down the hallway.

He opens a door, and we descend the stairs to a finished basement. The main room has doors leading off of it, so it must be sectioned into a few rooms. I look around. There's an exercise bike in one corner of the main room and a sofa that's seen better days. One of the doors is open, giving me a glimpse of storage shelves.

Miller opens a different door and flips on a light. "Here it is. Fancy, huh?"

I step through the door and take it in. It's sparse but cozy. A queen-sized bed with a plaid duvet takes up most of the space. The classic "dogs playing poker" picture is framed and hanging on one wall.

"Your selection or Lori's?" I ask, pointing.

Miller grins. "She picked it out, but I love it."

"It suits you." Poker and some sass. It's perfect for him, actually. I sniff the air. "It smells nice in here. I'm impressed. I thought your room would smell like old gym socks."

"Hey, the smell in my cabin this summer was from the campers," Miller protests, his eyes wide with mock indignation. "You should see my apartment. Or smell my apartment, whatever. It smells good, too. My mom's been sending me scented candles since I left for college. I'm as obsessed as she is at this point."

He points to a large candle that's sitting on a slim dresser. I pick it up and take the lid off to smell. Cranberry and... orange maybe? It smells amazing. I check the label, making a mental note to get one of these for my place.

"So." Miller pulls on the back of his neck. I've never seen him look nervous like this before. "The bathroom is in there." He points at a door that's cracked open. "And Mom said there's extra stuff in there, so I guess try the drawers. Do you want a t-shirt or something to sleep in?"

"Do you have any that the goat didn't eat?" I can't help it.

He cracks a smile and relaxes the smallest bit. "Only a few. Here." I step to the side as he pulls open a drawer. He rummages through the contents before holding up a ball of fabric that he tosses to me.

I hold it up in front of me. It's his University of Scranton t-shirt, the one he wore nonstop this summer. I'm glad it survived Lucy. I resist the urge to sniff it. "Thanks. I'll go change."

Miller closes the dresser drawer and steps closer to me. "I've missed you, Becs."

I clutch the fabric. "I've missed you, too," I whisper.

He steps even closer, and I tilt my head back to see his face. This close, he seems even taller, broader.

Miller's eyes fall to my lips. I dart my tongue out to trace them as his eyes darken. "God, Becs. I've-I've really fucking missed you." He ducks his head and presses his lips to mine.

His touch is dizzying. One hand traces my hairline, sending zings of electricity through me, while the other wraps around my waist. He guides me backward a step at a time until my back is pressed up against the door, then he moves the hand from my waist and brings it to the other side of my face, cradling my face gently with both hands.

Our kiss goes on forever. When he stops kissing me and takes a step back, my lips feel swollen, and my breath comes in short pants. I'm holding onto his t-shirt like it's keeping me afloat in this sea of sexual tension.

All I want is for him to take me to bed, to finally, *finally* relieve the ache that's been nonstop since our night together at the Nature barn.

And one look at Miller's face, his pupils dilated and one hand rubbing his jaw, tells me that I'm not the only one affected like this by the kiss. By this undeniable pull between us. But...

I swallow hard. "Can I, um..." How do I say this without being awkward? We're in the middle of the steamiest moment we've ever had and I *really* need to pee.

This never happens in the movies.

Miller kisses the edge of my jaw. "What do you need?"

My face flames. "I, um... bathroom?" Oh, God. That came out worse than I was expecting.

He smiles with amusement as he kisses my lips, soft and chaste. "Why don't you go slip into something more comfortable?"

Miller pulls back and winks at me as he points toward the bathroom door.

I close myself in the bathroom, leaning my back against the door to steady my breathing. After I take care of my pressing needs that brought our make-out session to a screeching halt, I stare at myself in the mirror, bringing his shirt to my nose and inhaling deeply as I replay the kiss.

It's his scent, the one I've missed: woodsy and sharp with a hint of something sweet underneath. It brings me right back to our time sitting together on the swing, to the night we spent together on the camping trip.

Jesus, Becca. The guy is in the next room. You don't need to fantasize.

I force my brain to function. If I stay in here too much longer, he's going to send a search party. Or worse, think I'm in here doing something unmentionable, like shaving my legs or going number two.

You know, all the things women aren't supposed to do.

I fold the clothes I was wearing into a neat pile and pull the soft cotton of his t-shirt over my head. The shirt falls to my mid-thigh as the material brushes against my peaked nipples.

I take a deep breath and let it out slowly. It's supposed to activate your parasympathetic nervous system and calm you, but there's no slowing my rapid heartrate. It's all I can do to go through the motions of brushing my teeth and washing my face, knowing that Miller is waiting.

Miller's mom wasn't joking when she said she stocked the bathroom, by the way. I doubt Miller's responsible for all of this.

One of the drawers is practically overflowing with travel-size items. Toothbrushes and toothpaste, of course, but there's also face wash—*nice* face wash—shampoo, conditioner, a face mask, hand lotion, moisturizer. A woman was definitely involved in this part.

And there's also a box of condoms, sitting next to three different flavors of lube, and from the way everything is tucked neatly into little drawer dividers, this seems like Lori's work, too.

Yeah, Miller's mom is the polar opposite of my parents.

I pull the little tubes out of the drawer to examine them closer. Sugar cookie, banana cream, and strawberry.

I shove the banana one in the back of the drawer with a shudder. I'm not entirely sold on the idea of putting flavored stuff in that region in the first place, but more importantly, I hate artificial banana flavor.

The idea of banana cream-flavored lubricant does bring up interesting philosophical questions, though. Like, what if you used it for a blowjob? Would it be like eating a real banana? Has anyone ever gotten so into the banana-flavored cock sucking that they took a bite by accident?

"You good in there?"

Miller's voice startles me from my banana musings, making me slam the drawer so fast the sound reverberates in the small space.

"Uh. Yeah. I'm good." *Don't mention the lube. Do not mention bananas. For the love of God, do not mention bananas and lubricant together.* "This place is, uh, well-stocked. I'll be out in a minute."

***

"Jesus, Mom," Miller groans from inside the bathroom as I settle under the covers.

He must have found the lube.

"My mother is insane," he says when he emerges from the bathroom. He's in plaid boxers and a dark green Camp Winnie t-shirt.

"You didn't stock that drawer yourself?" After much reflection while Miller did whatever guys do in the bathroom, I've decided that making a joke is better than ignoring the elephant in the room.

Or the banana in the room, as it were.

"I would have picked different flavors." Miller gives me a wink.

I'm curious which flavors he'd choose, honestly. I can't stop my gaze from dropping to the front of his boxers as I think of the intended use of those products.

I swallow. There's an obvious sizable bulge.

My face flushes, thinking of the first week of camp when he "rescued" me from drowning, pressing his crotch up against my ass in the process. About his body pressing me into the door just a few minutes ago.

He was hard then, there's no question, but in jeans his size wasn't so... obvious.

He flicks off the light beside the bed. "Need anything?"

You. "I'm good," I manage to get out.

Miller slides under the covers. He settles on his side

and props his head on his hand, just like he did when we were in the tent.

But this time, there aren't campers sleeping ten feet away.

"I'm glad you came over."

"Me, too," I say, turning onto my side to look at him. "I like your family." The covers bunch the t-shirt so it's barely covering my hips.

"Yeah," he says. In the dim light, I can barely make out the curves of his face. "I can't believe you're really here, Becs." He reaches out and brushes a piece of hair out of my face. "It's been too long."

His touch is electric, and everything we ignited with that kiss bursts into flames inside me. "I've missed you, too," I whisper.

Then he's above me, knees on either side of my hips, arms framing my head as he holds himself up. He captures my already swollen lips with his and kisses me, soft and slow at first, then harder, more insistent.

I moan into his mouth, my hips lifting toward him.

Miller pulls back, settling on his knees. He grips the hem of his t-shirt and pulls it over his head, tossing it to the floor. He studies my face as his fingers brush the hem of my shirt, dragging it slowly up my body.

When he pulls it over my breasts, there's a sharp

intake of breath. "Fuck, Becs." He pulls the shirt up over my head, biting his lip. "You're so fucking gorgeous."

My nipples harden even further in the cool air of the room.

Miller lowers his head, and I think he's going to kiss me again, but then he brings his mouth to my breast and sucks my nipple into his mouth.

My hips jerk at the sensation as electricity zings through me. He stays there, licking and sucking and biting until I practically come from just that, and then switches to the other nipple.

When he finally lifts his head, my entire body is so tight I'm about to snap.

"I could spend all night worshipping your body, Becs," he says huskily.

I'm not used to getting compliments about my body. I'm more round than skinny, and while I have decently-sized boobs, I've always been self-conscious of the roundness of my tummy, the size of my hips. But when Miller looks at me, I feel gorgeous.

He shifts above me, his fingers hooking in the elastic of my underwear. My heart beats faster as he pulls them down and then all the way off.

I keep waiting for a flash of disappointment to cross his face, some indicator that this is a mistake, but his expression just grows more reverent. When he settles himself between my legs, he's removed his boxers.

I swallow hard as I take in the sight of him. Yeah, he's as big as I thought from the bulge in his boxers. "Um. Miller."

His brows crease. "Yeah, baby? You okay?"

I nod. "I just... it's been a while."

I'm studying to be a doctor, so I know you obviously don't get revirginized or whatever rumor the high school kids started back when I was a teenager. But it almost feels that way. Or maybe it's just that this time seems to hold a significance as much as my first time. And emotions aside, Miller isn't small.

He leans down and kisses me. "Same, babe. I haven't been with anyone since I met you."

My situation isn't exactly the same. "I..." My cheeks flush. "It's been a couple years for me. So, um..."

His eyes darken with lust. "Two years?"

"Since my senior year of college," I whisper. "So like... two years and a few months."

Miller moves down, pressing my legs apart even further. "I'm going to take my time getting you ready then, Becs. Cause once I'm inside you, there's no way I'm going to be able to go slow."

35

MILLER

I push her legs even wider, marveling at her body. The body I've been imagining, fantasizing about, for months now.

And it's nothing like I imagined. It's so much better. Her curves are lush under my hands, her light brown skin soft as I run my palms down her sides to grip her hips, which lift eagerly in response to my touch.

It's just like her, I realize. She's all firm walls and sharp edges until you get beneath the surface. Then there's nothing hard about her.

She gives a small moan as I trace the contour of one hipbone until my fingers reach the spot where her legs meet her body. I keep my hand there, my touch light as I mirror the motion on the other side.

My fingers skim lightly down her inner thighs, getting closer to her core until I'm there, right at the spot I've been dreaming of for months. I part her with my fingers to open her up to me.

She's as gorgeous and addicting as I imagined. Pink, wet, perfect. I run one finger through her wetness, loving the way she shudders beneath my touch.

"Fuck, Becs. You're soaked," I murmur on a groan. I lower my head to press a kiss to her mound, and her hips jerk.

"Oh, God, Miller," she says, breathless. God, the way she says my name in that voice. It has my cock hardening just at the sound.

I need to hear that moan again. I swipe my tongue between her parted legs, earning me the blessed sound again. My dick is so hard it's fucking painful, and it's all I can do to hold off, to wait to bury myself between her legs.

Because this isn't about me. It's about Becca.

"You know," I say, murmuring against her and enjoying the gasp as my words send vibrations through her, "I appreciate the selection of flavors we have in the bathroom. But nothing compares to the taste of you."

I run my tongue next to her clit, up one side and down the other, so close to what I know she needs.

"Miller," she whines, and I dive in, consuming her.

She's the sweetest fucking thing I've ever tasted, and I don't think I'll ever get enough. Fuck sugar cookie and whatever other flavor options were in there. None of those choices could ever compare to Becca.

I flatten my tongue and trace the length of her. She groans as her hips buck beneath me. I press my palms to her thighs, holding her steady beneath the onslaught as I lick and suck and gently bite. Her muscles tremble under my hands.

When I slide a finger into her as I run my tongue over her in long, languid strokes, I let out a groan of my own. "Christ, Becs. You're so fucking tight."

I curl my finger against the front of her channel and take my cues from her, licking harder and faster as she gets closer to her climax.

"Miller. Oh, God. I'm going to—I'm going to come," she pants.

I slip my finger out and replace it with two, marveling again at how tight she is. My eyes almost roll back in my head imagining my dick inside her, gripped by her heat. "Come for me, Becs. Right now."

I suck her clit into my mouth and press the tips of my fingers against her G-spot, watching with reverence as she shatters around me.

I squeeze my eyes closed at the sensation as her

pussy grips my fingers, imagining what it'll feel like when it's my cock inside of her instead. The thought alone is almost enough to make me come right then and there.

While Becca recovers, breathing hard, I lift my head and slide my fingers out of her, landing a kiss on her soft stomach.

"Holy shit," she breathes as I settle on the pillow next to her. "Even my vibrator can't do that."

I laugh and nuzzle her neck. She's mine now to touch, really mine, and I can't keep my hands off of her. "I'm just getting started, baby."

I'm going to show her things no vibrator can do. After tonight, she'll know that there's no going back. To a vibrator or to any other man. Because she's mine.

As her breathing slows, I pull a condom from under the pillow and rip it open.

"Where did you get that?" she asks, her eyes finally opening at the sound of the foil tearing.

"From the stash in the bathroom." I roll the condom down my length and lean down to speak in her ear, my cheek brushing hers. "There's more where that came from. I don't think one will be enough for tonight."

Her eyes widen as I rub my cock along her pussy. Is there anything better than that expression on a woman's face? Lust and nerves and excitement, and knowing you did that to her. Knowing she wants you as badly as you want her.

"You know, it's almost too bad," I say casually, positioning myself at her entrance.

"What?" Her forehead creases with confusion.

I lean down again, loving the tremor that goes through her body at my touch. She should get used to it; I don't think I'll ever be able to keep my hands to myself anytime soon. "I was hoping to use some of that nice selection of lube that was in the bathroom. But you're so fucking wet we don't even need it."

That earns me a moan and a delicious flush that spreads across her face. Who would have thought that Miss Straight-Laced would be a sucker for dirty talk?

I press against her, just enough for her to feel the stretch. My arms strain from holding myself back. "You sure about this, Becs? You okay?" If she tells me to stop, I'll never recover from the blue balls. For the rest of my life, I'll walk around with aching nuts, knowing that no one in the world can fix it besides her. I grit my teeth, waiting for her consent.

"Yes. Please," she pants, pressing her hips upward.

I ease back and then push in, just the tiniest bit, not even the entire head, teasing her. "What do you want, Becs?"

"You. I want you."

Fuck yes. Those words. I play some more, holding back from what she wants. From what we both need.

A whine rips from her throat. "Miller, please. Oh God," she manages.

"Please what, babe?" The look on her face as I draw this out is worth the excruciating patience needed to hold myself back. My thighs burn with the effort of keeping myself from driving forward and right into her in one quick thrust. I lean in close. "And it isn't God's name you're going to be screaming in a minute. It's mine."

"Fuck me. Please, Miller. I want—" Her words die on her lips and turn into a gasp as I press further into her.

I'm going as slow as I can without losing my fucking mind. Her pussy grips me as I slide deeper inside her, and it's exactly what I imagined when it was my fingers. Better, even. Tighter, so much so that I'm sure this is stretching her uncomfortably.

It's all I can do to make these first few strokes slow, to let her get used to my girth.

Because while I'm just a little above average—I looked it up, of course, back in college, while using a measuring tape to compare my stats—the way our bodies fit together has me feeling like a fucking god.

Those two-plus years she's been untouched have made her as tight as a virgin. But she has the experience to give her confidence, and that raises this to another level entirely.

I watch her face closely as I move deeper, doing everything I can to keep myself in check, making sure she's adjusting to my size.

Because I wasn't kidding earlier.

Once I start moving, I won't be able to go slow.

I've been dreaming about fucking her for months. I have fantasies of taking her hard and fast, of pinning her up against the wall and fucking her, of making love to her with slow music in the background.

And the one thing I know for sure is that those fantasies can't hold a candle to the real thing.

But I want this to be good for both of us. Because I'd cut off my right nut before I'd hurt her. I don't care if I'm in excruciating pain, as long as Becs is taken care of. And if I have my way, this is the first of many, many times I'm going to be inside Becs.

"More," she pleads, her voice throaty as she presses her hips upward and angles them to take me deeper.

Another inch. "You ready for all of me, Becs?"

Her eyes widen.

"Yeah, babe. There's more." I smirk, pleased at the shock in her eyes. I'm about halfway in, and fuck if going this slowly isn't the hardest goddamn thing I've ever done.

"Don't go slow." Her eyes search my face. "I want all of you."

Her words are my undoing. I hold it together for a few more seconds. Half an inch back, then in one slow, smooth stroke I'm bottoming out inside her. Her body grips me like a glove, and I'm seeing stars.

"Oh, fuck! Miller!" Becca cries out.

I still, hoping I didn't hurt her, but when I look at her face all I see is rapture that matches the bliss that must be painted across my own expression.

Becca moves her hips beneath me, and that's all the encouragement I need. I pull back and thrust in, hard and deep, then piston my hips, driving into her over and over again, needing to hear her say my name in that voice again.

It's the best thing I've ever fucking felt, hot and wet and tight around me, and it's the only thing I want to feel for the rest of my goddamn life.

She's ruined me for any other woman. Hell, she ruined me for other women the first time she said my name.

Her pussy clenches around me as she pants. "I-I'm close again, Miller. Don't stop."

"Not a fucking chance, babe." The President or

the Pope or the second coming of Christ Almighty himself could appear in this room and it wouldn't make me stop.

I've been dreaming of this moment for months, and as soon as she starts pulsing around me, I know I won't be able to hold on.

"I'm going to come, too, Becs. God, you're fucking amazing." I thrust harder and deeper as her body starts to spasm. I want to lose myself in this woman forever.

36

BECCA

Holy shit.

I thought I was good with my vibrator, but clearly, I'm missing out. I'm still breathing heavily, trying to get all of my limbs to function as Miller takes care of the condom in the bathroom.

I still haven't regained the ability to talk when he reappears, so I just wave. He holds up a new foil packet and winks. "Just in case."

I think he's joking until I look down at his crotch, and there he is, ready to go again. I'm not sure how he's hard again this quickly after what I would consider mind-blowing sex. It's pretty damn impressive. Can all guys do that?

As a doctor, I should really know the answer to

that question. Maybe I should do some research right now, see how things work when you go for a second round this soon after finishing. I was ready for another orgasm pretty quickly after Miller went down on me, so maybe some guys are the same.

He tucks the condom under the pillow and slides under the covers. "Come here," he beckons, holding his arm out to the side.

Part of me wants to snuggle up to him, to see just what he'd do. Would he take me with the same energy, his alpha male personality taking over? Would it be slow and sweet? Quick and dirty?

There's a tingle between my legs at the thought of either of these options.

I chew on my lower lip as an idea forms. He completely dominated the situation last time, and god knows the alpha male thing was fucking hot.

But not this time.

This one is mine.

Wordlessly, I push on his shoulder until he's fully on his back, and then I straddle him. He has a foot of height and easily eighty pounds on me, but there's something hot about him letting me take control for a change.

Miller leans back against the pillow, an amused

grin on his face. "You think you're in charge now, huh?"

I sit back on my heels, my knees on either side of his legs. God, it's a heady feeling, isn't it? The man who could easily overpower you, laying back and letting you take over, like he's putty in your hands.

"For now," I say, my gaze raking over his body. I run my fingers down his chest, over the defined muscles. "How do you get muscles like this?"

He cracks a smile. "Lots of time in the gym. You should come with me sometime. I bet your ass looks fantastic in spandex."

My ass hasn't seen the inside of the gym in years, but now isn't the time to get into that.

I shift backward to get a better look at him. How is Miller hard again? His cock seems even more imposing from this angle. But I want this. More than want it.

I want him. And I want to make it good for him, to prove that I know what I'm doing.

I scoot back further to get the right angle. I may have been celibate for years, but I don't forget things. So this is like riding a bike, right?

I dip my head and swirl my tongue over the head of his cock.

Miller groans. "Fuck, Becs."

I smile. There's something about bringing a man to his knees, as it were. "Stay here."

I climb off the bed and walk to the bathroom. For the first time in all the times I've been with men, I'm not ashamed of my body. I know I don't have a flat stomach, my boobs aren't as perky as someone who doesn't have my C cups, and my ass is... generous, to say the least. But this time, I'm not grabbing for a robe or a shirt or a towel or something to hide my body.

Because Miller likes my body. So maybe I do, too.

In the bathroom I pull open *that* drawer, thanking God for Lori Quinlan. The lube might be a little over the top, but stocking condoms for her son? It shows just how close of a relationship they have, and also that we don't need to be embarrassed or make sure no one hears us.

I grab an extra condom from the box and one of the bottles of lube, double checking to make sure it's not banana. If I gag, it's not going to be because of the flavor.

I carry my loot back to the bed. The condom goes under the pillow with the one Miller brought back, *just in case*.

Miller is in the same spot, cock standing at attention as I straddle him again. "Find what you were looking for?" he asks, grinning.

I hold up the sugar cookie lube. "I did. Now shut up and let me enjoy myself."

He groans audibly. The sound does something to me, awakens something more inside me. I did this to him. I made him hard. I can make him lose control.

Fuck, it's a really good feeling.

I drizzle the slippery liquid over his hard cock. He hisses at the cold, then groans again when I use my hand to spread it around.

I lower my head and dart my tongue out to taste him.

Mmm.

So much fucking better than banana cream. Miller's taste all on its own is something I could get addicted to. The sugar cookie lube adds an interesting sweetness.

I take the head of his cock into my mouth and suck him deep.

"Fuck, Becs," he grinds out.

I pull off of him and smirk. "You like that?"

He gives me a heady look. "Get the fuck back down there and keep going or I won't be held responsible for what happens."

I kind of want to know what would happen. What he'd do to me if I pushed him too far. If he'd flip me onto my back, retake control, and fuck me into submission.

But I'm drunk with power as I take him deep into my mouth, his length hitting the back of my throat. I suppress the urge to gag and swallow to get him deeper.

"Christ, babe," he groans. "Fuck, that's so good. So fucking good, Becs."

I grin around his cock as I work my mouth up and down. Then, on a high that only comes from being in control, I move to his balls and suck those into my mouth, too.

"Fu—I'm going to—" Miller gasps.

I look him in the eye as I run my tongue along his length.

"Becs, if I don't get inside you in the next minute, I *really* can't be held accountable for what I do," he insists.

"Like what?" I lazily run my tongue over the head of his cock.

A muscle in his jaw ticks. "Like flip you over onto your back and have my way with you, woman."

"Really?" I make no attempt to change my rhythm, but my stomach flips at the thought of him manhandling me.

Miller's hips jerk. "Yeah. Don't tempt me. But

Jesus, your mouth." His head falls back against the pillow.

The sugar cookie lube is pretty good, actually. I could hang out down here, teasing Miller, for hours. But even I know you can only push a man so far.

I slide over him, gripping his hard cock with one fist, until it notches at my entrance.

Miller flexes his hips, and I move with him, controlling every movement.

"You want to be inside me?" I ask, my voice teasing.

"Don't fucking push me, babe," he says, flexing his hips again so that the head of his cock, the one that's covered in sugar cookie lube, presses into me enough to make me moan.

"Condom," I manage to say. I had plans of taking care of that myself, being one of those sexually experienced women who know what they're doing when it comes to protection, but right now all I want is Miller buried deep inside me, so I make no move to reach for the packet.

He reaches under the pillow and holds up the foil square. "God, I can't wait until I can take you bare. I can only fucking imagine."

I take the condom from him and open it, rolling it down his length as he lets out a groan. I position myself over him and let the tip of his cock slip inside me.

Miller's hands grip my hips. He pulls me down, impaling me on his cock as I moan loudly.

Fuck. I'm so... *full*, for lack of a better word. Not just physically. Somehow, this entire experience is filling me up emotionally, and maybe that's weird to say, but Miller's so *inside* me.

I hold onto his shoulders as I ride him, slowly at first, then moving faster. His eyes close as I grind back and forth, a groan slipping past his lips.

When his abs clench, I slow my pace, teasing him until hands grip my hips. His fingers press into my flesh—not enough to hurt, but tight enough that when he moves his hands, I move, and even though I'm the one on top, he's controlling our movements. Leading me.

I close my eyes and let him direct my hips as he brings them up and down, his length pressing against my clit with every thrust, until I'm wound so tight I'm about to explode.

I open my eyes, panting, and look down at Miller to see the same euphoric bliss written across his face. "I'm going to come," I say, breathless.

He doesn't respond, but he moves me faster and

harder against him, using my body to bring us both to another earth-shattering climax.

—

I've always needed my space when sleeping, but when I wake up, I'm still curled in Miller's arms. After we recovered, we had sex again, slower and sweeter, and after I came once more—I've lost count at this point of how many orgasms I had last night—I slipped into the deepest, most restful sleep I've had in years.

He opens his eyes and smiles at me. "Hey, Becs. Morning."

"Morning," I whisper back. I'm not sure what else to say, my brain spiraling with what-ifs.

"Whoa," Miller says, tapping my forehead. "What's going on in there?"

"Nothing," I respond quickly.

Miller snorts, but before I can say anything, he's flipped me onto my back and is kneeling over me, his hands holding my wrists gently by my head. He leans down over me. "You're getting in your head, Becs. We're good. Don't freak out."

I'm not freaking out. Am I freaking out? My heart is hammering in my chest, and my mouth is dry, but I'm pretty sure that's a result of the way he's holding me right now.

Does he want to have sex again?

I take inventory. My body is sore, but just thinking about him taking me again has the blood settling between my legs.

I flex my hips up. "Do you want to—"

Miller frowns, and my face falls as my heart drops to the ground.

Was it not good for him? Does he not want to be with me?

"I don't want to fuck you, Becs," he says, confirming what I already knew, but then he continues. "I mean, Christ, I *do* want to fuck you, over and over, but that's not what this is. I want to make you breakfast. Talk about things. Be there for you."

My heart beats faster as I try to figure out what he's saying.

"Becs, I don't want just a one-time thing, and I don't want to be friends. I want a relationship with you. This is serious for me."

My heart leaps, then immediately crashes to the ground. Because that's what I want, too. And because every way I've thought about it, I've come to one conclusion: long-distance isn't going to work with my schedule.

And so far, everything between us has been put on Miller. He's the one who made the first moves. He's the one who was there for me, at camp and at school, the one I leaned on. The one who always cheers me up.

And a relationship is supposed to be equal. It can't always be one person doing things for the other. If we try for something long-distance, it'll all be on him again. He'll have to be the one to travel to see me, to wait for my calls. It's not fair.

I swallow hard. "Miller, I want that too. But..." I bite my lip, something inside me dying as his face falls. "I can't be in a long-distance relationship with you."

37

MILLER

I can't be in a long-distance relationship with you.

The words keep circling in my brain. Isn't that what we've *been* doing, with the texting and the phone calls and the FaceTime chats? Or is it different now that there are feelings out in the open?

I slump into a kitchen chair with a sigh. Becca left a couple hours ago to drive back to Syracuse before the traffic got too bad. I already miss here like crazy.

"You want some French toast?" Mom asks, glancing over at me from the stove. "I'm making some for Jordan. I can make extra."

I shrug, not really all that interested in food. "I guess."

She pauses. "You okay? What happened with Becca?"

"She didn't like the flavored lube."

Mom's eyes widen. "What? Oh, shit."

I snort. "That had nothing to do with it, or at least she didn't say that. But really, three flavors?"

Mom turns back to the pan. "I like to offer variety. It's called being a good host."

I don't think an etiquette book would recommend providing three kinds of flavored personal lubricant and a thirty-six-pack of condoms, but that's Lori Quinlan for you.

"She had to head back to school," I say.

"So why do you look like your dog died?" She flips the egg-soaked bread. "It seemed like you two were having a good time last night."

Thinking about last night almost has me getting hard again. "She doesn't want to do a long-distance relationship."

"Oh." Mom slides the French toast onto a plate, her lips thinning into a line. "Jordan, your French toast is ready!" She looks over at me. "Can you get the syrup out?"

"No words of wisdom to offer?" I stand from the table and cross the kitchen to pull the syrup out of the fridge.

She soaks another piece of bread in the egg mixture. "Not really, actually. Being in med school has to be tough, and adding a long-distance relationship on top of it? I can see where she's coming from."

I set the syrup in front of Jordan, who has taken over my seat, and sit down in a different chair. "I can, too. I was just hoping she'd consider it."

"Well, would her answer be different if it wasn't long-distance?"

I pull on the back of my neck. "I don't know. I didn't ask. But she's kind of stuck in Syracuse for now with school."

Mom looks over her glasses at me. "And are you stuck in Philadelphia?"

CARD SHARKS

How was everyone's Thanksgiving?

Blake: Eh, it was fine. Went out to Denver to see Lawton and his girlfriend for a little bit.

I thought he was living in some small town now?

Blake: He is, up in the mountains. They came down to Denver for a few days. Apparently, there's nothing but snow and ice up there this time of year. Well, most of the year.

Maddox: Holly said that since she can't drink, no one could drink. It was a very tense Thanksgiving.

Cam: That's putting it mildly. Between pregnancy hormones and wedding planning nonsense from Addie…

Cam: But Judy's turkey is still the best, so I'll take it.

How many more weeks of this?

Cam: Till next fall.

Not until your wedding, you idiot. Until Holly has the baby.

Maddox: About two months. It feels like it might as well be next fall.

Maddox: You should get your girl knocked up so you can experience this joy, too.

Never been so thankful that Mom put condoms in my bathroom.

Blake: She bought you condoms?

And flavored lube.

Cam: What flavor?

There were three options. But now we're at another sticking point with my girl. And she's not my girl, not really yet.

Cam: What are you waiting for?

Cam: Addie and I were an item after like one week.

Blake: One week and thirteen years.

Cam: Same thing.

I'm not waiting, you idiots. I laid it all out there, told her I liked her, that I wanted a relationship.

Maddox: And?

She doesn't want to do long-distance.

Cam: Christ, you're an idiot.

And you're an asshole. What's your point?

Cam: Why would you give up now? You worked so hard to win her over in the first place. The distance seems easier to fix than when she hated you.

I slide my phone back into my pocket, thinking. Maddox and Cam's attachment to their women is clear, even over text. Maddox may whine about Holly's pregnancy cravings and hormonal mood swings, and Cam might bitch about the pains of wedding planning, but they both have stars in their eyes while they do it.

They're so in love with their women. And no little hiccups like cravings for pickles and chocolate sauce or dress-related meltdowns can change that.

And is distance really that much more insurmountable than what they're dealing with?

I spend the next couple of hours clicking through things on my phone while I let old episodes of JackAss play in the background. A frustrating number of businesses are closed the day after Thanksgiving, but there are a few of them open. Enough to get the information I need. And a lot of things can be scheduled or started online.

I don't know if it will be enough, or where this is heading. But I know what I need to do.

38

BECCA
DECEMBER

To: Rebecca.Patel@syracusemed.edu
From: AdamChenMD@elmirafammed.org
Subject: Following up

Rebecca,

It was great hearing from you. Jordan has told me a lot about you, all favorable. To answer a few of your questions, I did my residency in family medicine here in Elmira, which is a great program for you to consider. I knew I wanted to do exclusively outpatient medicine, and during my training, I had a few patients that really stuck with me; Jordan was one of them, in fact. Those experiences led me to focus my practice on being an expert for kids and adults with Down Syndrome. It didn't require any additional training, more so just marketing myself in that niche. It's led to a very fulfilling career thus far.

As you consider your elective rotations, I'd welcome you to rotate with us for a month and see exactly what we do here. If it happens to tickle your fancy, I'll throw in a plug here that my current partner plans to retire in about five years, so I'll be looking for a new partner to replace her.

Good luck in school, and keep in touch!

Adam Chen, MD

Elmira Family Medicine

It's only been a week, but it's love.

I slide my messenger bag off my shoulder and tuck it under a desk in the work room. I never imagined that I'd like family medicine this much, and I went into this rotation with some skepticism. But one week has opened my eyes: I think this is what I want to do with my life.

So much so that I got Dr. Chen's contact information from Jordan, via Miller, and sent him an email to see how he managed to set up a practice specializing in Down Syndrome.

I pick up the list of patients for the day from the

desk while I wait for Dr. Abrams, my preceptor for the rotation, to come in. Taking a moment, I scan it to see what patients are coming in this morning.

An infant doing a weight check.

A forty-year-old diabetic coming in for a medication check.

A teenager looking for birth control.

A fifty-two-year-old with back pain.

A six-year-old with an earache.

I grin at the variety, and the mostly benign complaints. It's not impossible that we'd find a cancer or other serious disease among the complaints, but unlike in the hospital setting, most of the patients we see are out there living their lives.

They're not sick and suffering. They're thriving, and we get to help them.

This is the magic my dad talked about, I realize. He's told me so many stories of his first day in the operating room: how he saw the surgeons and what they were doing and realized, *I want to do that, too.*

I figured that was something that was specific to surgeons, and when I didn't feel the same spark when I walked into the OR, I was worried that something was missing.

But now I know. That's the spark when you find your soulmate, the one you want to be with for the rest of your life. For me, it's family medicine. I can do this every day and be happy. And this month, I'm learning that I'm pretty darn good at it.

Not perfect by any means, and for the first time in my life, I'm okay with that. Because I can learn and get better, and I'm enjoying the journey. And because even when I'm not perfect, I'm still making a difference.

"Hey, Becca," Dr. Abrams greets, tossing his coat on a chair. "Do you want to see the baby or the diabetic?"

"Morning!" I say brightly, turning in the swivel chair to face him. "Either one is fine. Maybe the baby? I haven't seen an infant in a while."

"You got it," he says with a nod, taking a sip from his travel mug. "Ah, that's the good stuff."

"Coffee?" I raise a brow.

"Hot chocolate with two shots of espresso." He grins. "Best of both worlds."

"That's a wrap," Dr. Abrams says, setting a chart on the pile of completed ones with a dramatic flair. "Nice work today."

I look up from where I'm writing in a patient's chart. "That's it for today?" How did time fly like that?

On my inpatient rotations, it seems to drag, each minute feeling like an hour. Here, the end of the day seems to arrive before I can blink.

"Indeed." He sits back in his chair. "How do you feel like the rotation is going?"

It must be Friday, if he's giving me feedback. "I feel like it's going well," I answer honestly. "I'm really enjoying the mix of patients. I think this is what I want to do with my life."

A smile spreads across his face as he leans back, folding his hands behind his head. "I'm glad to hear it. You're doing a fantastic job. I'm looking forward to working with you more over the month, but even based on the last week, if you want a letter of recommendation, just say the word."

My stomach leaps. This has been the first week since I started my third year that I see potential for me actually liking a specialty, and I've already fallen in love.

With the feedback from Dr. Abrams, I feel like I can see my future taking form for the first time.

"Thank you," I say. I want to jump up and down and clap my hands, but I cross my legs at the ankles instead. More doctor-like, or something. "I think I'll take you up on that, but I'll let you know at the end of the rotation, if that's okay with you."

"Of course." He stands from his chair. "I'll see you Monday, okay?"

I'm alone in the workroom when he leaves. I don't feel the need to get out of the office the way I do when I'm in the hospital. I double check my work on the last chart before I place it in the pile.

My phone bumps against my hip when I pull my jacket on to leave. I pull it out, ready to tell Miller all about my day. He's the one I want to tell when something good happens, I realize. And he's the one whose shoulder I want to cry on when I need to get something off my chest. It's too bad he lives so far away, making a real relationship impossible.

MILLER

How's the new rotation?

Amazing, actually. I think this is it.

You found what you want to do?

Yeah. Family medicine is exactly what I was looking for.

Proud of you, Becs.

I stare at the phone so long my vision starts to blur. When Miller tells me he's proud of me, I get a warm, fuzzy feeling in my chest. What do you call that?

As I consider, my heart squeezes at another thought. My parents. Miller might be proud of me, but what about them?

I walk through the empty hallway as I type out a text, delete it, then type another one and stare at it. How exactly do I explain this? *Sorry, guys, I don't want to be a surgeon.*

Finally, I settle on a noncontroversial opening.

MOM

> Hi Mom, hope everything is going well. I'd love to tell you about the rotation I'm on now.

> I'm so excited for you, Rebecca! Can I call you? Maybe even FaceTime, with Dad?

> Sure. Can I text you when I get back to my apartment?

> *thumbs up emoji* Can't wait to hear all about it.

Once I've made it back to my place, I've fortified my resolve with a glass of red wine and reminded myself that it doesn't actually matter what they think about the specialty I choose. I need to make this decision for myself.

I keep my phone in front of me as I cook dinner:

spaghetti with jarred marinara sauce tonight. With the frozen garlic bread that's heating up in the oven, this seems like a step up from macaroni and cheese. And a nice merlot—*nice* meaning it wasn't from the $5 shelf —classes it up even more.

A ringing sound vibrates through the air. I set the wooden spoon down and swipe to open the video call, smiling as my parents' faces come into view.

"Rebecca! It's so good to see you," Mom says, leaning toward the camera, her dark hair falling over her face. This close, I can see the gray of her roots growing in. She's never quite gotten used to the idea that you don't have to speak directly into the phone when you're on a video call. "How are you doing?"

I smile as I wipe my hands on a towel. "I'm good. Really good, actually. How are you guys?"

My dad shifts in his seat, unlacing his fingers before folding them back together. "We are good as well. Have you done your surgery rotation yet?"

I shake my head, happy that I didn't cringe in front of them. I'm not exactly looking forward to it after experiencing the OR during my OB rotation. "I have that one right after Christmas."

My dad doesn't really care about Christmas, being Hindu, but we celebrated while I was growing up, because my mom is Catholic. She also convinced my dad that I should be baptized Catholic. I think that means she won.

"What rotation are you on now, love?" Mom asks with interest. "Do you like it?"

I take a deep breath. Moment of truth. "I'm on family medicine, and actually... I love it." I pause and take another breath. "I think this is what I'm going to do with my life."

I wait, holding my breath.

Then a smile spreads over my dad's face, and my mom's, too.

"That's great, sweetheart!" my mom says, leaning into the camera again to make sure I don't miss her words.

"That is wonderful, Rebecca," Dad says. His posture doesn't deviate from his perfect straight spine, but then again, it rarely does. "That is a wonderful specialty."

I open my mouth, ready to defend myself, then close it. Because they're not giving me a hard time. If anything, they're... supportive. "I... thank you," I finally manage.

"Where are you thinking about doing your residency?" my dad asks. Because he can't have a conversation that doesn't prompt some amount of stress in me.

I pick up the spoon and stir the Prego that's

starting to bubble in its saucepan. "I'm not sure yet. I'll let you know where I'm applying so you have a good idea before the Match."

The Match, with a capital M. The one day that determines the lives of so many medical students. We interview for positions, then rank the programs we want to train at; the programs rank the applicants they want, and all of it goes into a computer that spits out the matches, which are ceremoniously passed out one at a time on Match Day in early spring when we find out where we're going to spend the next three to seven years of our lives. And which are binding, at least for that first year.

No pressure or anything.

"You just find a program where you will be happy," Dad says, nodding somberly. "We will come and visit you anywhere. If you match in New York City, you can live with us, too."

Over my dead body. I love them, but I'm not moving back in with my parents in my late twenties. My mother would probably iron my work clothes the way she irons Dad's scrubs.

"I'll let you know," I promise.

With that, I end the call, marveling at the exchange that just happened. Are they really not going to try to talk me into surgery or, at the very least, anesthesia?

The idea that they'll support me in whatever I want to do is exhilarating.

The excitement carries me through dinner and an hour of studying, making sure I'm as ready for Monday as I can be.

I'm about to go to sleep when my phone buzzes with a text.

MILLER

I have some news. Can I come see you?

39

BECCA

God, I miss him so much. My vibrator, the one that used to give quick, reliable orgasms, is worthless compared to the memory of how Miller skillfully played my body like an instrument, coaxing orgasm after orgasm out of me.

And while we've talked almost every day since Thanksgiving, there's something empty in me. It's like I got a glimpse of how things could be—Miller and I together, our bodies fitting perfectly, his family around us—and now I realize ignorance really is bliss.

I'm a wreck at the thought of seeing him today. I've cleaned my place like ten times.

The laundry is tucked away in a closet. The bed is made. The throw pillows are arranged on the couch in a way that invites sitting, but that also says *the person who owns these throw pillows is a woman of impeccable taste*. I hope. It's also possible that they say *the person who owns these throw pillows bought them on sale at TJ Maxx*.

I've given up on seeming cool and casual. Now, I'm pacing the length of my small apartment, waiting for Miller to appear.

He says he has news. I'm not sure what it could be, honestly. Did he get a new job? He hasn't mentioned anything to me about applying for something, but maybe he doesn't tell me everything.

My stomach twists. Maybe he needs to tell me he met another girl.

I halt my pacing and sink onto the couch. Two of the throw pillows tumble to the ground. That's what it is, isn't it? He's too much of a nice guy to tell me via text.

I smile sadly at the irony. When I met him, I thought he was an asshole who didn't take anything seriously. Now that I know he's actually a good guy, I'm going to be subjected to an in-person breakup, or whatever you'd call this, since we're not really in a relationship.

It's okay, though. I said I didn't have time for a relationship, especially long-distance, and I meant it, because he deserves more. Miller deserves a girl who has time for him. Maybe one who thinks pranks are funny.

Okay, so I might have laughed when he hid all of his mom's spoons on Thanksgiving and we had to eat the butternut squash soup with forks. But most of his pranks aren't that hilarious.

I check my watch. It's 10:02. He said he was going to be here at ten.

Another reason he and I don't make sense together. I'm always on time. He's chronically late.

He hasn't told me he's met anyone. If anything, our talks have gotten more intimate, more heated. He seems determined to show me that he can do long-distance.

And that's not the point here. I know he can. But he shouldn't have to. I care about him, probably more than I should. I want to be there for him. But being there for him includes being *there*, and that's not in the cards right now.

There's a part of me that hopes he hasn't met someone else. That he still belongs to me. But there's another part, the logical side, that hopes he's happy, even if it can't be with me.

There's a sudden knock on my door, startling me from my thoughts. I stand up too quickly, sending another pillow to the floor. I start to pick one up, then stop. He's probably not coming in, anyway. This'll be a doorway conversation.

I leave the pillows where they are and cross to the front door. When I pull it open, the sight of him hits me like a gut punch.

"Miller," I say. It's all I can manage.

It's only been a month since I last saw him. Did my body react this way last time?

My gaze runs down his body. Shaggy blond hair peeks out from beneath a knit cap. His winter coat is hanging open, his University of Scranton t-shirt clinging to his chest. His dark wash jeans hug his hips.

I tear my gaze away from his crotch. "Hi. How are you?"

He smiles, and his crooked grin does me in even further. "I'm good, Becs. Can I come in?"

"Why?" I blurt out.

Miller tilts his head. He sets a hand on the door-frame and braces his weight on it as he leans in. "To talk, Becs. You okay?"

I'm not good. I'm an absolute fucking wreck seeing you and hearing you call me Becs and knowing we can't be together. "Yeah. I'm good." I swallow hard and step back to let him in.

He strides into my apartment like he owns it, taking it all in as he pulls off his jacket. He pauses by the couch. "Becs?" He turns back to look at me, his brows knitted together in concern.

It twists the knife in my gut even further, because I know he doesn't care about the pillows on the floor. It's that he can take one look at that scene and know what's going on in my head, and that kills me. It's one thing for the guy you're with to be able to read you like that.

It's an entirely different feeling when that guy can still see through you, even though you can't be together. I manage to shrug in a way that looks anything but casual.

"Sorry, I didn't clean up too well. I didn't think you were going to come in."

He crooks his finger for me to come closer. "Why would you think that? I said I was coming over."

I'm too close to him, my entire body at risk of bursting into flames, and I'm still a foot further away than normal conversation. "You said you had news. I figured you'd tell me about whoever you met and then leave. So... I didn't worry about the pillows."

"Whoever I met?" He steps even closer to me. The air thickens between us.

It's hard to breathe. Is he going to make me say it?

It all comes out in a rush, "I know it's my fault. I'm the one who said we can't be together, because of the distance thing. It's okay. But you said you had news. I figured you were going to tell me about someone new you met and that you want to pursue a relationship with her. I mean, it's what I told you to do, so I'm not mad. I didn't expect you to stay single. I just—"

His finger on my lips cuts off my rambling. "Becs, shut up for a minute."

"Okay," I whisper against his finger, because I'm powerless against his touch.

"I have two things to say. First, fuck the pillows." He turns away from me and uses his arm to sweep another three pillows to the ground. "And second? I didn't meet someone else. I don't want anyone else, Becs. I came here to tell you that I'm in love with you."

He pulls me into him and presses his lips against mine, kissing me hard while I try to process his words.

I'm in love with you.

He spins us around and lowers me to the couch. I bat away the one remaining pillow as he leans over me.

"It's you, Becs. You're the only one I want." He kisses me again, long and languid until I'm melting into the couch cushions.

I press my hips upward, against the hard bulge at the front of his pants.

"Christ, Becs," he groans. "This couch isn't big enough for the things I want to do to you."

Then we're on the floor, surrounded by the pillows as we both strip off our clothing like we're in a race against time. Miller pulls a foil packet out of the pocket of his discarded jeans.

"You came prepared," I say. I intend for it to be a teasing tone, but the words come out in a harsh whisper.

Miller rolls the condom on in one motion and positions himself at my entrance. "I brought enough for the whole weekend."

"I—" I'm about to tell him I have to study tomorrow, that I have things I need to do and that we need to talk about our relationship and what we're doing and if he's in love with me does that change things and all the thoughts that are muddling my brain, but then he thrusts into me, bottoming out in one stroke, and every thought flies out of my brain.

"You feel so good, Becs. So fucking good," he groans, pulling back and thrusting again.

My eyes roll back in my head, because he's right. It's so fucking good. All I can manage is a moan as Miller pistons his hips, picking up speed and fucking me harder and faster until I'm right on the edge.

"Oh God, Miller," I gasp. "I'm going to—"

"Come for me, Becs. Only me."

He reaches a hand between us and presses hard on

my clit, and my world shatters as I pulse around him.

"Fuck," he grinds out, slamming into me again as he comes hard.

We lie on my apartment floor, surrounded by throw pillows while we breathe hard. After a minute, Miller gets up and disposes of the condom. When he comes back, he grabs a blanket off the couch and lays right back down on the floor next to me.

"Don't get too comfortable, babe. I couldn't hold on any longer, but next time?" He runs a finger down my cheek. "I'm going to be inside you for hours."

He pulls the blanket up over both of us, pausing at my hips, where he runs his finger over my ladybug tattoo.

"I didn't notice this before," he says thoughtfully. "Is it for the Ladybugs at camp?"

"Yeah." I smile. "I got it the summer I was eighteen, a statement about independence and all that."

"I love it." He pulls the blanket up higher and tucks me into his side.

"My grandmother gave this to me," I murmur, tracing the blanket's pattern with a finger.

Miller tugs me closer, so my head nestles into the groove where his arm meets his chest. "Tell her it's great for post-sex cuddling. Thank her for me."

"She passed away when I was in high school, but I

think she'd roll over in her grave if she knew what we were using her carefully crocheted afghan for."

He laughs. "My apologies, then. Anyway, sorry again that I was so quick. I just couldn't hold back. I'll last longer next time."

I don't want to break the post-sex haze, but something is still tugging at my mind. He said he's in love with me, but there's still the distance issue. "So. Um. What was your news? Was it that you—the thing you said earlier?" My face heats.

"Oh!" Miller sits up in excitement, almost knocking me to the floor. "I got distracted."

I pull the blanket around myself and sit up to face him. "That's putting it lightly."

"We can do it again in a minute or two. Just let me recover," he says with a wink.

"Miller! We can't have sex all day. Besides, that wasn't the question. What was your news? Is everything okay?"

"Everything is great, Becs," he says with a wide smile. "You know how I was applying to grad school?"

A surge of excitement for him runs through me. He told me a few weeks ago that he was applying to grad schools to get his master's in special education. "Yeah. Did you hear back from one of the programs?"

His smile widens as he nods. "I got in. I start in

January."

His excitement is contagious. "That's amazing! I'm so proud of you. You'll be an amazing teacher."

His eyes sparkle with excitement. "Yeah. I'm so excited to get started. And I'll still be able to hit poker tournaments here and there, so I'll have some income if I can keep doing well there."

"Seriously, Miller. This is the best news ever. And hey, if you're a teacher, you'll have summers off, right? So you can go back to camp and hang out with the goats." I nudge him with my elbow.

Miller groans. "I never want to see that fucking goat again. If there's more than one of them next time I'm there, that just might push me over the edge."

"You're thinking of going back?" I'm surprised, but talking to him through the summer, it was clear he was happy up there. And despite his lack of experience, he ended up being an amazing counselor.

He'll be a fantastic father someday.

He nods. "Not next summer. The master's program goes through the summer, and I kind of just want to focus on that and get the classes done, so I'm going to be full-time. But I definitely want to go back." He shakes his head with a smile. "When I went up there last summer, I didn't think I'd make it a week, let alone the whole season, and I sure as hell didn't think

I'd consider making it a regular thing, but it grows on you."

"It sure does." I wonder if I'll ever have time to go back. My years of having a summer vacation are over at this point.

"So I booked the movers, but I have to decide where I'm going to be living." He looks at me, his eyebrows raised in question, but I'm not sure what he's asking.

"Like what town?" I realize I didn't even ask which program he got into. "Where are you going to be going to school?"

If at all possible, his smile grows even broader. "That's the best part. I got into my top choice program."

My heart swells for this man. He deserves this. "Congratulations, Miller. I'm so proud of you."

"And since my top choice was Syracuse, that means you're kind of stuck with me."

Something rises in me, light and joyful. *Hope.* Because if he's going to the same school as me, that means...

"Are you really going to make me ask?" He has the lopsided grin firmly in place as his eyes search my face.

"Are you moving up here?" I ask, breathless.

"That would make the most sense, wouldn't it?"

He waits, then lets out a long sigh. "Okay, I'll do the asking. Becca Patel, will you be my official girlfriend, and also can I move in here with you? That's about as anti-long-distance as I can do."

He wants to do *what*? "I only have another year and a half here." My brain isn't functioning.

A smile quirks on his lips. "Yeah. About how long the master's program would take me. And if I need to, I can finish it online wherever you end up."

"I..." This is obviously a dream. A very strange dream, where Miller is here and he's in love with me and he's moving to be with me.

All the things I've fantasized about. No wonder my brain cooked up this crazy dream.

A shadow of something crosses Miller's face, and I blink as I realize that maybe, I'm not dreaming. "Shit, I'm sorry, Becs. I shouldn't have come on so strong. I was just thinking that because you said you couldn't do long-distance that I could solve that problem, but it is moving fast, huh? I don't have to move up here or move in with you if you don't want me to."

I shake my head as I wrap my arms around him. "I want you to move in. And to be your girlfriend and all of that. I'm just... I wasn't expecting it. But I want all of it." I look up at him, my eyes pricking with tears. "Because I'm in love with you, too."

EPILOGUE

MAY

Becca

"When do you apply for residency again?" Miller asks, pushing off the ground to make the swing move.

I look out at Lake Winnipesaukee. The water is calm, quiet, just like the rest of camp. It's another week until the staff arrive to start getting everything ready, but Brett was nice enough to let Miller and I come up for a weekend before things officially open. "Next month. Then I'll interview in the fall and find out in the spring."

It's nerve-racking, knowing that I'll be making decisions in the next few months that will define my life. What specialty I'll choose, and where I move for residency training.

"You still thinking the hospital near my mom's house is where you want to be?"

I nod. "As long as they take me. I'd love to work with Dr. Chen some more." I managed to move my elective rotation to my third year and spent last month working in Dr. Chen's clinic. It has officially solidified my decision to do family medicine.

Miller grins. "Even if you have to live near my mom, huh?"

After living with Lori and Jordan for a month, I've gotten pretty good at Mario Kart—not good enough to beat Jordan all the time, but every once in a while— and I've gotten to be good friends with Miller's mom.

"I love your mom. I'd rather live with her than with you," I tease.

"Bummer. I was getting used to having mac and cheese for every meal."

I look at him with mock outrage. "I cook things other than mac and cheese. I vary the menu at least every two weeks. I made spaghetti last week."

He laughs. "You're just lucky I don't like you for your cooking skills."

"Yeah. That's definitely not my strong suit." I make a face, wrinkling my nose.

We sit in silence, looking out at the lake. It's strange to think it's only been a year since we sat in this very spot. Everything is so different now.

"Oh, I wanted to tell you something," Miller says.

"Mmm?" I glance back over at him.

He takes a deep breath and lets it out in a long sigh. "I don't want you to be my girlfriend."

My stomach plummets and I look at him, my eyes wide. "Miller?"

Slowly, his serious look fades to a sheepish grin. "I want you to be my wife." He pulls a small box out of his pocket and opens it as my heart starts to beat faster.

The channel-set diamonds glitter in the sunlight as my hands go to my mouth in shock. The diamonds alternate with sapphires. It's nontraditional and exactly what I would have picked out for myself.

He pulls the ring out of the box and holds it out to me. His hands shake the tiniest bit, and I love him that much more in this moment. "Rebecca Anjali Patel, will you marry me?"

I smack his arm as I nod, blinking back the tears that make my vision swim. "Of course. But maybe next time you propose to me, don't try to fake me out with something that sounds like a breakup."

"But it was funny, right? At least in retrospect?"

He can't hide his grin as he slides the ring onto my finger.

"Too soon," I say. I turn my hand back and forth, breathlessly watching the diamonds catch the sun. "I love it so much."

"I know you love sapphires cause they're your birthstone. And I wanted you to have a ring you could wear when you're working, too."

"It's perfect." And it is. The whole moment. Even Miller's prank is growing on me a little.

This one might even be better than the boxers up the flagpole.

Miller

We walk around the empty camp hand in hand. Becca can't stop holding her hand out to admire her ring.

"Hey, guess what else?" I say as we pass the Sports field. I almost forgot my other news, but proposing to the girl of your dreams will do that to you. I got this news a few days ago, but I wanted to keep it to myself until I was sure she was going to say yes to my proposal.

"You want to go see the goat?" she guesses.

There's not a chance in hell I want to see another goat ever again. "No. For real. I got offered a potential job."

Becca stops in her tracks. "Really? That's great. Where?"

"In my hometown. Teaching special ed, once I finish my master's and get my license. And they're willing to wait for me to give them an official answer, because they know you have to wait to find out about residency. So if you end up matching in Elmira, I can support you in the manner to which you've become accustomed." I gesture with a flourish.

"I'm accustomed to macaroni and cheese for almost every meal, so as long as you can keep up that standard of living, that'd be great." Becca grins at me. "I'm proud of you, Miller."

As we walk to the dining hall, my phone vibrates in my pocket. I slide it out and read the text chain that's coming in.

CARD SHARKS

Cam: Did you do it yet?

Maddox: What'd she say?

Blake: You didn't use the not my girlfriend anymore line, did you?

> I did, and yes, I used that line. She loved it.

> And she said yes. Thank you for the vote of confidence, though.

Blake: If she liked the prank, she's definitely the one for you. Congrats.

Maddox: That's awesome, man. Who knew you'd be headed down the aisle after Cam?

That reminds me.

I look over at Becca. "Hey, now that we're engaged, think you want to be my date to Cam's wedding? It's in November. In the Bahamas."

"Of course! I can't wait to meet all of these guys that have put up with you for so long." She gives me a wink.

> Not me, that's for sure. But Becca and I will be there for Cam's wedding. Can't wait.

Maddox: Now Blake is the only one who needs a date.

Cam: Want me to hire one for you?

Blake: I don't need a date. Just leave the plus-one off the invitation.

Hey, you never know if you'll meet someone by then. Maybe keep your plus-one just in case.

Blake: Doubtful. I'm starting my new job in August, so I'm pretty sure any time for dating is gone.

You got the gig? That's awesome!

Blake: Yeah. Professor at Ardmore College. Wild, right?

"Hey, it's my two favorite counselors!" Brett calls from the office.

I slide my phone back into my pocket to greet him. I'll have to talk to Blake later about this new job he has going on. I'm hoping to keep hitting some poker tournaments when I can, but I wonder what his plan is.

"Hey, Brett! Good to see you." I clap him on the back.

"Enjoying camp without the campers?" Brett asks with a knowing smile. "It's a different world, right?"

"It is. And guess what?" I hold Becca's hand out. "She said yes."

Brett whistles. "Amazing. And here I thought you'd eat Miller alive last summer."

Becca laughs, her cheeks flushing. "I hated him at first."

"I know." Brett chuckles. "He's an acquired taste. It's funny, though," he says, thoughtful. "You were running from something when you came up here last summer. I figured eventually you'd have to show your hand, but it seems like Miller was the one to call your bluff."

I put an arm around Becca and pull her close. "Hey, as soon as I met her, I knew I'd do whatever I needed to win her over. Becca's the easiest gamble I've ever made."

Blake's story is up next!

<u>Upping the Ante</u>
Betting on Love Book 4

When I gave up my days as a pro poker player for academia, I never imagined it would bring her into my life... or set me up for the biggest gamble of all.

My focus needs to be on establishing myself as a professor of game theory—not on romance. I have no time for a relationship, let alone interest in one. So when the girl in the bar needs someone to pretend to be her boyfriend in a pinch, I'm happy to step in—as long as she realizes it's a one time thing.

When I realize she works down the hall from me, though, a new plan starts to form: one that could help both of us, as long as we stick to the rules and keep real feelings out if it. Game theory only works if all the players have the same information and strategy, after all.

The more time we spend together, pretending to be in a relationship, the harder it's getting to walk away from her. But I haven't told her everything about me. I'll need to come clean if this is going to turn into something real—but when she finds out the truth, she might be the one walking away from me.

Read Now!